"The Last Dragon was just awesome! The author's storytelling had me hooked from the start. I highly recommend this author. I will buy books from her in the future."

— DebA from Night Owl Reviews,
TOP PICK AWARD

"This is a great read for anyone who likes paranormal romances that have a diverse group of characters. I have always enjoyed the shifter stories that had different groups having to work together to achieve success."

— Reviewed by LiaL for TheRomanceReviews.com
Amazon Top 100 Reviewer

"The story had moments of sweetness and serious moments of intensity toward the end that will absolutely keep you "IN" the story. I definitely look forward to seeing what happens next as Milchon set the stage for the next Omega to find his love and salvation."

— BookChick Blog Reviews

"Dragons, water beings, shadow movers plus their enemies all blend together to make this a really great book. "

— Long and Short Reviews, given a gold star and labeled
BEST BOOK

This was a great love story.

— Cranky Author's Book Blog

The Last Dragon

Artemis Milchon

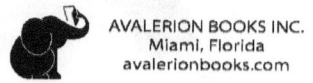

AVALERION BOOKS INC.
Miami, Florida
avalerionbooks.com

To Jayne, who started it all,

and

Libba, who makes all things magnificent.

For the dragon it shall salvation be,

Happiness is found in three.

Clearest sight is found below,

What was gone, must start to show.

Your armor will have to break,

The last will cause the big mistake.

Lay down your inherited power,

Do not stop in the final hour.

Your lives will grow again here,

When the Jewels provide the key to fear.

For the one who is my very own,

Your greatest destiny is alone.

❧ CHAPTER ONE ❧

Sally stood at the window looking out into the backyard. Anyone who thought magic was no longer possible had never seen rural Pennsylvania. It was late June, and the day had been especially hot. A cold system had blown in and gotten caught in the valley. It had pushed the clouds down so low it seemed if you climbed the highest, nearest peak you could touch them. The evening fog that came with the lowering temperatures covered the garden, a blanket of eerie pure white cotton that masked all the familiar features she knew as well as her own face. As Sally watched from her window, the fireflies began to rise from the fog, making iridescent points of light shine in the darkness. The stillness and enchantment of the moment made her hold her breath in wonder.

It was something out of a dream.

Sighing heavily, she turned back to the dinner she was finishing for her family. Some truths were self-evident to her.

If heaven was in her backyard, hell was in the living room.

"Sally, get your fat ass back in here." With a heavy sigh, she turned from the soothing pastoral bonanza and picked up the cheesecake she had prepared earlier. Entering the dining room, she froze as the gazes of her siblings pinned her to the spot.

"She's been daydreaming again," her sister Robin sneered.

Austin banged his hand against the table, "Dammit girl, how many times do we have to tell you to pay attention. Put the dessert down and get the blueprints."

Doing as ordered, Sally kept her resentment hidden behind her lowered eyes. "Be nice, Austin," Dawn tittered. "She can't help it if she's fat and has to be told how to do everything. It's really all her slut of a mother's fault."

"Dad should have dumped them both by the side of the road," Austin chuckled.

Sally brought the blueprints she had created, a feat she was very proud of. She had designed the front yard of the house they were building to cover every architectural flaw and defect. It would be a stunning effect when you looked at this property from the street. Less so when you went inside. Sally laid the papers out on the table, careful not to touch the rich dessert her brother had commanded her to make. The four of them stared at the plots of plants and bushes with little understanding. "This will look good," Mitch stated with an upward inflection, betraying confusion over what Sally had designed.

"Of course it will," Dawn confirmed, casting Sally a bewildered look.

She began to point out the features of the design, "I combined flowering trees and colorful bushes to create a mosaic of color. It will be stunning all year through. People will be so busy looking at the garden, they'll never think twice about the house."

"Just what I told her to do," Austin boasted.

Sally slid into her chair and began to cut the cake. Distributing the plates, she hid her satisfaction when everyone immediately started to dig into the dessert. She would receive no thanks for her efforts, but they would quickly make what she served disappear. Sally had learned long ago to take her compliments in silence rather than in empty talk. Knowing how many disapproving looks she would receive if she joined them; she chose not to cut herself a portion. If she were going to eat cake, she would have to do it when she was alone.

It was the only way she would be free to enjoy it.

At least, in her room surrounded by dragons, she would feel at home.

"Great," Austin trumpeted. Sally tried to pay attention to the plans and decisions going on around her. The company they owned and ran, the Triple Ease Constructors, was the creation of her father and should still be going strong. When he died, it was decided the siblings would work on it together. The Eversham family was a force to be reckoned with throughout the state. Austin was the CEO, Mitch served as head of construction, Dawn handled sales, Robin did marketing, and of course all landscaping was under her direction. It was the one area she could carve out of the close-knit family pie.

Sally looked around the table at the perfect dark haired and dark eyed siblings. It was a family truth that her father's second marriage to her mother had brought about a child, her, that just never fit in with the others. She stood out from them like a sore thumb. Her hair was pale strawberry. Her eyes a light green, sometimes losing all color, and turning to the wash of a watercolor. Her body ran more to fat than her brothers' and sisters' athletic builds.

She didn't fit. She never had.

Never would.

"Sally," Austin thundered.

"What," she shifted in her seat when she realized everyone was staring at her again.

"You're going out with Robin and Dawn tonight to party."

"I can't do that," she shifted back in her seat in fear. The one thing she hated the most was social situations. They all knew it.

"You have no choice," Robin pushed her half eaten cake away. "Dawn and I need an excuse to get out of there if the venture capitalists get too rowdy."

"Where are we going?"

"Simple," Dawn poured herself more coffee. "They want to see the rougher side of town so we're hitting the Underbelly."

"That's a biker bar," Sally gasped. "I can't go there."

"Why," Robin looked at her blankly. "Who'd mess with you?"

She buried her head down in the relative safety of her coffee. It didn't matter, she reminded herself. She would bring the number for a good cab company and escape as soon as possible. This meeting was important to the Triple Ease. These strange men that she had only caught glimpses of had promised the company a much needed influx of cash. The housing market was crippling them and without it, Sally was aware they were in jeopardy of losing everything. Dawn and Robin had been directed to get the three men in a happy and generous frame of mind.

It took her sisters two hours to get ready. Sally shifted around in her long cardigan and ankle length skirt as she watched her siblings walk down the steps in thigh high suede boots, mini-skirts made from leather so soft it looked painted on, and tops that were little more than glorified bras. "That's what you're wearing?" Robin sneered. "You couldn't find anything better?"

"She looks fine," Dawn waved Robin's concerns away. "We're late already."

"You know, you've been dieting for a year." Robin looked Sally up and down. "How can you be getting fatter?"

"Enough," Dawn pushed Robin towards the door.

The club was pulsing with music and bodies. The location in the middle of a cornfield gave plenty of room for the motorcycles, muscle cars, and SUV's its diverse clientele drove. Sally kept reaching into her purse to make sure she still had her cell phone and the taxi service business card. This was not a place she wanted to stay for long. And by not long, she meant five minutes was too much.

Her sisters threw themselves into the crowd with the confidence and enthusiasm of women who knew they were admired and sought after. Sally searched for a quiet niche she could hide in.

There was an empty booth in the corner. Heading over to it, Sally winced when she realized the space next to it was filled with two men that looked like something out of Robin's favorite sexual fantasy. She tried to avoid their notice as she slid into the booth and buried her head behind one of the greasy menus. "Five more minutes," she whispered to herself. "All I need, is to hold on for five more minutes, and I can be free." Sally tried to cheer herself up with the thought of the big piece of cake she would cut herself when she got home.

A harried-looking waitress came over and Sally ordered the drinks she knew her sisters would expect when they took a break from the dancing.

CHAPTER TWO

Sitting in the corner booth, the cousins were busy trying to drown their sorrows with as much alcohol as the waitress could bring. One of their own was dying. Again. Their despair was a heavy cloak on their souls that the bar packed with gorgeous women could not lighten. There was no understanding of this disease. No treatment, much less a cure. Their friends were sitting vigil while the greatest among them roared with agony behind steel walls.

Escaping seemed their only option to keep their pain from overwhelming their control and making them cry out as well.

Turbo opened his mouth to say something, when Mach grabbed his arm and squeezed. "What is your problem, brother?" Mach's eyes were mere slits; his head doing a slow turn as he tried to search for something in the gyrating throng that surrounded them.

"Don't you sense it?"

The two of them stood up, and began to turn around slowly trying to search for the thing enticing their noses. It was a rare smell, one buried in the back of their minds from another time. Home.

Spice and sweet earth; a streamer of memory delved into the deepest parts of their hearts.

Mach had it. Caught underneath the mixture of sweat, spilled beer, alcohol, smoke and the cheap perfume of the females looking for a hook-up for the night, he could smell the mixture of their home and this world. Mach turned to stare at the occupant in the next booth. He knew it was a woman from the smell and the little he could see of her. She was so unlike what usually attracted them it was a surprise.

"Can it really be coming from her?"

He shrugged away his brother's question. "You know it is."

Turbo looked between the female trying to disappear into the cracked vinyl of the booth and his bristling brother. "What do you plan?"

"You with me?"

"Always," Turbo felt a chill of dread in his soul when Mach gave him a slow smile. "Here comes the pain," he muttered to himself.

The two turned from the woman and took one of their favorite waitresses to the side. A few strategic questions gave them all they needed to form a plan. Mach slipped her enough money to pay off her car and he went to the alley to wait for the night to begin. His wolf-like grin was so wide it made his face hurt. It had been a long time since he had a reason to smile.

Hope was definitely a reason to exercise his facial muscles.

Turbo pulled the Range Rover around to the mouth of the alleyway and backed up so it would be easy for them to jump in when they had their quarry.

When the bar's door opened, Mach bit back his shout of triumph as the dowdy girl came wandering out. "Oh," she swallowed nervously as she peered around the darkened passage, "I was looking for my sisters."

"They split," Mach informed her softly.

She stood in the illusionary safety of the pool of light coming from the street. He took a long perusal of her outfit, and quirked his eyebrow. "Tell me," he asked her with deceptive mildness, "are you part of a cult?"

Sally shifted on her comfortable flats, pulling her sweater away from her stomach. "My clothes are chosen for function, not form."

"I would hope so," he mused. "There'd be no other reason to wear them."

He took a few steps to place one hand flat against the door and another on her shoulder, caging her within his arm's reach. "Your sisters wanted me to make sure you got home safe."

"What?" She looked up into the dark of the stranger's face. "Why would they do that? They never have before. I thought they were busy trying to work the investors."

Mach sighed heavily. *I tried to do sneaky. It's just not my style. Straightforward attacks are so more my thing.* His hand moved to the girl's shoulder and he found the nerve cluster he needed. Homo sapiens. So very easy to manage when you had a basic understanding of anatomy. "Sorry about this, love. My brothers and I need you, far more than anyone here. I can only guarantee you'll not be harmed." The look she gave him was empty as she tried to understand why this man was touching her. A sharp pinch and the female crumpled obligingly into his arms. He shrugged as he considered what they were about to do. "Well, not harmed much."

He lifted her up and a few steps ensconced them in the back of the vehicle. Turbo pulled out from behind the club and they were soon rushing down the road to home. "Did you get her name?"

Mach shrugged, "Who cares what her name is? If she cures Drake that's all we need to know."

CHAPTER THREE

The men standing vigil did not reveal how fazed they were by the bellows of pain echoing through the halls. You would have had to look closely to recognize their quandary. One gripped the dagger in his hand so tightly his knuckles were the color of paper, the hilt gaining the imprint of his fingers. It was the frozen stillness of the next that was the most unnerving. Only by peering deep into his eyes, could you see the flames of hell burning there, as he paid witness to the passing of his brother. The others just kept their heads down so none could see the shine of tears in their eyes.

All of them wished they could lighten the tortured man's agony.

Their friend was dying, and there was nothing they could do.

It did not matter that their brother was locked behind six inches of hard steel; they heard his cries as easily as if they had been next to him. It didn't matter what they had been doing before. Their lives would stay frozen at this moment, until their vigil for his passing ended. Together for centuries, they would not abandon one of their own to die by himself. The only reason they did not stand closer was he could take one of them with him as easily as breathing.

"Someone should go in there," Blade muttered.

Groans of frustration came from all of them. This was not the first time they'd had this fight. For Drake, it was going to be the last. Each was trying to hide his sorrow over the brother about to leave them. One who was the last of his kind, not that his clan had ever given him the respect or consideration he was due.

"He's more animal than man now," Luke cautioned Blade. "If he were standing next to us, even he would not suggest it."

"We could still try to find the cure," Stealth suggested.

The harsh laughter of their leader made them all wince. Luke's anger pulsed in the room like a physical cloud that battered against them. "We have been searching for the meaning of our riddle for generations. I am tired of watching the men I call friends die. I am more tired of feeling their pain. Do you think I don't long to return home? Do you believe I prefer this isolated and torturous rote we now call our existence?"

Aquos, Stealth, and Blade's eyes dropped to their feet. There was nothing they could say.

"Glad to hear you feel that way brother," Mach's voice cut through the tension in the room like a scalpel.

Turbo was walking in front of Mach, so it was difficult for them at first to tell what he was carrying. "We found Drake a present," he wrenched open the door and Mach tossed in the woman in his arms. They managed to secure the cell before their brother could get out, or the four others facing them could retrieve their offering. "What the hell have you done," Luke thundered.

"Saved our friend."

When Luke lunged towards Mach, it took all four to keep the two from battling. "If you fight within the Sanctuary, you will bring the wrath of everyone on both sides of the veil down on our heads," Stealth hissed at them.

"Can you go in there without Drake realizing it?"

Stealth shrugged, "You know I can. What do you want me to do?"

The weight of this moment bore down on him as heavily as had the choice to flee to this place in the first days of the devastation. He called up the points of the compact in his mind, and slowly nodded his head. "Keep him from killing her."

"That's all?"

Luke's gaze pierced through Stealth, "If she saves him, it will be the first sign our presence here is not without merit. Keep her living. No matter what. Let the rest play out as the Moirai wish."

"You put a great deal of faith in the hands of some fickle bitches."

"I do what I can for my brother."

The leader looked around the hall at the other men who had joined him in exile centuries ago. When not one gave any form of denial for the plan, he knew he was doing all he could to hold true to his word and still save his people. "For all of my brothers."

With a low bow, Stealth disappeared with a flash of light.

* * *

Sally woke up feeling as if a small truck had run over her, and backed up a few times as well. She had heard hangovers were brutal but this was ridiculous. *What did she have to drink?* The bottle of Jack Daniels she had ordered for the table must have been dumped in her coffee. Either that, or someone slipped her a date rape drug, but that seemed equally improbable.

A roar filled the room, making the floor she lay on start to shake like an earthquake. Not good. *They lived in Pennsylvania, not many earthquakes here.*

Not good at all.

Her eyes opened and she looked into a barrier of solid steel. Her body informed her the floor was more of the same. A slight turn of her head told her brain there was steel above her head as well. She was locked up. *Just what did she do last night, or get involved in?* Her mind remained as blank as the structure around her.

Another roar echoed around the chamber and she swallowed her squeak of terror.

So not good.

Turning her head some more she saw a man. Or at least, what was left of a man. His clothing had been ripped into shreds. He must have done it to himself; she could see the scratches marring the golden expanse of his body. The tattered cloth did not contain the movement of his skin. It was as if millions of worms moved under there. He arched off the floor where he lay, groaning in torment.

Sally used her heels to sit up into a corner of the room. Another squeak of terror slipped past her lips before she could stop it. The last thing she wanted was to attract the attention of whatever was making that man scream.

A rumble of awareness ripped through the male body, and she looked up in open-mouthed astonishment as the form bowing in painful throes across the long and narrow cell leapt up and landed at her feet, crouched on all four limbs. The noises coming from deep within his chest were more animal than human. The long, shaggy midnight hair fell in his face, making it impossible for her to see any of his features. His movements belonged to a mighty predator, his muscles and joints rolling with the power of the deadliest creature. She panted in fear as her mind took stock of the thick limbs and heavy planks of muscle covering every inch of this man. He sniffed her feet, then slowly moved up each of her legs, torso, and paused at her neck. Sally shivered at the sensation of his beard-roughened skin rubbing against hers, something she could feel with ease, even through her clothes.

His face nestled closer to her skin as he took slow, deep breaths of her scent.

Sally was torn between being turned on and insulted.

She felt the caress of a tongue lick at her jugular, and she shuddered. She assured herself there were no such things as vampires — no matter how much she liked reading about them. Her entire library was romance and fantasy books, with a heavy emphasis on dragons. The only thing that could be better was a fantasy book about vampires and dragons. Ok, *Sally... let's try to focus on the wild man now.* Another long slow lick at her neck, a burning hot tongue that felt rough like a cat's, and she almost had an orgasm. She was not so desperate that some crazy wild man was going to send her heart racing and body heating, she tried to assure herself. *Okay, she was that desperate, but she didn't have to admit that right now, did she?*

A slight press of teeth made her shake, "Please," she whispered. "Please don't hurt me."

The roar that ripped through the man was more about his own affront over her plea than pain. He did another one of those jaw-dropping leaps across the cell and huddled in the farthest corner from her. "Not. An. Animal."

She folded her legs underneath the drape of her skirt as she kept her eyes glued to him. "What's wrong with you?"

He fell forward as he clasped his arms around his knees. She swallowed with empathy as his misery tugged at her heart as little else could. The brief flashes Sally could see of his face, she could tell he was now clenching his jaw to keep his cries within. All to keep from scaring her. "Why isn't anyone here helping you?"

"No help." His cut off sob wrenched whatever fear she felt out of her soul. "No hope."

She inched her way closer to him, her heart thundering in her ears like an oncoming train. "There's always hope."

"Please," his voice broke as he tried to take in a deep breath, "stay away."

"You're hurting," she cocked her head to the side as she took her courage in hand. "I can't just sit back and watch."

"I could kill you."

"Believe me," her laugh was a harsh sound that was a contrast to the kindness of her smile. "There are worse things than death."

"Not to me," he backed away from the woman.

His continued attempts to protect her tugged at her heart as nothing else could, sending an open wave of emotion to him. She never could resist someone or something in pain. "What happened to you?"

He eyed her through the strands of his hair. "I am holding on for now, but can't for much longer."

"Let me help you."

"You are either very stupid or disturbingly brave."

Sally laughed low and gently, a sound she didn't know she could make. "I've heard the first one most of my life, but never the second." Reaching his side she could not resist extending her palm to smooth the wayward locks from his forehead. His face was on fire, and he was covered with sweat. The beads on his skin felt like oil against her fingertips. "Don't you have family?"

"My brothers," he said, as a low pained moan escaped his lips. "They are nearby."

"They should be here. By your side. Healing you."

He turned his head away as if her words wounded him. "Can't."

"Bull," she swallowed back any more of the words she considered spitting out at his relatives. It wasn't her business. It just hurt because their abandonment reminded her of her own siblings.

"So fierce," he mumbled.

"I guess I should apologize," she offered begrudgingly.

"I like fierce." His body writhed and he was thrown onto his back as if an attacker had flipped him. As he danced across the floor, locked in the pain of the disease gripping him, Sally tried to understand what she could do. When the episode seemed to subside, he turned onto his stomach and moaned softly.

It was then she saw the wound.

There was a deep puncture on the back of his neck. It looked fresh, almost raw. The red streaks shooting out from the hole told her this had to be the source of a serious infection. Green and yellow puss oozed out of the mark whenever he moved. A trace of sulfur burned her nose.

"Okay, here's the deal." Her voice was husky with a combination of terror and hope. "I'm about to try to help you, but I would really appreciate it if you wouldn't kill me. The truth is that I haven't managed to do much in my life, and would like more of a shot at some excitement before I'm dead."

Hell, even some happiness would be a nice change, she thought.

When there was no answer she made a quick prayer. As she brushed her fingers across the injury she could feel a hard substance underneath the skin. "Please be like the lion in that kid's story," she muttered.

"I. Am. No. Lion."

Her eyebrows rose at the affront in his voice. "Okay," she patted his shoulder, "no need to get all pissy." The growl at this statement made her smile. "I'm going to have to lean against this and it's going to hurt. So I am going to repeat my prayer that you not kill me."

She received another growl for her efforts. As Sally tried to press against the sides of the mark, she hoped getting out whatever was stuck in there was like removing a splinter. In her work she'd had plenty of experience with that.

When she felt the thorn start to move Sally let out the breath she'd been holding. He flinched at the feeling of her soft burst of air brushing against his skin.

More pressure wasn't making much difference, so she crawled over him to get better leverage. Sally ignored the rush of adrenalin she felt at the male body she could barely straddle between her knees. There was so much heat coming off him, and she was always cold. It was as if she had found a living-breathing heater that wouldn't singe her. She could feel his muscles spasm as she continued to work at the wound. Sally tried humming to soothe him, hoping he'd continue to control his response, and not kill her in a seizure of pain or confusion.

When the head of a dark object appeared in the hole, Sally leaned her elbows against his skin to grasp it with her fingers. Her nails were groomed into perfect square tips, the only sign of vanity she usually allowed herself.

Pulling out the thorn, she winced as she saw the five inches of razor sharp plant matter. There was a flood of pus when the object was removed. Pushing on the skin around it again she kept up the pressure until the viscous fluid turned into a healthy bright red blood. Tearing off her slip, she wadded it up to cover the wound. The cotton was at least clean, and that was the best she could offer. "Now let's hope you didn't just save the life of some serial killer, Sally."

"You talk too much," he gritted through his teeth.

Sally put the object next to the man's head. "That's what was wrong," she chided him. "This thing is so huge it was probably stuck in your spinal column." A single golden eye popped open to stare at the thorn lying near him.

In a sudden surge of outrage and betrayal, the man roared as he leapt to his feet. She could not have foretold his reaction to the display of the dart, so she never had a chance to get off his body. Her head made a loud cracking sound that echoed through the cell as she was catapulted into the steel wall. Sally slipped into the encompassing darkness to escape the pain she knew was coming.

CHAPTER FOUR

Luke collapsed to the floor as the final sounds of his brother's life came surging out of the cell. "It's over," he muttered.

All of the men's eyes shone in the darkness with their unshed tears. Another had fallen.

"We can't just stand around here and wait to die as well," Mach swore.

Turbo clasped his friend's shoulder, "None of us wish that."

"The burial ritual must come first." Blade reminded them with a voice as old as the mountains shielding the valley.

A knock made them pause in dividing the onerous duties before them. Luke looked around the hall. "What the hell is that?"

Stealth appeared before the others and gave a wide smile. "I've got good news and bad."

"Speak," Luke ordered.

"Our brother lives and I think we'd better let him out before he rips apart the isolation cell."

"Good and bad news together," Turbo joked. "Usually you make us work for it."

The door swung open and a sweaty, tattered Drake stood in the opening with a harsh glower. "We have a betrayer."

Stealth pointed to Drake with a wry smile, "That was the bad news."

Mach and Turbo shared a high five. "It worked."

"I will deal with the two of you later," Luke growled at them and made their smiles disappear.

Drake looked at the two youngest of the band, "How did you know?"

"She smelled like home," Mach explained.

"We knew we had to try," Turbo filled in.

"You have my clan's appreciation."

"Now the woman has done her work, she is to be returned." Luke's order was met with blank shock from the other men. "She is not one of us," he pointed out to them all. "She has no place here."

"I'll return her, when I'm done with her." Drake folded his arms across his chest as he stared at the ruler of Light.

Turbo stepped in to try to diffuse the simmering anger, "She doesn't belong there either."

"What do you mean?"

"She smells like home," Mach explained.

"If she belonged here, she would reek of the homo sapiens. Her smell is more indistinct. A combination of both."

"Did you know there could be half breeds," Blade questioned his leader.

"We were given no such data."

The others looked between them, hoping for some form of direction to guide their course. Drake decided it was time to make his feelings quite clear on the subject. "I will return the woman when I am ready," he informed his brothers with a quiet dignity incongruous with his devastated look. "No sooner or later."

"She is not your answer," Luke reminded him.

"I know that." Drake's stare was so hot it felt like a blade slicing through each of their stomachs. "Nevertheless, I am keeping her. If any of you have a problem with that, then my clan shall remove itself from the Sanctuary compact, and go our own way. This is not a negotiation."

They each allowed their eyes to slide from Drake as if they felt guilt for their thoughts. Drake's clan was one of the cruelest in their world. They could not imagine what this woman's fate might be.

Luke shrugged, his burdens once more making him sigh. *He was so tired of this. Running the Sanctuary compact was never meant to be his life, and yet here he was.* "Very well. The woman is yours, but you will return her to her people eventually, Drake, or the dragon clan shall bear the responsibility for your crime."

"Agreed." He stepped into the cell and lifted the woman into his arms; holding her close to his chest. Pausing in the doorway, his gaze seared each of his brothers as he let them see his continued rage. "Find the betrayer," he ordered them. "The proof is inside."

* * *

Drake flew through the halls, not caring what actions his brothers chose to take. His body was already expelling the poison tipped on the dart. As long as the delivery device was in his body there was no chance for it to heal. The girl's removal of it had saved him. It was his soul he needed to tend now. The woman pressed to his chest was just the answer to that need. She could not have braved him during his rage otherwise.

He pressed his face into the magical smell of her hair. "You are mine now, love. I only hope you agree.

Not that I plan on giving you any choice."

CHAPTER FIVE

The next time Sally woke up, it was the complete opposite of the last time she'd opened her eyes. A red brocade drapery hung from the carved posters of the massive bed where she lay. It was covered with sheets and pillows with a thread count so high she doubted she had ever even known such a thing was possible. The crimson chenille duvet was what she imagined being covered by a silken cloud would feel like. She could smell cloves and sage, tickling her nose and relaxing her lungs. Stretching in the warm cocoon, a slow satisfied smile spread across her face.

"That's a sight a man wishes to see each rising."

She began to sit straight up at the sound of the male voice brimming with amusement, but realized she was naked. Stark naked. That never happened before. Sally was sure her face was the same color as the bed hangings. Pulling the duvet over her shoulders she lifted her head enough to peer at the stranger with outrage. "Who are you?"

Drake made a rumbling noise from the back of his throat as her voice brushed over his skin like a seductive caress.

She was better than he imagined.

He never thought it would be possible.

Sally managed to get to a sitting position, while pulling the blanket up to her chin. "Why are you in my room?"

"This is my room, woman, and my bed."

"Fine," she snapped. "Why am I in your room?"

"And my bed."

"Semantics right now are not appreciated." Sally's voice was acerbic and she didn't care.

"I think the fact you're in my bed is very important."

She spotted the man across the room and swallowed several times to keep her mouth from falling open and panting with open need. *God, he was gorgeous. Not the so pretty he must be gay kind of hot, but more smoking hot, oh please tie him to my bedpost for three days, kind of hot.* His hair was to his shoulders and the color of ebony. His face was a cross of cowboy rugged and Greek god perfection. His body belonged to a warrior and was covered by skin proclaiming him as someone who lived in the sun.

It was his eyes that were familiar. The golden orbs, making her think of antique jewelry, were of her patient. "I know who you are," she whispered.

Drake grabbed her ankle and wrenched her down to lie flat ... where she belonged ... under him. A leap onto the bed, and he nestled in the cradle of her softness before she could do more than squeak. His body surged with need, hardening from shoulder to toe, as her form welcomed his weight. "And I know you," he purred. He pressed his lips to her neck, savoring the taste of her skin. "You are all honey and cream, my heart. You belong in my bed, in my room, and by my side at all times."

"I don't even know your name."

"Call me Drake," he purred, licking her again. "And I shall call you, mine."

Sally mentally reminded herself she was an independent, strong woman who deserved to be more than a mattress, but who was panting like a nymphomaniac. *Get a grip Sally*, she yelled inside of her mind, *we don't know what this is about, but no good comes from going after someone so hot. Time for a good dose of reality. Or at least a great number of anti-depressants to stop this hallucination.* "My name is Sally. You can call me a cab."

He chuckled and settled deeper into the comfort of her bounty. Drake growled low again as his body appreciated the way her female curves gave to the steel thrust of his. He already had a baseball bat between his legs and he could feel it move as it sought entrance to the haven they both knew was so close. A slow lick along her neck made his mouth buzz with longing for tastes of her body's other delights. "No cabs," he chuckled. "Not a one."

"There's always a cab, if you pay enough."

"I'll buy all the cab companies if it will keep you here."

"You look different," she gasped, as her entire being began to turn into a mass of pulsing need.

"I showered. You have slept for hours, my heart."

"That's what being knocked unconscious does to you."

Open-mouthed kisses ran up and down her jaw, taking considerable time on the spot behind her ear that was the most sensitive. "You have my eternal sorrow I caused you even a moment of pain, my heart. Will you forgive me?"

"You're forgiven." Sally turned her head to avoid his lips and shifted away from him. "Let me go."

"There are so many other things I would rather do." He moved again and stilled her escape efforts by a mere shift of his weight. It would be better if she understood a few truths at the beginning. He was strength. She was meant to be the softness in contrast to his power. "Stop struggling, woman. We should start out slow at first."

"I helped you," she whispered. "I deserve better than to get raped."

Drake's head fell to the pillow beside her cheek and took one last, regretful, deep breath of her scent. "You are right." He leapt off her, needing the distance to keep his body from overruling his empathy for her fear. "No harm shall come to you in this place, Sally. You are safe here."

She sat up once more, mounding the stack of pillows behind her. "I think I should go home."

He crouched by the wall, his eyes riveted to her face, taking in every nuance and response. "It would be my greatest pleasure, nay honor, if you should stay. No one shall interfere with you or cause you harm."

"Why?" Sally tried to clear her throat to loosen up the hoarse croak it had become. "Why me?"

"Verily, woman, have I searched for one such as you for thousands of years."

Sally's head fell forward to rest against her palms. "I must be dreaming."

He reached out a single hand, palm up. The entreaty in his eyes smote whatever defenses she had built around her heart. "Then dream with me, Sally. The rest of the world shall continue with its nightmare."

How could he know ... she cut off that line of thinking with a strength of will she didn't realize she had. There was no way he knew the truth of her home life. "What are the rules if I stay?" His eyebrow quirked, and a slow smile spread across his lips with the answers he had at his disposal. She put her hand up to keep him from responding. "I need to understand what you expect."

Drake eyed her as he considered the clothing he had stripped from her body before putting her in his bed. "Tell me something, Sally. When was the last time you did anything without worrying about the rules?"

Her eyes glittered like new grass as the tears sprung out. "Never."

"So why don't you start?" *Honest too*, Drake cocked his head. She was the bravest creature he had met in millennia. Her body was a bountiful amusement park that he was looking forward to playing in for months. Strike that. He would play for years, if he had his way. This woman was an unfolding turn on. "I give you my word on two things: you shall find neither pain, nor shame, in my bed."

"What if I don't sleep with you?"

He did another one of those breath-stopping jumps onto the bed and landed by her side. Drake cupped her cheek and licked the side of her neck, enjoying the dance of her pulse against his tongue. "We shall do little sleeping in my bed."

Sally pushed him aside and smiled when she realized he'd let her do so. "There will be none of that."

"You have the right to say stop, love." Drake grabbed her hand and pressed his hot lips against her knuckles. "I retain the power to decide when to start."

"You're about to hear 'no' a lot."

He chuckled and turned her hand over to nibble at the sensitive underside of her wrist. "I am sure I will, right before you climax." Her eyes closed and she swallowed several times as she tried to come up with some kind of retort. "And you will climax, Sally-mine. Again. Again. Again and again." Drake moved her arm so he could lick his way up to the shoulder that was bound to lead to even better locations. "Stay with me, Sally-mine."

"I don't even know your name," she gasped.

"Drake." As her mouth opened to say something else he covered her lips to take his seduction to the next level. "'Tis the second time I told you. Perhaps your brain is focused on something else?" He licked at the seam of her lips until his tongue could gain entrance to the moist cavern. He dueled with her, and longed to allow the lower part of his anatomy to do the same. She was addicting already. Tasting of ambrosia for him, his favorite food from home, the kiss grew more passionate. Soon he sensed her light-headedness, so he gave her his breath.

His soul soon followed.

"Nice to meet you Drake," she managed to groan before he covered her mouth once again. She had no resistance at this point to his gentle persuasion. Sally felt her hands go around his neck and she arched into the comforting weight of his body. She began to kiss him back, happy he made no notice of her obvious inexperience.

"Do you agree?" He pressed each word into the heated perfume of her jaw.

Sally swallowed several times, trying to get some of her blood running into the logical part of her mind. He wanted to know if she would stay, she reminded herself. *Get a grip, Sally. You keep acting like this much of an idiot and you are going to get in trouble. More than you already have.* "Yeah, I think I can do that." She winced at how ridiculous her attempt to be nonchalant sounded.

"Beware, lass," Drake outlined the shell of her ear with the tip of his tongue, "there is no going back on your word in the Sanctuary."

"I don't go back on my word. Anywhere."

He hid his smile of triumph against her hair. "Then you are sworn?"

She smiled as she considered how much she loved the way he talked. It was as if he'd fallen out of her favorite romance story. He certainly looked like he could be on the cover of one. "Consider me sworn."

Drake covered her lips for a kiss, equal parts triumph and possession.

Promising herself she would stop him as soon as she had enjoyed a few more of his luscious kisses, Sally settled in and allowed him freedom with her mouth. If a girl was going to have a serious make-out session it might as well be with a cover boy. He wasn't even gay. When Drake's hand began to move up her side she winced at the reminder of who she was. What she was. She was the overweight ugly sister of the enchanting Robin and Dawn. This man couldn't want her, no matter what she might be feeling between her legs, and pulsing across her thigh and stomach.

Oh wow. She didn't know they made guys like this anymore. Or you know ... like, ever.

Wrenching her mouth away she scrubbed her lips with shaking hands. "Please stop."

He made a leap from her body to land lightly on his feet at the foot of the bed. "I told you, sweet. You have only to say the word and I shall respond."

She wondered how he liked the word *more*. Or *harder*. Or *don't stop ever or I'll kill you. Oops. That was a lot more than a word.* Sally pulled her trembling body up to rest against the pillows piled at the headboard. Her dexterity at keeping the duvet high was a sign of how deep her shame ran. "Look," she swallowed so hard Drake could hear it, "you don't have to do this. I'll leave. I don't know if this is some kind of bet you lost, or a pity thing, but I'll just sneak out now and no one will know."

His eyes blazed the color of rubies and reminded her of the fires of hell. Drake shook his entire body to return them to the sherry color she was familiar with. "You stay."

"I don't mind going. You're under no responsibility for me."

"You are," he grabbed the posts of the bed so tight Sally could swear she heard the wood crack. "I warned you, Sally-mine. You gave me your word. Sanctuary does not allow you to go back."

"Why would you want me?"

"I promise to explain one day." Again she was stunned to see his eyes had changed to an orange color, reminding her of a tangerine. "You will not leave me. Say the words."

Sally was not sure, but she thought she caught a glimpse of extreme insecurity in the set of his jaw and shoulders. She bit at her lower lip as she tried to decide what to do. It was true. Her entire life had been dedicated to doing what was right for everyone else but her. Maybe just this once she should try something different. If it destroyed her, at least she could console herself with the fact she'd tried. "I will not leave."

He grunted his approval at her acquiescence. "You should rest."

When he took a step away she held out a hand to make him pause. "Where are you going?"

"If I am here for much longer I will want to get inside of you."

Her eyes widened with the shock of his statement as she blinked for several times trying desperately to process what he'd said. "Oh."

"When I return, I shall feed you."

That was a first for her. I mean, she hadn't ever dreamt of a man saying that to her, much less hearing it in person. "Most guys would say I could skip a few meals."

"I am not a guy."

As she watched the door close, Sally released a deep sigh. She collapsed against the pillows, her body exhausted in a way she hadn't known was possible. "More like a god," she muttered.

The room was a feast for the senses, and it was obviously designed by someone who savored everything sensual and seductive. This wasn't a dream. This was a hallucination. It was a slice of heaven or a bedroom from a temple on Mount Olympus. It even went beyond her idea of nirvana. "What have you gotten yourself into this time," she muttered.

"And how in hell are you going to get over it when he kicks you out?"

CHAPTER SIX

Drake kept moving until he made it to the Sanctuary council room. The chamber was hewn from the bedrock beneath the main house. It was a large space, forty-four square feet. There were small round daises set at equal degrees in a circle around the perimeter, the center filled with the tesseract which should have enabled his people to freely travel through the dimensional veils. When he had opened the portal to allow the Clan Lords to escape, the dragons had taken away his powers. Now they kept the portal guarded at all times, praying it would open one day and allow them to go home.

This was the reason all of the clans treated this spot as the holiest on this side of the veil.

He found his brothers where he'd expected. Each stood on their clan's platform as they held the conference over this unforeseen threat. They were not accustomed to working as one. There was no peace in this room. It was as if you could see the air's stress over the uneasy truce between ancient enemies. "What have you decided?"

Luke was the one who spoke, though he looked to the others first for confirmation. "Is there any chance you're wrong?"

"You saw the dart."

Blade sighed, "Our fearless leader is trying to explain the threat could be for the dragon clan and not the Sanctuary."

"So you abandon me a second time."

"That's unfair," Mach cried, "we were devastated at the thought of your loss."

"I declare there to be a threat to our compact."

"Is it from you," Stealth asked tightly.

Drake's jaw tightened at the slur cast against his honor. "I would never do such a thing. The fact you think otherwise saddens me. If the Sanctuary is no longer open to the dragons, I will go."

"Then you leave the woman behind."

"She goes with me," his eyes flashed red and glowed like a neon light.

Turbo shook his head, "I thought your kind stopped eating virgins."

"Nah, brother," Mach chuckled. "They just save them for dessert."

"The girl is mine," Drake folded his arms over his chest. "None of you shall interfere or see her."

"Why can't we see her?" Luke paled as the possibilities filled his mind. "By the Oracle's heart, brother, what have you done to the girl? She seemed harmless enough. Mach and Turbo said she isn't even pretty."

Drake's eyes grew brighter, and his threatening growl echoed through the room. "Should I hear any of you repeat such words, I will gut you."

"Okay," Luke drawled. "I guess we have our first guest."

"There is another issue here," Stealth reminded them with his quiet way. All eyes snapped to his face. He wasn't known as a vocal contributor at these meetings, and was prone to stay even quieter when the issue dealt with the dragons. The animosity between the two families was one of the oldest and most virulent. "Drake's guest reeks of home. The first woman any of has found with such a scent."

Blade cleared his throat. "We were each given a riddle to solve when we decided to come here. The Oracle promised the answer would be the key to resurrecting our world."

"What's your point?" Mach interrupted.

"We never considered the answer might be people and not things."

"What does that mean?"

The others shrugged to Turbo's question. It was a good one. None of them had any answers. "Perhaps its time to ask the Oracle," Blade suggested.

"Nej," Luke shook his head.

"You are the only one who can go," Turbo prodded their leader.

"I do not care."

The other men sighed as Luke glowered at each of them in turn. Stealth could see pushing him was not going to work. "We could try to speak with one of the guardians of this planet," he suggested.

"They've been so helpful in the past," Mach drawled.

"Do we have any other choice?"

Turbo watched with satisfaction as each of them shrugged their approval of this path. "Look, this world may not be perfect, but there is still life here. We were the last children born to our planet. If there is a chance, even the slimmest hope, that there are some women here who could exist in our world ... women who could bear children, healthy babes, and thereby resurrect our civilization for all the clans ... is there any plan we shouldn't pursue?"

"What would you have of me?" Luke rubbed his eyes, trying to push away the hopelessness he sensed on each of the paths before them.

Drake hid his frustration. This was always the way. The one clan Luke would not listen to was the dragon. He would take counsel from all others. It was only when it came time for destruction that he'd be called.

He wanted more.

He deserved it.

"So fearless leader, what's your decision?"

"We split up." When all of the other men waited for more instructions, Luke allowed himself a small grim smile. Perhaps the compact and Sanctuary had begun to change them. When they first arrived in this world, any such pronouncement would have been met by loud debate. They were so lacking in trust, the mere thought of separating would have had them running for their weapons. "Stealth and Blade shall investigate the possibility there are some of our women living in this world. Turbo and Mach shall focus on detecting whatever and whoever might be trying to harm us."

"What of you and Drake?"

Luke shrugged, "Drake will be occupied with his toy."

Drake considered taking umbrage at Luke calling Sally his toy, but chose to pick the battles he fought with more wisdom. There was one more in their midst that had not been given an assignment. "And Aquos?"

Looking at the final member of their contingent Luke could not hold back his sigh of frustration. "I do not dictate to him."

"That's because he can't catch me."

The others laughed at how true this statement was.

Aquos waited until their amusement died down before announcing his choice, "I shall protect the Sanctuary." Turning to Luke he couldn't resist asking, "And you?"

"I shall be considering how to discuss this with the Oracle."

Drake joined his brothers in the middle of the room as they watched Luke depart with his head so far forward, it was as if his neck had been broken. "Should one of us go with him?"

"He wouldn't welcome us."

"True that, Stealth. Still, I wish I could help."

Mach nodded his head to Turbo's comment. "Can't be easy being Luke."

"When your mother is a god, you've got to have some childhood issues."

The five of them laughed deeply as they made their way through the underground passages to the house above them. When Sanctuary was designed it was placed in the heart of forty untouched acres in the center of

Pennsylvania. The structure was designed in the pattern of a star, with each of the six wings belonging to a different clan. That way, their preferred habitats could exist within the one building, without infringing on one of the other's territory.

It was far more effective than their previous choice of living in separate homes on islands off different coasts of Europe.

Much more convenient, too.

The main hub was designed for them to play and train as a team. It was also where their servants, the elementals from home, slept. This co-living had formed more bonds between them than generations of inter-marriage and coalition treaties. It was the greatest irony that just when their culture had collapsed, and their way had slid into the nothingness of the ruin, they had finally found a way to get along.

Entering the living room, each of the men sprawled in a different chair to put their feet up on a cushioned stool set in the middle. The seven-foot flat screen television was clicked on, and Turbo found a football game they could watch. He left it on mute so they could still talk.

Violence. One thing they all had in common.

Blade looked at the two men that lived for all things fast. "So. How do you plan on finding our enemy?"

"No clue," Turbo shrugged.

One of the servants brought in the first of many trays of food for the men to enjoy. Mach snagged the bowl of kettle corn and began to munch out. "Why Luke chose us to play detective is a mystery."

"You got any direction on how to find us some more women?"

Blade shook his head at Turbo's query. He looked at Drake with a considering frown, "Your toy might be able to help us."

"She has sisters," Mach inserted recalling what he had learned at the bar.

Drake winced as he recalled the snippets of Sally's family he had picked up from the flashes of memories he had taken from her mind. "Not a possibility." When the others frowned at him, he shook his head. "It's really not. The two are naught more than vipers. If they were as she is, I would have found it in her thoughts."

"They would also have cared when we kidnapped her," Turbo added.

"Speaking of which," Drake looked for a long time at the two men that had brought him his missing half. "My clan has much to thank you for. Your actions saved my life and brought me something I needed."

Mach was the one who answered for them both, "You owe us naught; we did no more or less than you would for us."

"Still," Drake rose, considering what he should bring to his woman. "You have our thanks. I shall leave you to your conference. Your success might mean the difference between life and death for our world. I would suggest you get started."

"Remember, dragon. You gave your word you would release the girl to her family."

The smile he gave them made each of the men's breath freeze. This was the legendary beast that still put a cold knife of fear through their hearts. "I never said I would leave her there. Sally shall be returned to her clan, but if I have chosen her as my mate, I'll get her back. Never doubt that a dragon protects its treasure."

He would have found it comforting to know he left the four men each nodding their heads with approval at his announcement. They would do no less.

CHAPTER SEVEN

Sally had investigated every space, drawer and cupboard in the room and come to several conclusions. There was no sign of the clothing she had worn when she had left her house this evening.

There was also no way of getting out of the chamber.

She couldn't budge the one door she'd tried to open. Years of watching crime shows had taught her little in the ways of picking a lock.

The one possible escape route she identified was the fireplaces. There were four in the room and she considered trying to climb up through the chimney. This would have to be a last option, only used in the most desperate of situations. For one, they were really narrow and she knew there had to be a flue somewhere she would have to navigate around. *Like she would fit.* For two, she had no idea how to climb.

"Like I said," she muttered to the empty room. "Last most desperate option."

She sat on the bed with the top sheet wrapped around her in a cross between a toga and a shroud. *I can't believe he saw me in my white bra and granny-panty set. That embarrassing moment was not going to be dealt with until I have ice cream cake nearby.* She adjusted the folds of the sheet to cover her as much as possible. No reason to make the man nauseous when he reappeared. She needed him to be in a good mood and open to letting her go.

Right. Because staying one minute more in this luxurious sensual feast was too close to torture.

If she kept reminding herself of that she might actually start to believe it.

The door opened and Sally cursed. *He was as beautiful as she remembered. Bastard.* "Hello."

Drake paused in the doorway and smiled. It would have been better if she'd been lying in the bed with nothing on, but he'd take this as well. She was like a present he was eager to unwrap. He held out the delicacies he'd assembled for her. "I brought some food."

She uneasily eyed the tray that was as large as her dining room table. It was more food than she would serve her family of five. "That's for me?"

"It is." When she looked down in shame he set the tray on the dresser and moved to her, "What's wrong?"

"I'm not that fat," she whispered.

He recoiled as if she had struck him. *Why did she think he was complaining about her size? Any smaller and he would fear crushing her.* He sat next to her and tried not to be insulted when she shifted away from the press of his leg. "The standard of beauty in this country would have been insulting to my kind. You look like a healthy weight to me, and that's all that counts."

"Most men wouldn't look at me twice."

"I personally have never dreamt of having sex with a plank of wood."

She giggled and slapped her hands over her mouth. Drake smiled at her and let one eyebrow rise. Sally let loose a long series of chuckles that he soon joined. He hid the flare of triumph he felt when she leaned her body against him. She felt like a cold trickle of water against his burning skin. She was so cool on the outside and warm inside. He had never met a woman with fire in her heart that could hold up to the dragon's flames. "You're bad," she teased.

He turned and began to nibble at her neck, heading to her ear. "Let me take you to bed and you'll find out just how very good I can be."

She couldn't keep herself from turning into him and giving him greater access. "Please," she whispered. "If this is a dream, never let me wake up." A hand cupped her cheek and turned her face so her mouth could be captured by a kiss that burned through all her reservations and fears. As she gave herself up to the wave of passion lifting her, Sally began to hear the voices in her head.

The voices of her siblings.

Each statement over the years cut the sensual haze this dream-man was wrapping around her like a sharp knife. "Who would ever want you?" "Why are you so fat?" "Why can't you do something with your looks?"

She broke away from his hold and backed up until she was pressed against one of the walls. When it looked like he was going to follow her, Sally held up her hands at him. "Please stop." His gaze was far too knowing and sure for her peace of mind. She let her knees give out and she slid down the wall, covering her eyes with her hands. "I can't do this. I just can't do this."

He rose and placed the tray on a table, drawing up two chairs. Drake lit candles through the room and bath, letting his woman have some time to get herself together. When he had the chambers arranged with a romantic glow, he moved back to her side.

Sally looked up at him when she felt a hand rest on her knee. "Quite a turn on, huh? I knew I had self esteem issues, I just didn't know it was this bad."

Drake cupped her elbows and guided her to her feet. Moving her closer to him, he wrapped his body around her. Resting his cheek against the silk of her hair he rubbed his palm up and down her back. He had to clear his throat several times to get words past the lump her distress had put there. "Your issues, as you call them, do not scare me. I think there is a treasure in you. One I would hold most dear."

"I don't know what I think about you."

He brushed a kiss against her forehead. "I believe you think far too much."

Her chuckle made him smile. "No argument here."

"You have a choice, my lady," Drake leaned back so he could look deep in her eyes. "We could stand here and wallow in fear and insecurity, or we could put it aside, and enjoy the meal."

Sally shifted away from him. "I'm not hungry."

He chuckled at the squeak she made when he tightened his arms around her and lifted. "You are not telling the truth."

"I really shouldn't eat this late."

Drake tried to hide his frustration over her belief her size was an issue. "Sally-mine, it is a few moments before dawn. It would honor me beyond measure if you allowed me to feed you. Do not insult me to refuse."

She bent her head to rest her forehead against his shoulder and prevent those penetrating eyes from delving too far into her soul. *Well, too much farther.* "I'm a real pain."

"No, love. You are a treasure. Just one that's been knocked around a bit."

When her eyes met his, he let her see his flare of triumph. Sally giggled and released a deep sigh. "Breakfast sounds great."

* * *

Drake could not resist twirling her around and joined her laughter. Her enjoyment in anything made his body harden and his mind flare. His nose was almost twitching as he kept catching different tones and notes in her scent. *I bet I look like a damned rabbit.* He regretfully settled her in her own chair. At home she would be in his lap, and he would get to feed her by hand. Here, he did not know the rules or what her expectation might be. The mightiest and most powerful creatures of his home were answerable only to their mates, God, and their clan.

In that order.

Lifting the silver covers from the dishes, Drake was glad the elemental that prepared the tray had seen to it there was plenty to choose from. "I did not know what you would like."

Sally hid her shock what was before her could rival a buffet on a five-star luxury cruise. "Do you eat like this all the time?"

"No. This is only a snack to my friends and me."

"Who would they be exactly?"

Drake clenched his teeth as he resisted the impulse to bellow his insistence she never see them. Mach and Turbo with their humor, Luke with looks that made even men's jaws drop; any of the others could take her away. Stealth, who had a mind that surprised even their kind, and Aquos, with his shy withdrawn charm. He'd kill them first, but the mere thought she might prefer one of them to him was unacceptable.

Breaking the ice, Sally picked up Drake's plate and began to fill it. He took it from her and growled. "You are not here to serve me."

"I thought if you'd eat you might be able to pay attention to my questions."

He put his plate down and picked up hers. "My friends are no concern of yours."

She dropped her gaze at his words. Fine. Once again she was an embarrassment. *Go hide in your closet Sal; no one wants to see the slob.* Looking up she swallowed painfully and then realized he was about to pile her plate with some sliced steak. "I don't eat anything that bleeds red."

Drake looked at the steak and then at her in confusion. "How do you live?"

Taking her plate away from him, giggling, Sally finished it from the vegetables and grains. "It's not really difficult."

"I do not understand why you live in such a manner."

She shrugged as she set the plate down. "It's not hard. I like to grow things. Seemed like a natural way to live, eat only what you've raised or made. You should see my garden. It's like paradise."

A vision of scorched and barren earth filled his mind. *She would hate his home.*

"I don't care if you eat meat in front of me. I made the choice for myself; no one else has to join in."

"My apologies," he spoke gruffly as her kindness struck him anew, "you surprised me."

"You must not date often," she joked. "I don't know many women today who don't live on sushi and lettuce."

"I believe I established my opinion of sleeping with wood boards."

She smiled as she shook her head. When Drake lowered his head to pray over his food, she followed suit. As they began to eat, she noticed his manners were impeccable and formal. "Do you live here with many others?

And are you married?" Looking around the sensual bedroom she scowled, "You'd better not be married."

"I am not mated." He caught her hand and raised it to his lips. "Not that your jealousy does not please me."

"I'm not jealous," she snatched her hand away from him, "much."

He chuckled and retrieved her hand to brush another kiss against it. "My friends each have their own wing in Sanctuary - what we call this place. It would be better for many if you did not meet them."

"Right." Sally's eyes dropped to her food but she pushed it around with a heavy heart.

Drake didn't understand her change in mood. He kept stealing glances at her from beneath his lashes. They finished dinner in silence, though Sally barely touched her food. When he uncovered the dish of tiramisu she reeled away from it as if it had bitten her. "You do not like this?"

"I'm full."

He sighed. Realizing his being patient was not helping the situation, he gave into his true nature. Standing up, he wrenched Sally from the chair and sat in it. She gave him a dumbfounded look, which Drake met with a winsome smile. "I do not understand what is wrong." He picked Sally up and settled her in his lap. "Now," Drake pushed Sally's head down onto his shoulder and wrapped his arms around her, "speak."

"Let me go."

"No."

"Drake, this whole thing is insane."

"No." When she started to pick up her head to look at him, he moved it back to the place he liked best. "Outside is insane. What I feel for you is natural and right. I am a bit behind what most men you know are like, Sally-mine. Please tell me what I have done wrong."

"I was kidnapped."

"Not by me," Drake shrugged. "Though I cannot say I regret the choice of my friends."

"They should have left me alone."

"If they had I would be dead."

"Why is that exactly?"

"The men where I am from have been struck down by an illness. We have been so far away from our home for so long we grow ill and die. None of my brothers can tend those who grow ill, in fear of catching the disease. If you had not pulled the dart with the poison from my skin I would have died. Alone. Screaming in agony. Is that what you would have preferred for me?"

"No. Of course not." She swallowed and released a heavy sigh. Sally shifted in his arms and felt the clear evidence against her butt, her proximity was affecting him. *If all that was him, she should definitely be running for the hills.* "Just let me go, Drake."

"Sally-mine, if I truly thought that was what you wanted, I would."

"Why do you want me to stay?"

"Something in me has been broken for a very long time. All I can explain is you healed a part of me when we met. I'm not willing to return you to your life, when you have done so much for me."

Rather than relaxing her, this just made her stiffen more. "You don't owe me anything."

"Sally-mine, I think there is no other woman in all the universe that would ever be able to accept me. I owe you everything for that alone."

"What's so horrible about you? Really Drake, you look like a Calvin Klein model."

"Is that good?"

She struggled to get off his lap at this comment, feeling like he was making fun of her.

Drake squashed her efforts with little movement. "What? What is it I said?"

"How can you not know what a Calvin Klein model looks like? Their underwear ads are everywhere you turn."

"I don't wear underwear."

When that statement froze her as if she had fallen into an iceberg's run-off, he turned her head to look into his eyes. "Sally-mine, I don't know your rules. Your standards. Outer beauty means nothing to me. Courage. Kindness. Intelligence." Drake leaned forward so he could nibble behind her ears. "Passion," he whispered the word in a low guttural voice sending chills dancing over her spine. "Those are the qualities that last through the centuries. That is how we choose our mates."

"Why do you keep talking like you are from some ancient country?" Sally was very proud she managed to ask the question in a reasonable voice.

Drake had to blink several times as he tried to come up with the words needed to answer her query. He had two ways he could go. Wrap his woman in a sensual haze and keep her there until she was willing to mate with him, or be singed by the desire he could send galloping through her body ... or, tell her the truth. Let her see all the truth of who and what he is and hope for the best. The thought of lying or hedging went against everything in him. They were, as a rule, a very direct clan.

He could not hide from whom he truly was if he wanted Sally to do the same.

He just did not have to do it this day. When she gave a huge yawn he saw a way out. "Are you tired?"

"A little."

He hid his smile by burying his face in the crook of her neck. Her hair tickled his nose and her smell made his mouth water. "Could we not rest before you force me to reveal my secrets?"

A stab of guilt pierced her self-pity. "I don't want to force you to do anything you don't want."

"I would do anything to make you happy."

Sally's head snapped up as her eyes opened and closed while her brain tried to understand what he had said. That he had meant it. It was the first time anyone had put her desire first. "What is it you would like to do?"

He sighed. She was so self-sacrificing. His existence was for her now, how could she not understand? "I am tired."

"Then you should go to sleep."

Drake looked with pointed purpose between the bed and her anxious face. When it clicked in her eyes, he barely kept the chuckle from escaping his lips. "I cannot sleep without you beside me."

"Why?"

"You saved my life. How could I be sure you would not be handy should someone attack again?"

Sally rested her head against him. "No sex?"

"Not now." He could feel the tenseness in her body.

"Let's go to sleep."

Drake picked her up and settled her on the bed. Tucking the duvet around her body he lay down on top of the covers and wrapped his arms around her. "You do not mind if I hold you?"

It was like she had a body-sized heater. She had never been so warm. "No."

He heard her sighs and felt a surge of triumph when she cuddled closer to him. "Could I even say you like it?"

"Your head gets any bigger you're not getting through the door."

The two of them chuckled and went to sleep listening to the other breathe. It was the best sleep either of them ever had.

CHAPTER EIGHT

Luke wandered through the mansion, avoiding the harsh, cheery light of the sun. He was in no mood for happiness. Everywhere he looked, he felt as if he could sense reminders of what they had lost. Home. Now there was this interloper in their sacred retreat, a painful and fragrant piece of proof they either had spent centuries searching for the wrong thing or worse. They had been sent into exile by the Oracle, alone and forlorn, knowing they were destined for ages of solitary, debilitating grief. Either option broke his heart.

Once he believed he lost that most useless of organs.

Now his men were asking him to make just as impossible a choice as the Oracle had forced upon him in the beginning.

He drew near the library doors, and hearing noise within, gave it a diffident knock.

"Enter, Lord of Light."

The confident voice brought a smile to his face. Inside the cavernous space, lined with mahogany bookshelves stuffed with tomes that covered every age, was the one being that might have the power to grant him some answers. Standing near one of the windows with a Bible in his hands, the pale face was as lined as the pages he was studying. He wore a pair of dark blue dress slacks, white button down shirt, with shining Italian loafers on his feet. His dark hair was cut short, and to Luke he resembled a Wall Street banker on the way to a three-martini lunch. "King James did much to take the magic out of these stories," he mused to Luke.

"Wise One," Luke bowed from the waist and waited to be welcomed.

"Rise, Son of Light. There is no need of formality between two true fans of knowledge."

"I seek your counsel."

"That would be why I am here."

Luke blinked as he tried to understand. It was rare for the guardians of this world to try and help them. Even rarer was the idea one of them would admit to paying attention to their plight. "My brothers feel we need counsel with the Oracle."

"You mean your mother."

"I have no proof of that belief."

"Have you ever asked for it?"

"No, Wise One."

"Until you do," the Archangel chuckled, "I suggest you not deny it."

"Wise One, I ..."

When Luke seemed incapable of continuing, the Archangel's steely-eyed stare softened. "Sit, Luke. Call me Uriel and let us discuss your burdens. We have had many such conversations over the ages. Why is it you resort to this cold-hearted way of speaking when you are faced with the connection to your dam?"

"I apologize, Wise One."

Uriel shook his head as he settled his large lanky frame in one of the two Chippendale wing backed chairs flanking the window. When he looked with pointed intent at its mate, Luke sat down, his back as straight as a poker. In close proximity to the angel, he could smell the scent of ancient parchment and knowledge; it burned in the back of his nose like charred toast. Such was the effect of the archangel most associated with wisdom and education. "Luke, speaking with your Oracle is not possible while you are on this side of the veil."

His shoulders slumped as his regret added an additional burden. "I apologize for bothering you with a request. I suspected it was impossible."

"There is another you could speak with."

"An angel?"

"Your Oracle was an extension of God. Such a being has an equivalent in this world."

"I am not worthy of such an honor."

Uriel sighed. Some of his brethren were resistant to these refugees. They were granted the right to the places on the planet they themselves used, being given a set of laws to live by that would have broken most mortals. It was only due to the fact the Omega lived somewhere between immortal and mortal that they had survived their expectation. He was one of the few that had sought to cushion the change from one dimension to this. He feared he had failed. Surely these creatures deserved the same welcoming understanding homo sapiens were given. They were all made from the same God, why should they not be loved as well? "You are worthy if you deem it so. You know you have much in common with him. He will not come if not asked, but should you entreat him, this solitary pain will be eased."

"I have no right, Wise One."

"If you do not uncover the information you seek, what shall you do?"

Luke shook his head. "I don't know." He hoped the Archangel would not hear the way his voice cracked.

"Luke, call to him. He may have the answers you seek."

"Does he?"

"I can only pray."

The leader of the Omega chuckled at the idea. When Uriel continued to gaze at him with his steady, endless eyes, he coughed back his amusement. "You pray?"

"Of course."

"Why would an Archangel pray?"

"My friend," Uriel stood and whirled the dust motes dancing in the sunbeams around him as if they were a cloak of fabric for his hands to command, "Who else would pray more?" Luke joined in his laughter, though both knew he did not feel it in his heart.

CHAPTER NINE

Drake was surprised when he rose at sundown. It was not his way to rest for long; he always awoke to wander the confines of Sanctuary, restlessly searching for something. Now he had that missing treasure wrapped in his arms.

Making the sweetest snuffing noise.

He wouldn't call it snoring even in his mind. He might not know much about females, but even he knew they took offense at the silliest crimes.

Entering their main part of the building, he paused to ask one of the many faceless servants flittering from shadow to shadow to prepare a first meal for him and his woman. Waiting in the living room he was shocked to see Aquos slither in, his skin a pale translucent crystal-like sheen sending prisms of colors bouncing around the room. "Bad night?" Drake asked his friend.

"The fevers are brutal."

I remember." When he uttered the words he closed his mouth with a loud clap that sounded more like a lion's response. His shock at his restful night hit him anew. It was true. This was the first slumber he hadn't been hit by the fevers racking each of them since they came to this planet of possibilities.

"You're cured?"

"I don't know," Drake admitted with reluctance. "I know this was the first time I slept in peace."

"Perhaps this woman means more than you thought."

He snorted. "That's impossible." At Aquos' arch look Drake explained, "I'm already terrified at how much she means to me. Don't make it worse."

Behind them a squadron of servants passed carrying buckets of water, mops, towels, and chagrined expressions. The two men watched them all go by without saying a word. When Drake stared at Aquos, he shrugged. "I told you I had a fever."

"Looks like a flood."

"Let's just say a great deal of water was released in the process."

Drake shook his head, "I thought I had it rough."

"So did I." Aquos kicked his feet up on the table and folded his arms behind his head. "Tell me about the girl."

"Her family treats her like dirt."

"When are you going to kill them?"

Drake smiled. Here was the one man that understood how his mind worked and approved of it. "I can't."

"Why not?"

"She would not be pleased."

Aquos shrugged again, "Don't tell her."

"I think she'll notice when I bring her home and there is nothing left but smoking embers."

"Why would you possibly take her home?"

"You mean to let her go?" Blade asked as he entered the room.

"I gave my word to Luke I would take her back to her family."

Aquos stood, his body hardening to the look of silver and blue glass. "Let me be clear, Draco. Should you give up that woman she will not stay free for long."

"Don't threaten me ice-boy."

"It's a promise."

Drake watched his best friend leave the room with thundering footsteps reminding him of a winter's storm. Aquos barely saw her. *Why was he being so territorial about Sally?* Not that it really mattered. There was no way he would ever let her go. He just didn't know how he was going to keep his word to Luke, yet still keep that which belonged to him.

Thinking so much about Sally alone made him edgy. He jumped off the couch and made his way to his wing.

His Princess in the Tower.

She would be his Queen as soon as he found his loophole.

Entering the bedchamber he swore softly. His Princess had disappeared. He heard the sound of her panting breaths and the scrabble of rocks falling. Looking at the north fireplace, he could not help but laugh.

His Princess was trying to escape.

By climbing the fireplace.

He hoped she didn't get stuck.

"What are you doing?"

What he could see of her, two feet covered with thick wool socks, stilled. A small voice answered his question, "Escaping."

"I see. How's that going for you?"

"Not that well," a wry answer was given.

"Need some help?"

"You'd help me escape?"

"I thought you'd given me your word you'd stay."

He hadn't thought the feet could get more still. "I forgot," she confessed.

"What's your choice, Sally-mine?"

"Help me down," she whispered softly, but somehow he could still hear her.

With a wrench at her ankles, Sally tumbled from the chimney. He suspected she figured he'd let her fall on the piled logs always kept in the grate. Catching her with ease, he hid his smile when her eyes flew open, surprised there was no pain. He held her out by the shoulders. "Is it truly so horrid being with me?"

Her heart caught in her throat when she saw the pain in his eyes. He looked more hurt than when he had the dart in his neck. "I'm sorry," she offered him with haste. "I just feel wrong being here."

"Why?"

"I have a family. People will miss me."

Drake decided it was time to be as cruel to her as she was being to him. He opened a high cabinet and took out a cell phone from a secret compartment in the wood. Handing it to her he grunted, "Call them. Tell them you are going to be gone for a few days."

Sally took the phone and sat down on the bed. Looking at it she was frozen as she tried to decide whom to call.

"Problem?"

"No," she told him. Taking a deep breath she started to dial the number for Austin. He was the one brother who seemed to rely on her cooking skills the most. The phone rang twice before it was picked up. "Austin," she began.

"Sally? Where the hell are you? I'm waiting for my dinner."

"Austin I'm not ..."

Speaking over her without mercy he continued, "How could you be so thoughtless? I haven't eaten at all today and now you're so inconsiderate to not even try to have dinner on the table on time? I swear I should kick you out on your ungrateful fat ass. I thought you'd be more responsible by now, but you are still such a child."

Feeling as if each one of his words were a barb in her soul, Sally tried to angle the phone away from Drake, so he couldn't hear. His saddened expression made her think she was failing miserably.

"I'm sorry, Austin. I decided to take a little vacation."

"What kind of vacation? You don't have any money. We took it all."

Well. That was news. Last she heard her money went into a savings account. Apparently that wasn't true. Looked like she had a lot to deal with when she got back to the real world. "We'll discuss it when I return. If I return."

"If? What about the Bucks county property? Sall …"

With a strong feeling of satisfaction, Sally hung up on her oldest brother. Her blood. And turned to a man whom she had known for barely twenty-four hours. It was nothing like any choice she had ever made before. It made no possible sense. Probably the height of stupidity and rashness, and she didn't care a bit.

Drake pulled her into his arms, resting his head against hers. "I shouldn't have done that."

"No. It was good for me."

He cringed with unease, "If you want to cry you can."

Sally burst into laughter. Looking up she took note of the horrified expression in his eyes, as she expected. "Thank you for permission."

"I've noticed on television women find it cathartic."

"We do," Sally shook her head and rested it back against his chest. His heart made such a pleasing rhythm. At the moment it sounded like a reggae drum to her. Almost as if there was more than one heart beneath the body builder chest she was snuggled against. "It's just not as much fun when you give me permission."

"Good. You have my permission to cry whenever you wish."

She burst into laughter and punched at his solar plexus. The pain this caused her hand made her hop up and down shaking her fingers. One problem. Hopping on polished wood floor in wool socks can be very slippery. Sally felt her feet fly out from under her and would have ended up planted on her ass had it not been for Drake's quick reflexes. He carried her to the chair and sat with her on his lap. "What was that?"

"Me hitting you," she confessed while she tried to wiggle her fingers.

Drake pulled her fingers to his lips so he could kiss every inch of them. To make sure they were fully functional, he began to nibble on them next. He enjoyed the way her breath froze in her lungs. It would be soon, he consoled himself. She would let the calls of her body drown out all of her insecurities soon enough. He just hoped he didn't lose his mind in the meantime. "That's probably not a good idea."

"I've never felt anyone so hard," she muttered as she continued to glare at her throbbing hand.

He tried not to laugh. He almost choked on it. When she realized what she had said and what she could feel, she hopped off of his lap as if he were on fire.

"Is that permanent?" she pointed to his lap.

"It is with you around."

"Drake," she paused to swallow, "you don't have to do this."

"If you understood how much I need to do this," he moved closer to her so she could feel the pulsing heat coming from him. "You'd be running from this tower as if the hounds of hell were on your heels."

"No," Sally held her head up with pride. "I would never run from you."

The words had barely cleared her throat before she was caught in a passionate embrace. *This man should give kissing lessons to everyone.* No, strike that. If all men kissed like this no woman would ever be able to get anything done. He released her with a suddenness that would have sent her to the floor in a boneless heap if he had not caught her and held her close. "Breathe, baby," he chuckled in her ear. "Air in and air out. A very good thing." She took a shaking breath and ignored the vibrations of his laughter against her skin. "This is only going to get better."

"Death by sex," Sally murmured. "Just what I always dreamt of."

"Nope. You'll be awake. I promise."

There was a mechanical sound of moving machinery that broke their cocoon of peace. Looking around, Sally tried to determine where it was coming from. When she recognized it was one of the fireplaces she could not keep the scowl from crossing her face. "Tell me there was an easier way to escape."

"You're not still considering that, are you?"

She was saddened at how much hurt there was in his question. Sally put her hand against his cheek and shook her head. "I gave my word and will keep it, but you in turn must keep yours."

"They do not appreciate you."

"I still will expect you to take me back to them. Eventually."

"Eventually can be a long time."

"Serves them right," she quipped.

When the machinery noise stopped Drake drifted to the southern fireplace. Moving the grate, she was shocked to see it was a very large dumb waiter. There were two shelves. One was filled with a silver tray with covered dishes like the one he had brought their dinner up on. The other was stuffed with clothing and boxes of toiletries.

"Breakfast is served."

Looking at the clock she was forced to point out something, "Isn't that more like dinner?"

"We look at meals more in terms of numbers. This would be first meal."

"Who are *we*, Drake?"

He knelt by the dumbwaiter and began to pull out the clothing.

When she saw he was not planning on speaking, Sally put her hand on his shoulder. The heat was so soothing against her ice-cold hands she could barely resist running her fingers over his skin to warm her. "Drake, I said I would stay. Nothing you tell me will change that."

"Please," his voice was hoarse to the point of sounding strangled. "Let's eat first."

Sighing heavily, she gave in with ill-concealed grace. Sitting at the table, Sally watched as he unloaded the mini-elevator for her. Most of the packages were taken to the matching wardrobe she had found empty when she had investigated. Drake made a dramatic show of picking out clothing and small crystal bottles before returning to her.

Dumping the items into her lap, he gestured to the bathroom, "I thought you'd like to shower before we ate. Don't worry about the food keeping warm."

"Okay," she stood up and paused when she caught sight of her face for the first time.

She was covered with soot.

And leaves.

"Damned fireplace." Catching his eyes in the mirror, she smiled when she saw he had a good amount of soot on his face as well. "You should have told me."

He chuckled at the horrified look on her face. "I think you look cute." When she jerked to move away from him he wrapped his arms around her to hold her in place. "Besides, there was no reason to send you into the shower until I had a change of clothes for you."

Looking at the top and pants he handed her, she sighed. "There is no way these will fit."

"You'll see."

When she'd showered, using shampoo and soap the consistency of liquid silk, Sally was chagrined to find out he was right. The clothing fit. It fit perfectly. She'd been buying clothes three sizes too big. The burnt umber top and pants were like no sweat suit she had ever seen before. It's color brought out the gold tints of her eyes and the caramel in her hair.

She lingered at the mirror to note it was cut for her curves perfectly.

Her smile was radiant. She looked like a woman.

Even better, she felt like a seductive female.

Drake had no idea what he'd let himself in for.

His first meal proceeded in almost silence. She kept his plate filled and relished his open mouthed response to how she looked. The staff of the estate had supplied even more vegetarian dishes for her to pick from, for which she was grateful. When they were done, Drake pulled her from her chair and wrenched her into his tight embrace.

"I must ask something from you."

"Okay."

Drake took a deep breath before he leapt. "Don't scream or run away."

Sally's jaw dropped open at this request. Her head tilted to the side. "Drake, what could be so terrible you would ask such a thing?"

"I am not what you might expect."

"You already proved that with your decision to take my ugly clothes and feed me."

He chuckled and buried his face in her hair, not wanting her to see the tears in his eyes. Sally stiffened when she felt one drop to her skin. "I can't stand the thought you will be frightened of me," he muttered into her shoulder.

She forced him to lift his head and look at her. Sally leaned forward to brush a kiss against each of his cheeks and take the crystalline drops away. "Do you hurt children?"

"Never."

Sally released a deep sigh. His answer was given so quickly and with such fierceness she could not doubt his word. "Then I'll be fine."

"I'm not of your world."

"At the moment I'm thinking that is a very good thing."

Drake hissed as he tried to make his point to her, but he could not come up with an explanation. Words were not his specialty. Action was. "It would be better if I just showed you."

"Then show me."

"I am still concerned that you'll be disgusted."

Her smile was as pure and bright as the summer sun breaking through a hurricane's gloom. "Drake, I think under the circumstances, I'm the only one who gets to have an inferiority complex in this room. Mine is large enough for both of us."

"You have nothing to be inferior about."

Sally ran her hand over his face until he smiled at her. "I know that. It doesn't alter the damage done by those years of people telling me otherwise, though."

"I think I should hunt down your family and kill them."

He made the statement with such mock fierceness she could not help laughing. "No, you won't. But I do thank you for offering." Sally measured his look for a moment. "If you hate my insecurity so much, you could always return my clothing and let me go."

"Do you truly wish that?"

Her eyes closed on reflex. She had been asking because she thought she should.

"It would be easier to let you go now rather than later."

Opening her eyes she had made her decision. *Try it, Sally. Just once, take a leap and try it. There are no siblings here to tell you what you can't or shouldn't do.* "No," she stated slowly. "I want to stay." The flare of triumph lit his eyes and made them flash from gold to red to orange and back to a Spring sunset. "Not that I'm guaranteeing I'll sleep with you."

Her words were a challenge to everything in him. Drake's mouth ran up her throat, over her jaw, tasting and nibbling as he went. "Oh, Sally-mine.

You will indeed go to bed with me, though once again … sleep is the last thing on my mind."

She would have responded. She really would have. It's just that next his mouth covered hers and took every coherent thought in her mind. *How does he reduce me to this shivering, gasping, quivering puddle of desire with a kiss?*

Right. Like he couldn't do that with a mere word.

It was Drake who ended the kiss. He wanted the truth out. He needed her to know everything about him before they mated. At home he would have just kept seducing her until she could not breathe without his kiss. Could not stand without his touch. Here he was a slave to other laws, well, at least to some of them. There was little chance he would go back from here. He wanted her too much. If times had been different, he would have thought he was in heat. The last eight hours he had spent with a permanent hard-on between his legs. He was beginning to think it was damaging his sanity.

"First thing first. I would have you know the real me."

"Okay," she was helped to her feet by his assistance, though her legs were so shaky from the roller coaster of desire he'd placed her on that it was evident to both of them. Her body felt like a pulsing force of endless need. Sally decided it was wiser to ignore his laughter over her weakness. "Just hurry this up, funny man."

"I pray you continue to think that when we are done."

Sally tried for sheer bravado to deal with the simmering cauldron of terror she had in her gut. Her imagination was providing her with one more nightmarish sequence after another. "Drake, the suspense here is killing me."

"I pray your reaction does not kill me." Drake pulled out a new thick pair of socks from his dresser to add to her body. It might be summer but the night was chilled. She would not suffer from this experience. He guided her to the bed to sit and knelt before her. Sally put her hand out to stop him, "Drake, what are you doing?"

"You need something for your feet."

"I can put on my own socks."

His eyes glowed neon orange as he gazed up at her. "Tending you is my honor and right, woman." Sally leaned forward and brushed a kiss against his lips. He had to tense all his muscles to keep from leaping on top of her. His response was an out of control fire with a mere hint of a spark from her. This was another sign his patience was wise; she was beginning to initiate contact. Reach out to him. "Your feet will grow cold if we do not cover them."

Sally let him continue, her toes wiggling in the thick wool of the socks as he secured them. "Where have you been all my life?"

"Looking for you," his answer came so swift he could not keep it back.

When she was covered, Drake stood and seemed frozen for a moment. This next step would decide everything. He had never felt such fear in all of his life, and considering the length of it, that was quite a statement. Drake paused to say a prayer to the Goddess that made them, and then took his woman's hand. She gave it with such a willing and eager smile; he could not help but pray once more this would not be his last chance with her.

Sally held her peace as Drake guided her to the portal from which he entered the chamber. "I tried this door before but it was locked."

"That was for your safety."

When he said nothing and the two of them stood in front of the door not doing anything, Sally thought his inferiority might be rearing its head. Sally tried to bite back her sigh. *What was she doing? Why did this beautiful man twist her up like her soul was being braided into his? Was it his beauty? Or because he seemed to look at her and see something worthwhile?* Sally shook her head. It didn't matter. What did was that they were here. Together. "Drake," Sally was about to do something she rarely did, and that was trust. "Drake, whatever happens won't change how I feel."

"I don't know how you feel."

"Neither do I."

He turned to her with eyes an equal mixture of warmth and humor. "That is what I am afraid of."

"I know it's not bad, what I feel."

"That is what I am counting on."

Sally tossed her hands up, "So what do we do?"

"Would you let me blindfold you?"

Her mouth began to do that landed fish thing, opening and closing futilely as she tried to come up with an answer to that question. "Why would you want to do that?"

"It would be easier for me."

With a curt nod, she gave in to his request. Sally closed her eyes as Drake fastened a silk scarf around her head. If he noticed her lips moving over the words of a silent prayer, he kept it to himself.

His prayer he said within his heart.

For both of them.

CHAPTER TEN

Drake kept his words locked behind his teeth as he positioned Sally in front of the door once more. This was a huge chance in so many ways. A bet of immeasurable proportions. There was a reason why dragons had so much treasure; they were excellent gamblers. He had just never put the future of his heart on the turn of the dice before.

He took the few steps past the threshold to stand at the outer portal. His part of Sanctuary had a high tower on the end. The aerie was the closest he could get to his natural habitat. His hand was firm on her arms as he guided her to stand at the edge of the platform beside him.

Sally took in a deep breath of the air whistling past her face. "That's what was missing in your room," she gushed. "Windows."

"You like the outdoors?"

"Love it."

Drake took his shirt off and lifted Sally close to his chest. He grunted with approval when she twined her arms around his neck. "That will make this easier," he whispered in her ears before he stepped off the ledge where they were standing.

"What ..." The rest of her words were cut off when she felt the drop. Her arms tightened around his neck in reflex. "What are you doing?" she yelled at him.

When he was sure his wings had opened, Drake whispered in her ear. "Remove the cloth." Sally wasn't willing to let go of him for an instant. Drake found a strong up current and managed to snake his hand around to pull the blindfold. He could not resist his laughter as she continued to keep her eyes tightly closed. "Be brave, Sally-mine. Feel the wind as we soar."

He juggled her in his hold as his wings took them higher into the air to ascend over the clouds. As soon as he began to sail, the dimensional veils dropped around them to mask their movements from most humans. There was no way for anyone looking up to see them, so he was not concerned about witnesses. He just wanted her to enjoy everything she saw.

Sally tried to tell herself she was dreaming.

Or hallucinating.

Or delusional.

Anything would be more acceptable than the idea her dream man had just sprouted wings out of his back and taken them flying. Over farms. "What are you doing?"

"Showing you who I really am."

"Can you stop?"

He immediately sent them plunging down to land with a gentle thump in the middle of a bean field. Sally staggered away from him, her eyes open and mouth gaping. "Drake," she took a deep breath. "Please tell me what this is?"

"Sally-mine, this is who I truly am."

She tried to process, she really did. Everything felt real. She could see the moon, hanging above them like a spotlight. She could feel the crunched and bumpy snap beans beneath her feet. She could even taste the corn in the wind as it came wafting from the fields on the other side of a nearby stand of ancient oaks.

The only thing she couldn't understand was how her dream man had wings coming out of his back.

"What are they?"

"My wings."

"Did you always have them?"

"I do. My transformation is only partial right now."

"What do you look like when you have a full transformation?"

Oh no, Sally … why would you ask that? What possible good could come from going there?

Drake shrugged and then switched. There was no great flash of light as you saw in movies. It was a simple cracking and movement of shadows gathering and redistributing around him. When he was done, his size eclipsed the trees. He was so proud of her. She did not scream. She did not faint or even run away. Instead his woman's mouth opened and her eyes got a dreamy look.

* * *

Standing before her was a dragon.

A very tall, fierce, powerful dragon. Bigger than a large Colonial suburban home, it shone with all the colors of oil on water.

Sally loved dragons.

Her room was filled with every dragon book, statue, and poster she could find of them. She stumbled forward and touched the side of one of his legs. She always imagined a dragon would have feathers. Instead he was covered with gills that were soft, with little tiny hairs on them, reminding her of velvet. Running her hand over his black, crimson, and blood-red leg, Sally smiled when her dragon made a low whirring song of approval.

With the sound of breaking twigs Drake turned back into her dream man. Not that she got to see him for long, for he pulled her off her feet and into his arms. Her gasp gave him the perfect opportunity to taste her mouth fully.

When he sensed she was going to pass out from loss of breath he released her. "You are not afraid?"

"Well, opening my eyes to find myself flying was a shock, but no, you don't scare me."

"Why not?"

She laughed when he gave her a look of mild disgruntlement and confusion. "I love dragons."

"You hammer me about wanting you in my bed but my turning into a dragon is no problem?"

Sally shrugged. "I must be insane."

"You are not insane," he snapped.

"You say tomato ..."

Drake ran his hand through his hair. "Impossible girl."

"My Indian name I believe."

He shook his head. "Sally-mine, can you really be so accepting of this?"

"Drake, I'm a woman who cleared thirty a while ago. Yet, I have never understood people. I prefer to spend all of my time with plants and animals, or my books. Every moment since meeting you has been a dream. Why shouldn't you be a dragon? How come your clothes came back?"

"The magic of the transformation returns me to my state from before the change."

"Makes sense," she allowed.

Accepting her ease with the idea was harder than deciding on ways to calm her misgivings about who he was. Pulling her back into his embrace he gave her another scorching kiss, making them exchange breath several times to survive. His woman pressed her body into his unyielding frame and made him rethink how fast he could get her back to his chamber. "I want you, Sally-mine."

"And are you planning on having me in the field?"

"My plan was more for the bed in our chamber."

Sally eyed his male form with appreciation. "Before we do that ..."

He smiled eagerly at her considering look. "Yes?"

"Couldn't we go flying some more?"

Drake moved to pick her up in his arms but she stepped away from him. "No," when he looked at her with a raised eyebrow she shrugged. "I was hoping we could fly with you in your dragon form."

He flashed into the other as he chuckled at her. Sally's mouth was filled with saliva as she ran her hand over the muscles in his neck. He moved his head under her caress as if relishing the contact between them. When he settled down closer to the ground Sally found it was easy to climb onto his shoulders. She could not come close to wrapping her arms around his neck, but two of his gills on either side grew very long and gave her a handle to cling to. "I don't want to hurt you."

In her head, she heard a rumbling noise as if a doorway had opened. "You won't."

"You're telepathic too?"

"Just slightly, as a man. Dragons have few limits to their powers."

"And I thought you couldn't get more sexy," she muttered.

His chuckle was something she felt beneath her legs and in her mind. Without further discussion, Drake took three lurching steps forward and they were soaring up through the air. She looked behind to marvel as his ruby wings glinted in the moonlight and sent a glow everywhere she looked. It was as if he put rose-colored glasses on her, and it changed the world in the process.

Pennsylvania had always seemed beautiful to her. Now it was perfect.

They moved so fast, dipping and gliding through the air currents as if they were on jet skis in the ocean; she could soon see they were leaving the Delaware valley. "Aren't you worried about people seeing us?"

In her mind she could hear his words as if they were whispered in her ear, "When I am even close to dragon form there is a dimensional veil created that cloaks me."

"So why are there so many stories about dragons?"

"There are always a few special people that can see me."

"Am I one of those people?" Sally perked up at the thought she had some undiscovered talent.

"You are even more special than they."

His murmur sent chills of desire through her as if he had hummed the words against her skin. Sally could not keep herself from running her hands over his neck, and enjoying the ripple of tendons and muscles in response. The whirring sound she felt and heard in her mind seemed to indicate he enjoyed her attentions, as much as she did in giving them to him. "Are the others who live with you like this?"

His barking laugh made her clutch at the reins to keep from plummeting to the ground. "No," he explained. "They are different."

Just then he did a banking turn that made her throw her head back with laughter.

They spent what felt like hours soaring through clouds and diving down to skim over the earth, with his wings slicing through corn stalks and sending wisps of plant matter to puff up like fog. Sally was glad she had never had allergies.

Drake decided it was time to turn them back for home when he reached the Atlantic Ocean. There was no reason to get into major air traffic patterns.

It had been years since he played chicken with a 747.

Sally laughed as he made several tight turns over the ocean to send spray cascading over them both. The only thing dragons loved more than their heart's treasure was water. He always suspected that accounted for his tight relationship with Aquos' clan.

As they started back for Sanctuary, he felt Sally let go of the reins he had provided.

Looking back he could see her arms thrown up to the sky and her face turned up to heaven. She shone with such joy her incandescence outdid the moon, sun and any spotlight ever created. Drake made sure his pace was steady and fast, so she could savor every moment of the wind whipping past her face. He just didn't want to make any sudden moves and possibly throw her from her perch.

When she saw the familiar fields of home, Sally reclaimed her reins. As soon as he knew she was secure again he made the adjustments in their course to land on the Sanctuary perch.

Morphing back into a man, Sally threw herself into his arms. "Thank you, thank you, thank you."

Drake carried her through the doors, shutting them with his mind. Her clothes were soaked from the ocean. He kept going until they were in the bathroom; the rooms were still awash from the flickering magic of the candles he had lit before they left. His mouth covered hers and her taste sent a bolt of hunger through him. Knowing he was so close to his release made the need into a flood tide that swamped most of what made him human.

She was not even aware of his intent until she felt a shivering of cold through her soul as her skin felt the air around them. With a sudden clarity Sally recognized she was now wrapped in his arms, naked. "Wait," she wrenched her mouth away from him, panting from her mass of rioting senses.

"No, Sally-mine. No more waiting. Your body screams yes to me, I can smell it. Feel it." His eyes blazed like a fire as his hand cupped her between her legs. She colored a pink blush from her head to her toes when he rumbled his approval at her liquid heat. "I just showed you my true self. The being I keep hidden at all times from the rest of the world. Will you really deny me the same right now? Can you?"

Backing up until she touched the bathroom wall, Sally snatched a towel from the rack and draped it around her body. Her eyes burned with unshed tears as her body continued to call out to this man who set her every nerve on fire.

What do I do? Oh God, what do I do? The chanting in her mind almost drowned out the voices of her siblings that kept warning her this was a mistake. A trick.

Looking up, her breath froze as she realized the fire in his eyes was desire. The man she was looking at was a tower of hunger for her. Her eyelids shut like the slam of a door as she realized she could not walk away from the wanting she saw so clearly in his expression.

"Can you get rid of the lights?" she asked without bothering to open her eyes.

Without a word all of the candles were extinguished. Drake hummed with satisfaction. Darkness meant nothing, he could see in any kind of illumination with his other senses. If it made her more comfortable he was more than willing to provide.

"Do you say yea or nej?"

"Nej?"

"It means *no* in my language."

"What would happen if I say no?"

Drake almost moaned at the thought of being denied once more. "I would be saddened, especially given your eagerness as we soared. I would not take you with force, love, you have my word."

"Then my answer is yes."

His eyes flashed with an iridescent surge as he smelled her acquiescence in body, mind, and spirit. "Take off the towel."

"What?"

Her squeak of a question made him chuckle. Her eyes were dilating, her breath coming in brief pants, her mouth open slightly as if already anticipating the surge of his tongue. "Drop. The. Towel."

"How can you tell I haven't?"

His chuckle made her take a half step away from the wall toward him. Drake waited, hoping she would find the courage to release her body into his care in all ways. "I can see in the dark, Sally-mine. My hearing is also extraordinary in comparison with humans. Regardless of my abilities, I know you still have not dropped the cloth."

"I asked you to turn off the lights so you couldn't see me."

Drake ripped the linen away from her body, no longer caring if she flinched. "Sally-mine, I have seen you before." He wrapped his arms around her body, groaning as her flesh met his. Taking the few steps needed to reach the large glassed-in shower he groaned again as the hot spray washed over both their intertwined bodies. Their mouths met and sealed together as their tongues started a battle both were destined to win.

His mouth running down her throat, she could hear her panting over the beating of the water against the marble floor. "I don't usually do this," she gasped. "I'm not real sure what I'm supposed to do."

"There are no rules, sweet." He scraped his teeth over her pulse as he kept moving his hands over her body, trying to ease some of the tension. Right now, making love to her would be more pain for her, and if he was going to entice her to stay with him as long as he wanted, it had to be perfect. "Baby, please relax."

"I can't," she moaned resting her head against his shoulders as she stood within the circle of his arms.

He swallowed difficultly. Regretting it deeply, Drake used his mental powers to turn off the water. A towel appeared in his hands, which he wrapped around her body, and continued to try and soothe her, by caressing her body through the safety of the cloth. He was still so aroused he felt as if he would break from the amount of pain it was causing him. Lifting her in his arms, he carried the two of them back to the balcony.

Sitting down on the ledge he rocked her back and forth. Regulating his body temperature, Drake made sure his woman would be warm enough even with the chilled breeze wrapping around them.

"So I guess we're not doing this?"

"I think we should talk."

Sally knew tears were streaming down her face but she hoped if she could keep her breathing steady he would not notice. "Look," she took a deep quivering breath. "It's fine. We don't have to have sex."

His jaw clenched as her words ripped across his sense of honor.

"Sally-mine, when you are with a man, the only rule is to do that which makes you both feel good."

"Thanks for telling me. If you let me go I'll get dressed and leave."

He nodded with a curt jerk of his head; as his eyes seemed to shutter his thoughts from her searching gaze. "Okay, Sally-mine. I tried to be gentle and patient. I tried to find a way to talk you through this. You liked the dragon in me, and now you shall have to accept all of it. Every bit of me."

Standing up he strode back inside, closing the doors behind him as he went. With a toss of his arms, Sally found herself bouncing into the middle of the bed. The towel disappeared with a blink of her eyes, and next both her arms were wrenched back and tied with silk scarves. "What are you doing?" Invisible hands caught her left leg and her ankle was tied to the end of the bed, "Drake, what's going on?"

"No more talking, Sally-mine. I want you. I need you." He crawled up her body as he brushed feather-light kisses against her skin in a random pattern. "And more importantly ... you need me."

"This is how we do it where I'm from." Reaching her face, Drake settled his body against her, groaning when he rested his hardness into the cradle of her legs. He purred with satisfaction when he heard a catch in her throat and her hips began to undulate against him. "One more thing, before the verbal portion of the evening erodes into a series of one word sentences like more, and yes, and oh my god."

"That's three words," she gasped as he began to nibble on her ear.

"This is us ... making love. Not sex. Not a one-night stand. The only way you can use that term with us, concerns a part of me that would stand up all night long with you in my bed."

Sally turned her head away from him as she tried to get enough oxygen into her lungs to keep from passing out. "I thought when you turned off the shower you changed your mind about the whole thing."

"I don't think you're very good at figuring out what I'm planning, or not planning, to do. You should probably stop trying."

"It would help if you weren't so confusing." Her mouth caught in another one of his soul-searing kisses, Sally put aside all her misgivings and fear and tried to focus on just feeling. His skin was warming her in ways and places she never imagined could be more than frozen.

Willing the lights off in the room, Drake took a moment to lean back and survey the woman laid out before him like a feast for a starving man. He breathed over her and watched with satisfaction as Sally shook from head to toe with need. "Oh my, Sally-mine. Would that I could make you see you through my eyes."

"What do you see?"

The tremulous note in her voice reached out to him as nothing else ever had before. "Perfection," he shrugged, helpless to find the proper words to encapsulate everything she was to him right now. "You are incandescent to me, my heart. Something no woman has ever been before."

She purred with need, and undulated in a sexy wave that made his breath hitch. Looking down he felt all of the saliva abandon his body. She wanted him. All of the physical signs were there. Her eyes were turbulent with emotion and need. Her nipples were hard, perfect raspberries poised on the very top of two plentiful mounds of cream. *He'd always loved cream.* Her tongue made a slow sweep of her lips as her head began to toss on the pillow. And her smell.

God, he could die tomorrow knowing he'd gotten his lungs full of pure heaven. Her hunger made a perfume that was his home on a high Spring night when all the flowers would burst and the land was bountiful with new life.

His favorite time.

Well, was his favorite time. Right now, this moment, when he proved to this indomitable beautiful woman she belonged with him, was going down in his history book as his new favorite moment of all time. Dipping down, he cradled her jaw, slanted her face, and kissed her, long and deep. He was still clothed in the leather pants he wore when he flew, and would stay that way until he had her ready to accept everything he was prepared to give her.

For he had so very much to give.

He kept nipping at her kiss-bruised lips, tasting her with long firm sucking pulls. He trailed kisses over the edge of her jaw to her neck. His hands massaged the rampaging pulse in her neck as he followed the line of her throat down to her collarbone. Her skin was so fine, like velvet combed with silk.

Not able to wait another moment, he moved further down to gaze at the breasts that had become such fascination for him it approached being a drug. The moan bubbling from her throat made him chuckle as he let his eyes feast. "Sally-mine," he whispered over her trembling chest. "How you please me."

She tried to come up with an answer, a comment. Some pithy statement that might make him smile. When she felt his sandpaper tongue lower to take one, long, delicious lick along her nipple all she could do was moan.

He chuckled at the sound, but then she sighed into the hot sanctuary of his mouth and made him moan as well. His hand cupped her breast, kneading it while he suckled. Drake scraped his teeth along the hardened ridge, then brushed his tongue against the sensitized bud to sooth it. Sally's gasp combined with shock and need, her hips making small circles as if reaching for the thing that throbbed with each of his heartbeats.

Drake sent his fingers sliding over the swells and dips of her body until he could cover the cauldron of fire. Gateway to his own private heaven. His teeth closed on her nipple, giving her a small edge of pain as his fingers played in her slick center. His head reeled as she oozed another wave of scent that made his mouth water.

She could feel his moans vibrating through her body. His penis jerked as he rubbed it through the buttery softness of his pants against the side of her leg. He was engorging so much he felt as if he would explode and he knew he needed some relief soon. His mouth switched to her other breast, determined to turn it the same pleasing shade of burgundy he had the first. His teeth teasing at her nipple to keep her walking the edge between pleasure and fulfillment, he took a moment to sit back and look at her. "Do you understand now, Sally-mine? This is where you belong."

A wail of desire ripped from the bottom of her soul. "Drake," she panted, her head tossing back and forth. "Stop teasing."

He rewarded her with a series of pulls on her trembling breasts that had her close to tears. Drake's felt as if half of him was covered with sweat and the other was turning to ice. She was killing him, and he was loving every moment of it.

Sally rattled the bedposts as she tested the length of her restraints. "Let me go."

"Nej, sweetheart. If I give you an inch you will let all those dark thoughts from the past drown out my cries of need for you now."

"I want to feel you," she cried.

His laughter made her groan with agonizing pleasure as he buried his cheek between her breasts. "You will soon feel me, baby." He positioned his body against her again, "you will soon feel every aching part of me."

When she groaned her desire and undulated against him in the sexiest unashamed act of need, Drake felt a type of madness overcome him. She was his. This female would never again walk near any male and not remember the moment the dragon came home to her. He began to move down her neck, tiny kisses that left fire dancing over her nerve endings. His fingers caught at her nipples and rolled them until he had her sobbing with desire. Sally didn't know how pain and pleasure and overwhelming need could combine together, but her skin was so hypersensitive even his breath was driving her crazy. She felt as if he were galloping her toward the edge of a cliff and she did not care if she fell to her death. He shouldered his way between her legs, his breath catching at her shining, jewel-like look, in the ambient light that his eyes could detect.

"I am going to make sure you never doubt your beauty again."

His voice was so harsh she shuddered. "If I tell you mission accomplished, would you believe me?"

He hummed as his hands pushed her one free leg farther out. "Now baby, I need you to stay very, very still." Without warning or discussion, Drake took one long perfect lick along her core. If it had not been for the ties, she would have flown off of the bed. He smoothed his hand along the knotted muscles of her lower abdomen while he waited for her to calm. "You're not going to come until I tell you," he growled into her. Her sobbing panting was the only answer she was able to give.

Drake was more animal than man right now. He was burning with his own need, but more important to him was to make sure she never forgot this moment. She would rise from this bed a phoenix. Remade with an understanding of how desirable she truly was. He would sear his name into her soul with every orgasm before the morning came. Taking her core in his lips he licked, sucked and nibbled. The taste of her slid down his throat and made his toes curl with satisfaction. Using his longest finger, he slid into her depths, grunting when her channel locked down on it. He steepled his fingers and scissored to widen her for later. His cock yearned and bucked in his pants, demanding its own satisfaction. First he was determined to take his woman to the stars. He burrowed in to capture her clit and nibble it between his teeth, chuckling when she began to scream out for mercy from her very torturer. He ignored her and continued molding his woman into the seductive goddess he knew her to be.

Looking at him, Sally felt her body tensing and relaxing in waves. His eyes were glowing in the night, shedding a crimson light over their bodies. Her hands kept opening and closing with the need to touch him, but all she could do was grasp at the silk binds he'd knotted around her wrists. Her leg was pulled so tight; she was surprised she had not cracked the furniture.

Drake lowered his head again as his mouth took possession of her most intimate lips. His tongue thrust deep inside her. With that one action, she seemed to explode into a million pieces. Glancing up, satisfaction flooded him at the dazed look on her face, a single tear shining like a ruby.

Moving up her body they groaned in unison when he was cradled by her legs. A thought was all it took to make his pants disappear. His erection pushed between her thighs, and a moan escaped her lips again. He captured one of her breasts, massaging the nipple as she shook from a perfect combination of pleasure and pain. Her stomach was quivering, sending lightning bolts through her body and making her eyes feel like they were rolling in her head. Drake bit her neck and then licked along the artery as he nibbled at the pulse he found. His fingers grew rougher against her breasts as he began to purr again, a sound of such need and pleasure that Sally no longer cared she sounded like a panting dog.

Their bodies were so illuminated by the glow of his eyes she could see his features peeling back from his face as he tried to control his lust. "By the light of the Oracle, baby, I need you."

"Well," she paused to try and pant some more breath into her lungs. "What. Are. You. Waiting. For?"

A finger entered her suddenly and her need was so great she lifted them both when she arched into it. Drake hissed as he added a second finger and rotated them within the burning heat of her core. "Just a little more, baby." Her panting made him feel like he was omnipotent. A third finger entered her and pierced the hymen she had never mentioned. He rested his head on the pillow beside her head as buckets of sweat poured out of him. "Did you really think I wouldn't have noticed?"

Sally tried to think. She shook her head several times trying to make some blood and oxygen get to her mind. "I never thought you'd go through with it."

He growled as he shifted over her, his staff pressing at her entrance. The heat coming from him seemed to be burning through her. "You will soon lose all doubt," he swore to her and smiled at her whimpered response. Drake rubbed his cock back and forth in her cream, spreading her liquid silk over him. He noted with satisfaction the way she twitched with desire, small squeaks escaping her lips.

"Drake," she managed to pant. "Please don't make me wait anymore."

He began to enter her with a slow deliberate erotic slide. Her whole body convulsed as she tried to push him into her heat with one leg, desperate for something to ease the tension gripping her. He was so long and wide. Thick. Drake pushed forward but paused, as he could see the burning feverish need in her mind was outpacing her body's call. "Hold on, baby," he purred against the perfume of her neck. "Just a little bit more. Can you take it? Just a little bit more?"

"Yes," she panted.

"A little bit more?"

"Yes."

"No matter how much? Hard? Fast?" Drake couldn't believe he could manage words past the boulder of ache filling his throat.

"I will take whatever you've got," she swore.

Looking down, he let out his breath in a rush past his clenched teeth. "Good answer," he praised her before sinking in to the hilt. His balls were bathed in silk fire as they felt the overflow from her center, and the two of them groaned with satisfaction. He rested his head against her forehead, noting proudly that her eyes were mere slits, like a cat's. "Baby. Sally. My own," he gifted her with a searing kiss as he waited for her body to adapt to his possession. "Are you ready for more?"

"There's more?"

His low chuckles was all it took to start to send her over the edge. She wrapped her fingers into the ties, the only things that felt as if they were keeping her from splintering apart into a million little pieces. They were now the ties that held her physical body to the world while her spiritual one joined Drake in every other way.

It took Drake several long strokes before he joined her, plummeting over the precipice of control, into the whirlpool of completion. With no reason to hold back, he came over and over, pumping his flow into her. Whether it was the heat or the drawn out foreplay, Sally joined him for another round, her sheath clenching like a fist around his burning shaft. Their combined orgasms were a wave neither of them wanted nor tried to escape. Their ecstasy had no end, there was no way to stop it, and all their locked brains could understand was that it began in the eyes of the partner staring at them with absolute adoration.

It felt like hours before either of them could move. Drake staggered from the bed to the bathroom and she could distinguish the sounds of water running. When he returned he washed her between her legs, taking care to sooth the ravaged skin shining with their combined fulfillment. He made sure to remove each drop of blood, and hoped she could not see the deep pride he felt at this proof no other man had ventured here before him.

Crawling back into bed, Drake could not believe how rubber and noodles had replaced every one of his bones and each of his muscles. He summoned enough energy to release his mate's limbs from their ties and drape her on top of him. Her body was returning to its cool state, and felt like a soothing caress against his skin.

"Wow," was the sole word she managed to whisper from her swollen lips.

His low chuckle was the music that sent her off to sleep.

CHAPTER ELEVEN

It had to have been around noon when Sally woke. The night had passed in a haze of pleasure, hunger, and fulfillment. Drake had woken her three times to take her on another trip through the wonders of making love.

She wasn't sure she could walk.

Ever again.

Not that it wasn't worth the sacrifice.

Each time when they were through he would get a cloth to sooth her flesh. Drake would make jokes that he always tended that which he valued most. Sally suspected he must have been healing her in some way, for though she hurt, she was in no real pain.

Her eyes opened first and she smiled to realize the covers were still a tangled mess on the floor some place. The warmth she was feeling was entirely due to the living male heater wrapped around her. Drake was holding her so tightly, it was as if he feared her disappearing. She rubbed her chilled feet against his leg. This was one guy who would never need an electric blanket. There were a lot more benefits to having a dragon in her life than she had ever imagined.

Toe-curling, mind-numbing, breath-stealing endless orgasms were at the top of that list.

Moving the heavy arm wrapped around her middle, Sally figured out she needed to slide out of the bed to get her hair free of his cheek. She had to shimmy her legs from underneath the one holding her down. When she could sit up free of his restraint, she looked back at the man who had rocked her world. All night long. He was more beautiful when he was asleep. *Like that was possible.*

Walking on her toes, she sneaked into the bathroom, wincing with every step she took. Her dragon might distribute climaxes with a free hand, but her body was definitely paying the price for it now. Running a hot bath she hoped he wouldn't be awakened by the noise. It wasn't like she knew how to say no to him once he started kissing her. *Or touching her. Or, you know, looking at her.*

A long soak took some of her aches and pains away. The Jacuzzi jets did a great deal to move the process along. Easing back in the marble tub she took a moment to gaze around. Since arriving she had been so focused on leaving this place she had never taken the time to really see the suite.

Her dragon came by his love of sensuality in an honest fashion.

This bathroom was a delight for every one of the senses.

The majority of the room was marble. Grained with silver and gray, it covered the walls, countertops, and glassed-in shower. There was slate on the floor that was several shades of lead. Someone had distributed white fluffy small rugs over the floor so one could walk from one to the other without touching the cold tile. The brushed nickel fixtures continued the feeling of male luxury.

It was the smaller features that kept the chamber from being harsh and unyielding. The towels were the same stark white as the floor rugs, and were so large, she was sure she could use one to cover her bed as a blanket. There were pink and lavender scented candles throughout the room. One of the counters had an assembly of silver-topped crystal jars housing different soaps, bubble bath, lotions, and large cotton swabs. She had even taken some time before slipping into the hot water to smell the vanilla scent of the potpourri in the corner.

Then of course the shower and the tub were both almost large enough for Drake to use while in dragon form.

After taking her bath, she was feeling so good, and the toiletries Drake had arranged for her were so luxurious, she decided to take a shower as well. It also meant she could shampoo and condition her hair with some creams that left it smelling like cinnamon buns. Sally paused with a slight smile on her face. She was starving, and for the first time in her life, she felt as if she deserved to eat. A quick blow dry, some light make-up, and she was almost ready to face the world, or the smoking hot man who was sleeping like ... a man who had spent the entire night making love to her.

Peeking around the door she frowned.

He was still fast asleep.

Tiptoes took her to the closet where she rifled through until she found something that would be suitable to try and hunt her man up some food. Khaki pants with multiple pockets, a white collar t-shirt, and a long dark sweater on top. Sally gathered up her outfit, the silk bra and panties set, and returned to the bathroom to pull it all on. She winced when she caught sight of her body in the mirror. Being with a dragon was hard on the skin. She had dark bruises on her thighs and hips, razor burn on her breasts, and hickeys on her neck.

She chuckled as she examined the love bites in the mirror. It seemed her life had been a series of firsts since meeting this man.

If only her sisters could see her now.

Thinking over how fast they tended to manipulate all men around them, she shook off that thought. Better she stay Drake's secret, and he remain her fantasy.

Leaving the bathroom she considered the exits from the chamber. It was not as if she could call for someone to bring them food. Even the cell phone Drake had given her yesterday had disappeared. The dumb waiter was still there though. Crouching down next to it, Sally realized it was so large one could call it an elevator. The controls inside the small box looked simple enough.

Folding her body into the structure, she pressed the button that had a down arrow. With a slight lurch the platform began to lower through the dark tower to some unidentified location. She closed her eyes and began to pray her weight would not break it. *Great*, Sally, she muttered to herself, *now you think about your size, when you are already in the chamber and on your way down.*

"It's okay," she swore to herself. "We'll be fine. After all, God is never cruel. No way he's giving you a man like that and killing you in a dumb waiter. Think of the headlines. It'd be ridiculous."

The lurching stop almost sent her sprawling out onto the floor. Sally caught her body on the lip and surveyed where she had landed. There was a long hallway before her. Dark polished wood on the floors, intricately carved wainscoting, a series of landscape paintings of what appeared to be an alien planet, and tables with vases of Asian influence were all she could see. Hopping off the platform, Sally continued to ease her way down the hall as she tried to imagine what she would say should someone find her.

At the end was a large room with a flat screen television that was longer than she was tall. There were several different large easy chairs and leather couches distributed around a tufted footstool. It was a chamber designed for big men to watch their bigger television in comfort. For some reason, it made her smile.

"Hello," a male voice spoke in a soft and courteous tone.

She turned around so fast, Sally almost grew dizzy from the movement. In the corner of the chamber, near a large case of books, was a man. One with coloring she had never seen before. His skin was tinged a watered down blue, his eyes were the color of sapphires and his hair was cobalt. The features of his unusual coloring were so fine, it kept his weirdness from overwhelming. It was as if she were looking at a grown-up Smurf who happened to be a cover model. "Hi," Sally began to back away her heart pounding with fear. "I am so sorry for intruding."

"I'm not," his voice rolled in waves from very deep to a sensual purr.

"I've been rather bored, so you are a pleasant change."

"Drake told me I shouldn't bother any of you," she confessed.

Aquos breathed out in a slow and steady rhythm, concerned any quick movement would send the beauty running for her life. Her smell was a combination of spice and vanilla, with an additional undercurrent of cinnamon. He didn't know if he should eat her, lock her up to keep her safe, or send her far from the building so his peace of mind was not permanently disturbed. "That's because he was worried one of us would steal you away from him."

Her mouth was opening and closing as she tried to understand what he was saying. An answer popped in her mind and she gave the stranger a small smile. "Oh, you're teasing. That's very nice of you. I'm Sally Eversham, by the way."

"My friends call me Aquos."

She bit back the observation the nickname was obvious. "It's nice to meet you."

"Are you running away from Drake?"

Sally looked down uneasily, recalling the fact in her haste to find some food, she had neglected to put on shoes or socks. Her feet were ice. Aquos looked down and hid his smile behind his palm. He gestured to the couch. "Perhaps you should sit down before you freeze. I fear we are keeping this room colder than usual for me."

"Why do you like it so cold?"

He stayed motionless as she began to move to the place he indicated. "I don't as a rule. It's just I was fighting a fever most of the night."

"You're sick, too?" She sank down on the cushion and tucked her feet under her body.

"Drake is ill again?" Aquos asked so quickly Sally jumped up and began to slide back to where she came. "Wait," he held up his hand to stop her. "Please don't leave."

She trembled at the threshold, longing to flee with all of her heart. There was something so unyielding about this man. Foreign. Just when she was about to return the way she came, she saw a flicker in his eyes; a flicker that reminded her of … herself. Loneliness. Regret. Insecurity. All emotions she knew very well. "I'm not running away," she confessed.

His smile was a mere quirk of the corners of his lips that turned into a full-fledged beam when she slid back to her place on the couch. "We were," Sally wrapped her hands up in the oversized sweater as she tried to explain. "We were busy last night and I thought I would try to find us some food."

"I'm afraid when I have a fever the elementals are very busy the next morning."

"Oh," Sally released a deep sigh. "I could cook. I like cooking," she brightened with enthusiasm. "I think I'm good at it."

He chuckled at her hopeful expression. "I am sure you are."

Sally felt tears spring to her eyes at the kindness she identified in his smile. "You're a very nice man, aren't you?"

"No," Aquos shook his head with regret. "I am not a man."

She smiled with interest, "Are you a dragon, like Drake?"

Aquos found he was sitting on the couch next to her as his knees gave out. "He told," Aquos sputtered with disbelief. "Drake told you what he really is? In truth?"

"He showed it to me," she confessed. "Why are you so surprised?"

"I've lived with him for centuries and I've never seen his true form. The idea he would reveal it to you after a mere heartbeat of acquaintance is unbelievable to me." When she recoiled from him he put his hand up, "not because of anything wrong with you. Just from his tendency for secrecy."

Sally shrugged, "I liked it. You should fly with him. It's amazing."

He gave her a shy smile and then laughed when her stomach suddenly erupted with a loud growl. She covered her middle with her hands and colored bright crimson. "I've never seen a woman turn neon red before," he teased.

She lowered her head and jumped off the couch, backing away from him. "I apologize. It doesn't mean anything, you know. I should be dieting, but maybe later I'll get some exercise in."

Aquos shook his head. "Why would you need to diet?"

"Boy, I could have used you guys around over the last … oh every day of my life," she muttered to herself.

He didn't quite grasp what she was saying or why she was saying it. "Sally Eversham, why are you changing to the color of a steamed lobster?" When her eyes grew wide as a jellyfish he held his hand out to her in entreaty. "Not that it isn't a very pleasing color on you. It brings out the ruby in your hair."

She put a hand on her locks and looked down. In her haste to get some food before Drake woke, Sally had neglected to do anything with it. By now, she probably had a cloud of frizz around her face. Her head fell forward with defeat. It seemed that femme fatale was never going to be in her job description. When she caught those flickers of pain in his eyes she tried to explain her upset. "I just didn't wish to insult you with my body needing some food."

"Why would that insult me? If I know anything about Drake he kept you up all night making love to you. I would be astonished if you weren't hungry."

"I'm really going to have to stop liking you guys."

Aquos shook his head in confusion. "Why?"

Sally sighed as she tried to blink away the tears in her eyes. "If I don't stop now, when Drake kicks me out, it's going to destroy me. Liking two of you might kill me."

He clenched his jaw at the mere thought they would lose the treasure this woman revealed herself to be. "If my brother is stupid enough to send you away, I will keep you. There is no way you should worry about liking us, as you say."

She giggled at the idea they were treating her like some kind of precious possession. "What do you mean … keep me?"

Aquos' eyes blazed, the fire turning his soft look into one of unyielding strength. "I would first make sure you wanted to be kept, Sally Eversham. But rest assured, if I had the choice I would never let you out of my sight."

Her tremulous smile disclosed her feelings of pleasure and unease without any need of words. She didn't know what to say. How could she? It wasn't like she'd had any experience with men before last night, and now she was having another man throw himself at her. It made her want to have someone to ask to pinch her, for she was sure she was dreaming.

Only problem was she had never dreamt this well.

"Well, that's uhm, very nice of you."

When her stomach let rip another noise of annoyance, they both laughed at her discomfort. Aquos realized she needed food, and probably had not realized how to get it. "Sanctuary is an unusual home. We are served by what are called elementals. They are spirits of our home world who work on a telepathic basis. Most of them are occupied at the moment, but all you need do is think of what you need, and state it in a clear and matter-of-fact manner."

"What do you mean?"

"Normally, I would have you say 'we need first meal' but because they are so busy, I would suggest 'thank you for providing something to curb our hunger.' No matter where you are inside the building, someone will come here with a tray of whatever your body had need of."

Sally threw her head back with her laughter. When she saw he wasn't joining in, she guessed he hadn't just been kidding her. Wiping her streaming eyes, she asked, "Aren't you joking?"

"Nope," Aquos winked at her.

"Aquos, with a sense of humor? That would mark the end of our days."

Sally jumped up and whirled around to face four other men who had entered while they were speaking. Years of insecurity and mental abuse made her step behind her new friend, hoping he wouldn't mind her need to be protected from unknown forces.

"Hey," Mach called as he strode in the room and collapsed in his favorite leather lazy boy. "It's Drake's toy."

"Toy?"

All of the men froze and looked at her with interest when her squeak came out with a gasp. "He calls me a toy?"

The horror and tears in her eyes made Aquos long to put an icicle through his younger brother's forehead. "No, Sally Eversham, he does not. This is Mach and he has a dubious sense of humor at best." Aquos made a studied effort to point out and introduce each brother, while continuing to keep her sheltered behind his body. He sent enough mist into the room to keep the others from getting a good look at her. "The other miscreants are Blade, Stealth and Turbo. You will remember Mach and Turbo as the ones who found you."

"You mean kidnapped me."

"Doesn't look to me like you are any worse for wear for the experience," Stealth snickered.

Sally swallowed back her tears and stepped back again to put some distance between her and these strange men. The two that had taken her were normal enough; if normal was over six feet tall and so gorgeous it made your toes curl. Stealth was uncomfortable to witness with his glowing eyes and washed out color. The way he seemed to fade away when he was done speaking was a new level of freaky for her. Blade reminded her of all the pictures she had seen of Archangel Michael. His golden hair and blue eyes, and shining sword hanging from his side, made him look like he just stepped off the podium of a church icon.

Aquos positioned his body to stand before her, "One more word, brother, and you will be the one feeling the burn. You getting me?" The two men faced off. Turbo looked down in shame as Aquos refused to blink away from the standoff. "One of you say one word to make her cry and I will drown your asses. Am I clear?"

"Come on Aquos," Mach teased. "Stop showing off."

Blade leaned to the side to look at Sally, but Aquos shifted so he was denied the right. "You have to pardon my brothers, Sally. I fear it's been decades since we had a visitor here. We're rather lacking in certain social niceties."

"Decades?" Mach turned to Turbo. "Who was the last visitor we had?"

"He means Turner."

Mach shrugged, "He was a prisoner."

"No one else has ever visited here," Turbo reminded him.

Blade shook his head, "Brothers, it is rude to have a conversation that excludes the guest. How about if everyone puts on his nice face and we talk to the lady?" When Aquos refused to give an inch from his protective pose, he sighed. "Sally, perhaps you would join us. The elementals are bringing some kind of drink for all of us to curb our appetites while they finish cleaning the flood."

"Flood?"

Stealth gave a low round of laughter at Sally's question, setting all of their teeth on edge. "Guess Aquos and Drake haven't revealed all of our secrets."

"Watch it, brother," Aquos warned.

"Or at least," Stealth continued as if he hadn't said anything. "All of *their* secrets."

Blade kicked his feet up on the stool and crossed his arms behind his head. "Come on you two, can't we all just get along?"

Mach turned on the television and Turbo turned it off. When Mach glowered at him, he shrugged in answer. "We're supposed to be making nice. That means no porn or football. Women don't like those things. Or at least I don't think they do." Mach was going to grab the remote from his hand when they heard Sally sputter, trying to conceal her laughter. "Hey," Turbo drawled. "She speaks."

The two turned to her, and she helplessly shrugged her shoulders. "Sorry," she tried to explain to all of the piercing glares turned her way. "It's just I'm guessing neither of you has ever seen a romance book."

"You mean one of those novels with the woman wearing the ripped clothes on the cover?"

Mach scowled, "Why would we care about those?"

"They're female porn," she explained. Sally almost jumped back when all five sets of male eyes grew bright with interest. "You never heard of that before?" she asked them.

"No," Blade admitted.

Stealth took a step forward and froze when Aquos tried to block him. "What do you mean?"

"Romance books speak to the deepest dreams and fantasies in a woman's secret heart."

All the men moved to make a loose ring around her. Sally sent a smile at Stealth, the one directly to her right, who was looking at her with a much softer look, making it easier for her to breathe. Turbo and Mach shared a pointed look and she hid her smile when she heard Mach mutter, "We need to get some romance books right away."

"I don't understand," she looked between them. "Don't you know about all this?"

"Why would we?" Blade asked.

Sally held out her hands, "I hate to state the obvious, but you guys are like the living embodiment of every female wet dream."

"Girls have wet dreams?" Turbo questioned with excitement.

"Well no," Sally said. "But you get the idea."

The guys looked at each other, studiously avoiding her eyes. Finally, when he sensed she was getting nervous again, Aquos confessed the truth to her. "Women were a forgotten resource from where we come from. In our lifetimes, there was one female born to the elemental clan before we left our home. Though we have all found our own ways of enjoying the female of the species on this planet, I fear we have little real experience with your kind. It leaves one at a disadvantage."

"What about moms? Who raised you?"

"We were the last children to be born," Blade explained with a gentle tone.

"There were no moms," Stealth finished.

Sally gave each of them a tremulous smile. "Then I guess we have more in common than I thought."

"What do you mean?" Aquos was standing on her left, still ready to shelter her.

"My mom died when I was young as well. I kind of ended up raising myself."

The men all smiled at her, each sure she had no clear idea of how rough their lives had been before they came here, but not one of them was willing to question her statement. Her empathy touched each of them, deep inside the most hidden recesses of their souls. "Looks like you fit in here more than you know," Aquos shared with her.

"I've never fit in anywhere else," she quipped, "might be a nice change."

"We don't usually blend either," Mach boasted to her. "You picked the right bunch of guys to be kidnapped by."

Sally rolled her eyes as the others broke into laughter. A small man, stooped with age and toil, entered the room carrying another one of those manhole-sized trays, like what Drake had used the night before. On it were seven jeweled goblets, which looked more like they belonged in a museum. "Forgive me, sires; I did not realize there was still a guest."

"It's fine," Mach waved. "Luke and Drake are asleep."

The man seemed ill at ease, but Sally chalked it up to his five-foot height in the midst of the gang of seven-foot tall men. Not to mention the fact the servant was barely one third of one of these guys' individual weight. He handed out the cups to each of them, giving her the last one with a regretful look.

Mach glanced at the others as he cupped the beverage in both palms, "So are there more like you?"

"Women of average look with above average weight?"

When the guys shared confused glances Sally felt her head drop forward, uncomfortable at letting her true nature out again. She tried to break the mood by taking a sip of the beverage in her hand. It was a tantalizing blend of coconut, pineapple, banana, and strawberry. Delicious. Aquos was the one who broke their silence. "No," he cleared his throat several times before proceeding. "He means are there any other women who smell like you?"

"What do you mean smell?"

"That's why we took you," Turbo explained. "You smell like our home."

"You smelled me?"

"Of course."

Sally felt the blush fill her cheeks again, and gave Aquos a sharp look before he could comment on her resemblance to crustaceans. "What do I smell like?"

"Homo sapiens smell kind of like copper," Mach blurted out. "You're a blend of spice and copper."

Turbo put a hand on his arm to keep his brother from pouncing on the girl. "Your spirit carries some of the scent of our planet. We're hoping there are others like you. We think that's one of the reasons why Drake is so much better. You have just enough of the materials of our home to cheat the physical laws of this world to help him stay here."

"This is the disease you have mentioned to me?" She took another long drink from her cup.

"Yes," Blade put his cup down, for he was uncomfortable trying to talk without using his hands and he needed to keep one on his sword. "There were many of us when we first came here. We've been slowly dying off over the years and more women like you might be the answer we seek."

"To cure the disease?"

Stealth shook his head, gaining solidity with the force of his emotion. "No. We were each given riddles to solve when we came to this world."

"What happens if you find the answer?" Sally felt her stomach clenching and took some more of the beverage, hoping it would ease the tension. "I mean, there are a lot of great minds who might be able to help you if they understood the stakes."

"Our Oracle," Aquos cleared his throat and put down his cup. The last thing he needed was more liquid. "Promised us when we find the answers to the riddle we will be able to return to our world and resurrect it. You see, there was a horrible war and our planet's ecosystem was destroyed. Until we find the answers, we will never be able to go home." When he noticed her cup was empty he took it from her. "I am glad you liked it. I can call for more if you want."

Blade shook his head, "Remember, they already brought too many." He grabbed one of the unused cups and handed it to her. "So are there?"

"More women like me?" When all of them nodded their eyes, Sally smiled. "I don't really know. Until you said something, I had no idea I was even different."

Two arms snaked around her waist as a purr of a voice sent her senses soaring. "You are not just different, Sally-mine. You are perfect." Drake pressed a hot, open-mouthed kiss against the crook of her neck, right where it met her shoulder.

Stealth handed him a goblet as all of them rolled their eyes. "Give us a break, Drake. None of us needs you rubbing what you've got in our faces."

"I propose a toast," Blade declared. "To the perfect Sally Eversham."

As all the men raised their cups, Sally felt an acidic burn flood her system. Her stomach clenched, bucked, and cartwheeled, as her body was covered with an ice-cold sweat as if she had been dunked in a bucket of glacier water. Her eyes grew as round as two moons as she jumped to an uncomfortable conclusion when she recalled the dart she had pulled from Drake's neck just a few days before.

Looking up she felt as if the world had slipped into a slow-motion parody of life. Each man was bringing his drink up to his mouth to toast her name. She lunged forward managing to smack the goblets out of Stealth and Aquos's hands right before her body fell to the ground to writhe in agony.

Drake dropped his as he lunged to gather her against her chest. "Poison," she managed to whisper before she threw up everything in her stomach onto both of them. Her cheeks grew cold as the tears streaming down her face.

The gaze he turned to them flared with the fires of hell as he roared like a great African cat. "Find the elemental," he demanded.

If she had been conscious, Sally would have enjoyed the sight of his wings bursting out of his shirt. She would have rejoiced with the feeling of the wind streaming past them as they went soaring through the halls to his aerie. Sally vomited twice more before he even got them to the room. He willed the sick to disappear and cleansed them, taking particles from the air and demolishing any residual smells. When they reached the bed he settled her in the softness and covered her with the blankets, hands clenched in helpless terror as he tried to figure out how to help her.

As soon as she was settled, the fever started.

Drake dashed to get a damp cloth and tried to wipe it over her skin to cool her. He knew how to make things hotter, not colder. A knock on the hidden door sounded and he opened it with his mind. Luke came in and witnessed the scene before him with dismay. "I am sorry, brother. The elemental that did this was dead by the time we got to him. There was no one else to question."

"It was meant for us," he whispered as he continued to try and cool her face.

Luke nodded once. "All of the goblets were dosed. We would have been dead in an instant if we had consumed it. She saved our lives."

"You should have seen her," Drake's eyes were pinned on her face as he spoke to his friend and technical leader. "She knocked the cups out of my best friend's and most hated enemies' hands at the same time. Managing to get just the one word of warning out, before she was carried under, by the toxin meant for us."

"Our brothers told me," Luke assured him.

Drake folded in on himself as he buried his face in the pillow next to her trying to hide his tears. "Do you know she has no confidence in herself? Her family has made her feel like she is so much less than she is. It makes me want to cry every time she looks around in confusion when I compliment her."

A hand grasped his shoulder and squeezed. "You have much in common."

"She is meant to be my mate."

Luke winced at the statement. Drake was trying to force him into a situation that would never be tolerated by the rules of Sanctuary. There was no way he could keep a female meant to be in this planet's dimension. "I am sorry, brother. We cannot break the rules of this house."

"I know," Drake's shoulders squared and he shrugged away from Luke's hand. "That does not mean I won't try and avoid them."

Without knocking, the other clan leaders of Sanctuary entered Drake's room. Blade, Aquos, Mach and Turbo looked devastated. Stealth's head was down so none could see what was in his eyes. He carried a small chest made from worked metal that had the sheen of something ancient and rare.

Drake moved his forehead to Sally's, longing to give his breath to keep her going. "We need to get her to a hospital. A doctor. Someone has to help her."

"We can't," Luke sighed when everyone turned murderous glares at him. "She was doused with poison from our world. If we took her to an earth place of healing they would recognize the components as being extra terrestrial. We learned when Mach's older brother decided to play with saucers in New Mexico how costly attention can be for us."

"She'll die if we don't help her."

Aquos stepped forward, "There has to be a way."

Turbo cleared his throat, "She's holding on, so far."

"That has to be a good sign," Mach finished for him.

It was Stealth who broke the silence gripping all the men crammed into the dragon's rooms. "I would dare to suggest a solution."

"We are not killing her," Drake roared.

Luke stepped between the two men, "Give him a chance to speak, brother."

Stealth faced Drake and Aquos with a quiet dignity that had always marked his bloodline. "I have brought a potion of my people. It should eradicate any residual toxins infiltrating her blood."

"This could heal her?" Luke tried to hide his disbelief, but knew he did a poor job of it. Of all the brothers, the hatred between Stealth and Drake ran so deep, and was so old, he was sure the last ones to assist the girl would be the people of the air. "Brother, you must be sure. I will not endanger her more than she already is."

"I am," Stealth nodded his head. "If my oath is required, you have it."

"What are the risks?"

All of the men turned to Aquos. Out of all of their number to be suspicious or doubtful, it was the water clan that was the last. They were usually far more giving and understanding than any of the brethren. Stealth's head came up with pride, "She might have some powers when we are done. Nothing major, but this will add more of our world into her body. I cannot guarantee the outcome."

"Will she die?"

The sheer desperation in Drake's eyes were understandable to every man in the room. He had found the one thing they were searching for the hardest; the concept of losing it after so little time together was inconceivable. "No," Stealth swore to him by placing his fist over his heart. "I swear it to you."

"Give her the potion," Drake commanded.

Turning back to his woman, he tried to drape his body over as much of her as he could reach. The fever had disappeared and turned into something that scared him even worse. *She is so cold. It was as if no matter what he did, no matter how much heat he radiated into her body ... she was just so cold.*

"Hold on," Luke shifted on his feet as he tried to consider the repercussions of what they were about to do. "You can't just send this poor kid into our world without considering what might happen."

Aquos sneered, "Bullshit. Her dying will only get us in more trouble."

"I like her," Mach offered.

Turbo gave them a shy smile, "She might help us find more like her."

Luke shook his head, "We should ask the Oracle."

"Who you won't speak to," Blade chided him.

Stealth opened the box and grabbed the emerald vial inside of it. He tossed it to Drake and jerked his head at him. "Do it."

A nod of thanks was all Drake had time for before he bit off the cork and poured it into Sally's mouth. He rubbed her throat to make sure she swallowed every bit of it. As soon as the last drop was in her stomach, he tossed the vial back to Stealth. It was obviously from their home, so he suspected it was treasured. He was going to owe him big for this.

That was, if she lived.

Merciful Oracle, he prayed, let her live.

Sally opened her mouth and let out a scream as she turned in one wave from endless cold back to searing pain. Her body began to levitate off of the bed, and Drake had to pounce over her to keep her Earth-side. "Hold on, baby," he muttered.

"Did you know she'd turn into one of the characters from *Ghostbusters*?" Mach asked Stealth.

"Shut up and help me," Drake ordered as he continued to try to keep Sally safe on the covers. Each of the men moved to add his hands to try to hold Sally on the surface of the bed. Stealth gazed at the problem with unease and returned to the chest. "I might have some sedative tea in here as well."

"After the last thing we tossed down her throat, is that a good idea?"

Stealth returned to Sally's leg and grasped at her ankle to try to keep her from floating away. Next, her body began to writhe, as she was hit by a series of convulsions. Each of the men grunted as they tried to keep the female they cherished from doing any kind of permanent damage to her body, or any of their own. It was like trying to catch a bucking bronco with bare hands. "I'll say one thing for her," Blade panted as he tried to capture her hand again. "This chick has some kind of strength."

"Reminds me of you," Turbo nodded at Drake.

"She is perfect," Drake tried to blink away the tears burning the inside of his skull.

A surge in the transformation sent her body bucking and two of the men felt the clip of her fists against their jaws. "She is perfect," Mach joked as he tested his mouth to see if it still worked. "The perfect right hook."

"Definitely like you," Turbo drawled.

"What's next?" Drake demanded of Stealth.

His brow furrowed, Stealth surveyed the woman he seemed to have given an express train to hell. "It should end soon." When her body twisted and once more shook off the combined weight of six men, he grimaced. "At least, I hope it will end soon."

A scream ripped from her throat and went echoing through the chamber and into their souls.

In that moment her body stilled and she seemed to release the deepest breath any of them had ever heard. Her scent, that elusive smell of home, intensified to make all of them rub at their noses. Drake glanced at his friends, and was not surprised when none of them could look him directly in the eye. They would each be affected by the odor and probably as hard with need as he felt himself. "She seems better." He looked around again, "doesn't she?"

Blade was closest to her head so he placed his hand over her nose and mouth. Her breathing was strong and steady. Turbo reached over to cover the pulse of life in her neck, and nodded with a large smile when he felt the rhythm beneath his palm. Luke covered her foot in his two palms and smiled as well when he felt her skin returning to a normal temperature. It was Stealth who spoke. "Feels like she's on the mend. I am pleased for you ... brother."

All of the men stared at him in shock, and then looked at Drake to see how he would take this comment. As the last free dragon rose from the side of the bed they all began to back away with concern. When Drake lost his temper he tended to spit fire, literally and figuratively, hence the reason why they had so many fireplaces in the house.

By the time he had reached Stealth, the others were all lined up next to him. Without a word, Drake dropped to his knees, and lowered his body until his forehead was pressing the floor. "You have my thanks for my mate's life."

Stealth looked at his friends, trying desperately to understand what to do. What to say. The act of submissive contrition was an offering rarely given on their world, and never outside your family. If he wished, he could claim the great dragon as his own personal slave. Drake would be a servant to his wishes for all time.

For a moment, he considered it.

The thought of being the first of his kind to gain a dragon's obedience would set his name in the sacred rolls. It was power beyond his imagination. Freedom. Total and complete freedom. It was the very thing his people had sought as they were seeking a way out of the final war that had destroyed the planet.

With those words Stealth felt his sense of triumph fade.

Sally Eversham had tried to save him. It was his hand she had knocked the cup from; he had been the closest of all of them to having the fluid touch his lips. He owed her his life, how could he not do anything needed to return it to her?

Stealth lowered his body to the floor, and matched Drake's pose. "My clan owes your mate, my life. You have my thanks."

Each of the other men did the same thing, and offered up the ritual words. For the first time in the history of their people all of the clan rulers had found a peaceful area of co-existence. Luke found he had to fight back tears. Through all the hardships and war, all the fighting and years of endless loneliness, this was the first time he had ever found a reason to believe they could make it.

They rose together, for the first time united.

Drake looked at the others, "The elemental that brought the drink couldn't have been working alone. They are placid and peace loving. There is no way they came up with this thing on their own."

"So someone wants us dead."

"Now there is no doubt."

All of the men nodded their heads to Luke's statement. "We need to warn the other enclaves." He looked up, and pinned Blade with the mission. "Make sure they recall all the scouts."

"I think we should share the fact our search has changed," Aquos suggested.

Mach and Turbo glowed with pride, "We're looking for women rather than things, now."

"We are," Luke gave them a small smile as commendation for their unwitting act of genius. "Everyone needs to go into lock-down. We protect our own, and the only way to do that is to stay close to home. Each of the elementals will need to get mind swept for us to find the traitor. Someone needs to call in a mage."

Stealth said, "I am the best clan for that."

The others all grimaced at their brother's sacrifice. None of them liked the mage clan, they kept to themselves and that tended to be better for everyone involved. The forces mages commanded could take out whole continents in this place. Even their displeasure could cause small problems. Like earthquakes. Tsunamis. Stock market crashes. "There is one more thread to take care of," Luke reminded them with an ominous glower.

Drake stiffened with outrage. "We are not evicting my mate when she is ill."

"As soon as she recovers," Luke stepped closer to the great dragon. "I will have my way in this. The girl belongs on Earth and you gave your word." When Drake made no further comment he swept the others with an encompassing look. "We all have things to do. Leave Drake here to deal with his woman."

They left without a word, though Aquos paused in the doorway to glance with longing at the form huddled on the bed. It was Blade's hand that reached back and pulled him out of the way of the closing door.

"At least he acknowledges you are my female. My mate." Drake returned to the bed and snuggled down closer to Sally. He put his hand on her forehead and smoothed the tendrils of hair back so they did not annoy her eyes when she awoke. "He is right," he whispered to his heart's still face. "I'll have to return you to your world. I just don't have to leave you there."

* * *

As Luke stalked off away from the others, Turbo paused. "You don't think he means it, do you? Drake won't really send her away."

"No way, my brother," Mach promised.

Aquos gave a smile that sent a shiver of dread through all of the men surrounding them. "If Drake sends her away, there's nothing to say we can't take her back. We like her, too."

"So we can keep her?"

They all laughed at the enthusiasm in Mach's voice. Blade nodded his head, "We can, indeed." When Stealth cleared his throat, everyone turned to him with concern in their eyes. He was the one brother, as connected as he was to the guardians of this world and the mage, who could stop their current plans.

Stealth smiled, "Not only can we keep her, but we will. She's the first woman we've found who carries a trace of home. No way we're letting that go."

The others were not sure if they should be relieved or terrified that he agreed.

They had just finished one ancient war. It seemed bad timing to start a new one.

CHAPTER TWELVE

Drake refused to leave Sally's side for one moment while she slept. Recovered. His hands kept fluttering between her pulse and her mouth to watch over her vital signs the only way he knew. He had seen some television shows that dealt with human healing but they never had enough violence for his taste. Now he regretted that life choice with every fiber of his being. If he knew something, anything of value, maybe he could help her.

His vigilance was so great he guarded her through each phase of her sleep.

He sensed her waking even before her eyes opened.

Smoothing her hair from her face, he waited for her to make some sign of being on the mend. When she just stayed frozen in place, blinking at him with no attempt to communicate, he could not hold his peace. "Sweetheart … Sally-mine … please say something. Anything? I cannot live without your voice."

Sally tried to get her tongue to settle into place so she could respond. Even so her brain was unwilling to provide much in terms of vocabulary. "Ow," she wailed as her stomach and muscles began to send data to her reawakening nerves. It felt as if someone had cleaned out every inch of her arterial network with hot pokers, and given the rest of her insides a wash with pure acid. Her arms and legs were pummeled, the bones within them the consistency of broken balsa wood. "What happened?"

He began to sob. Tears from his eyes cascaded over her cheeks like a benediction as he gathered her with gentle hands and cradled her body close to him. "Sally-mine, you gave me quite the scare. Don't ever do that again."

"Believe me," she wrapped her arms around him, happy to have him to hold. "I will try to avoid it." For her, no sign could be greater of where she stood in his life. A man so large and commanding was not used to revealing any weakness. This break in his impregnable façade was like a balm for her quaking heart.

Drake was ashamed of himself. *Crying like a sissy.* He should just torch himself, as his clan requested, and end his pitiful existence right now. *Way to impress the girl.* He tried to dry his face in the sheet without her realizing what he was doing but her arms tightened around his neck before he could withdraw. *Didn't she realize how difficult this was for him? How wrong this made him to the dragon clan? How he would be exiled by any dragonswan should he ever reveal such failing?*

Why was she at his side?

"Where do you think you're going?" she rasped.

"I should get you something to drink," his voice was so hoarse it sounded like someone was strangling him.

Sally nestled her face closer to him. "The only thing I need is what I'm getting right now."

"I almost lost you," he confessed, still shuddering with untapped grief.

"No way I'm leaving," she whispered. "Things just got interesting."

Drake released his breath as he crawled over her and wrapped his body around her, closer than a second skin. He knew he was probably holding her too tight but he just could not bring himself to let her go. "I was very frightened," he felt the words burst from his lips before he could consider how she would accept them.

Her hands tightened around his neck as she let the comforting double time beat of his heart lull her to sleep. "So was I."

"Please don't leave me."

Sally felt tears seep out of her eyes and drop down to mix with his. "I have no desire to do any such thing." He moved over her so he could stare directly into her eyes. "I have no desire to leave you – ever." She repeated with full intention and purpose.

"You remember the rules of Sanctuary don't you?"

Her smile was luminous in spite of her ten-miles-of-bad-road feeling. "I do."

Drake shuddered with need when she used the words associated with marriage. "I will keep you to it," he said against her neck.

"I fully expect you to," she teased him.

Drake stood up and staggered into the bathroom to get her a drink, hoping the reprieve would give him a moment to assemble his composure. He felt as if he had been shattered into tiny pieces by a sledgehammer. The cabinet in the corner had a hidden refrigerator with drinks and snacks.

Pouring her a glass of ginger ale, he brought it to her. The one thing he knew about humans was the fizzy soda pleased their stomachs. It also tended to get him drunk, so he kept a large inventory on hand. Helping her sit up by reclining her against his body, Drake brought the fluid to her lips. He fed it to her in small sips, hoping this would not react negatively with the potion they had given her to counteract the poison. When she began to push away his hand after a small third of the glass, Drake growled. "You are dehydrated."

Sally turned her head to avoid the returning glass. "What I am is tired," her voice was so sore it hurt to talk and more to drink. "Please, Drake."

Drake's sigh was heavy as he gave in. How could he try to insist she do something when he had just come so close to losing her? He also knew little of healing; perhaps sleep was the best medicine for her at this moment. "I will leave it by the bed so you can have it as soon as you wake."

Her face was contorted with a frown until he shed his clothing and crawled back into the bed to drape his body around her. His warmth dispelled the chill still clinging to her bones. When she felt the trembles rocking his frame, she snuggled closer to him. Her head was on his chest, with her legs on either side of his. His arms were tight on her back, one high near her shoulders and the other angled closer to her behind. "If I am sleeping when you wake up you must just shake me," he commanded her. "Why were you even in the main building?"

"I was hungry," she admitted to him. "I went looking for some food. It was my intention to surprise you."

Drake chuckled, "Well, that certainly worked."

"Glad to be of service," Sally drawled.

"How did you get out of the aerie?"

She shrugged, "I used the dumb waiter."

His entire being froze in place. "You used the little tiny lift the elementals utilize to send food and supplies up to me? The one made for small trays of food and bags of fabric? That dumb waiter?"

"Hello," Sally was very aware if she did not get him off this subject she was about to be stuck with a very long and tiresome lecture. "Injured woman here."

He gritted his teeth as he tried to settle down. "We will discuss this later."

Not if she had anything to say about it.

Drake rubbed his cheek against the silk of her hair as he continued to pulse his body heat to keep her warm. "Please don't do that again."

"Oh, baby, no way I can refuse you when you use the please word."

He chuckled and held her closer to his body as he tried to fight down the hunger hardening his cock. He felt as if he would burst apart with a harsh breeze he was so full and aching. The only problem was there was no way he was going after an injured woman, or one who had just lost her virginity the night before.

Some rumors about dragons were drastically overstated.

Thinking about rumors, the magic and abilities associated with Stealth's clan suddenly popped into his mind. "Sally-mine, there is something you might need to know. The poison that almost killed you, and would have taken all of our lives, was meant for us. It was from our home world. The only antidote was also from our world."

"What does that mean?"

"In saving you, we may have changed some parts of you. Forever."

"Will it make me skinny?" Sally glowed with the idea of changing into some perfect size-four who could eat whatever she wanted and not have to exercise.

He scowled at the idea of any part of her changing on a physical level. "Why?"

"That would be great."

Drake's eyebrow rose, "I don't think so. Sally-mine, how could you change what is already perfect?"

Her breath caught and tears sprang to her eyes. Laying her head back against his wide muscled chest, she sighed as she felt her body sliding into unconsciousness. "You know," she mumbled. "It is so going to hurt when you break my heart."

"I know the feeling," he confessed, knowing she had already slipped away into the world of dreams.

CHAPTER THIRTEEN

Beneath the main room of Sanctuary was the gathering hall designated as their ceremonial chamber when they first built over the final active gateway. The large stones had been crafted from a quarry a few miles away and had the smell of ancient earth energy that made each of the Lords glow with their individual power. The torches, set at equal distances around the hall, filled the chamber with living light, and provided the element of fire. A pool in the center was their water, and the air moving through the long, soccer-field sized hall, finished the mixture.

It was a place made with the powers of home provided from their new world. A poor substitute for their planet but the best Luke felt he could provide his people in this place.

Gazing out at the assembly, he grunted approval. Sending a telepathic message to Stealth, Luke encouraged his brother to hurry. None of his people appreciated being crammed into this space, even if they had been picked off over the years and now barely filled a third of the space. The only one who would not be present for this meeting was Drake who was still keeping watch over his woman.

Oh Oracle, what the hell am I supposed to do about that? A mated dragon was one of the most territorial, protective, possessive entities in the known universe. If Drake got any closer to that woman it would take death to separate them. Even then, he guessed it was iffy.

The elementals had lined themselves up for them in an orderly fashion without any direction from any of the brothers. Luke had called them to the lower gathering hall with the rumor they were to make an announcement. The three reds were grouped together in the northeast corner, the only clan that did not have over twenty members. Mach and Turbo lingered near them, convinced it was the healers that were to blame for the plot against them.

In the middle, was the clan in deep green. Elementals of the earth relished cleaning and gardening. They tended to be the simplest of any of the beings serving the noble families for generations.

To the far left of him were the blue clothed members, the elementals of the water. Their specialty was the arts. This included cooking, music, writing, and painting. It had only been in the last few years they discovered other forms of art, including sculpture and metalwork. Their beautiful jewelry had become some of the most prized examples of antiquity in this world. For Luke, it was the blue elementals who were the most likely to have caused this dilemma. They certainly had the most access.

Finally there were the goldens. Here were their protectors and guardians. Their sunlit colored robes were ludicrous against their muscled bodies. Tallest of the elementals, some of them topped over five and a half feet. As a rule these house knights were bred for their stamina and assistance to the higher clans in their pursuit of warfare. Here, Luke had set them to guarding the Sanctuary boundaries and representing them to the outside world.

This was the first time he had ever gathered them all together at once.

It was also the first time he realized not one of them had ever considered marrying with the humans. He understood relationships could grow tricky when you were immortal, but you would think one of them at some point would have bonded with a local woman. This seemed odd to him.

He just could not grasp what it might mean.

Blade stood behind him, his hand caressing his sword as usual. Luke tried to hide his amusement at his brother's glower and almost eager clenching of his weapon. The intimidation seemed to be working; everyone in the hall was glancing at him with concern and unease. It would have been funny if it weren't so telling of how dire this situation truly was.

Stealth entered with the mage and Luke could hear half the people stop breathing, and the other half start to pray.

The mage was dressed in floor length black robes that seemed to slither and slide around the being within them as if the fabric were made from living snakes. The shadows, as the mage passed by his stance on the platform in the front of the room, seemed to reach out to him as if recognizing a creature that was a part of their own.

"I have arrived," the man's sibilant breathing made the small hairs on the back of Luke's neck rise.

A few murmured words from Stealth sent the mage to the red healers. As the great psychic passed in front of each of the men they dropped to their knees in agony. Luke bristled with affront that he would cause hurt without motivation. "Mage," he barked. "We believe in innocence until proved guilty."

The attack was cut off with his command, though the mage made no effort to respond audibly to him. When he turned to the green elementals, Luke stepped down from the platform and moved between them. "You will not cause pain."

Stealth shifted with unease as he sensed the insult his leader was giving Altea, the man who had been called to run this investigation. "Luke."

"You will not cause them pain."

When the mage gave him a slow nod he moved out of the way. Luke drifted over to the red elementals and tried to help some of them gain their feet. "I am so sorry," he murmured to each of them.

"Sire," one man whom he remembered from when he was a child. "We would never harm any of the Lords."

Luke clenched his jaw. He had called in the mage, for that was what was expected. He could not tolerate the destruction of these people. Years of living in a country that had created the concept of rights had taught him in many ways, his people had neglected the very building blocks they might have stood on to survive the flood of wars and hatred.

When one of the women in the green elementals let out a cry of terror, he realized he could not tolerate anymore.

"I apologize, my people. Mage, you will hold."

Luke returned to the dais to give himself some time to consider his choice and how he should proceed. At home, he would set the mage to torture and investigate each suspect, until the culprit was found and killed. There would be no consideration for rights or trial. He couldn't tolerate his plan any longer.

He knew these people. They lived together. Over the eons of time most of them had become as dear to him as his own family once had been. This was just plain wrong.

"Can you conduct this investigation without causing pain?"

The mage gave a slow and ponderous shake of his head as if communication with the disciple of the Oracle's own was beneath him. Stealth moved to flank his other side from Blade, and Luke was again struck by how much had changed. The positioning was on purpose, and he appreciated his friends' silent statement.

"Do you understand how terrifying this is to them?" When the mage made no response he guessed that meant he did not care. "If you stay here for a few days, in the retreat cabin, could you continue the investigation from a distance and identify the culprit in a less obtrusive way?"

Another nod was all he received, though the length of time it took for him to give it was more than enough information for him.

The mage would do as he asked; he just did not wish to.

Stealth looked over to see the little green elemental clinging to her husband with a desperation that smote his heart. "Altea, he is right. We cannot harm these people in this manner. It is a new age; it is time for our attitudes to change as well."

Without a word to any of them, the mage left the room without looking back.

Gazing out at the gathered elementals, he prayed the light he was seeing in their eyes was one of hope and not of derision. "It has been a long, hard road we have walked together. Once we stood in separate groups, our loyalty to clan and Oracle alone. Too many years have passed since we came to this place, where we live and work together. I will no longer think of you by bloodline. I see you each as a member of my clan. The Oracle's children, one and all, perfect and equal in our own ways."

His little speech caused a smattering of applause and beaming smiles.

Luke shifted on his feet, still hesitant and unsure in the role of leader. "There is someone seeking to end us. We have sustained two attacks that we know of."

Blade gazed at the reds, "The first was against our brother, Drake. He was given an aster dart."

The reds began to confer amongst themselves and one of them shook his head as he stepped away from the others. "My Lord, it was Lena who tended the dragon. None of us were even aware she had ignored such a thing. It is against everything we believe in not to prevent pain."

"I appreciate that," Luke accepted.

"The next thing that almost took us was a poison slipped into our ceremonial goblets. If an earth woman had not consumed the asper venom first we would have been killed as soon as it touched our lips."

One of the older blues stepped forward, his robes singing as he moved his arms. "We live to make beauty in the world, my Liege. Why would we take any action that might cause such an ugly response? It is our gift to grant the physical senses ease and illumination. An elemental can never go against his nature."

"Or her nature," the little green elemental added without looking up from her husband's embrace.

Mach and Turbo left their supervisory position to join their brothers on the dais. Mach cleared his throat, looking as guilty as he felt. "I hate to intrude, but they really do have a point. The only way the elementals would do this, is if they were ordered." When his brothers gave him disbelieving looks, Mach shrugged. "Sorry, I don't mean to intrude. I know I'm kind of a bonehead."

"No, brother," Stealth chuckled. "You're right."

"Exactly right," Blade added with awe.

Luke nodded his head, "They had to have been ordered by one of us."

"I apologize to you," Luke added. When he was about to say more,

Blade put a hand on his arm to stop him. "We all apologize to you," Luke amended. "We should not have accused you without thinking it through. You deserve better than that from us."

"What do we do now," one of the goldens asked him.

"We lock down our borders," Stealth said with a hard glint in his eyes. "We just lock everyone out not present at this time."

The elementals rushed out of the room to do their bidding as the five remaining men continued to reel at the implications. "This means one of our own has to have declared war against one of us," Turbo's mouth remained gaping with his shock.

"No," Luke barked. "You declare war on one, you declare it on all."

They left feeling even more disquieted by their choices than before. It was one thing to know your enemy was amongst your friends, quite another matter to know your enemy was with you and you had no way of knowing who he was.

May the Oracle help them. Only God knew who else would.

CHAPTER FOURTEEN

As soon as Sally opened her eyes, Drake was leaning over her, peering into her face with clear anxiety. She tried to give him a smile, which only seemed to make the fear flare brighter in the glow of his eyes. Reaching up, she cupped his cheek, "Please stop worrying. I am right here, and feeling just fine."

He brushed his lips against the corner of her mouth, and would have withdrawn if she had not guided his face to give her a true good morning kiss. Sally opened her mouth just a little to ask him to slow down because her heart had started to pound like a freight train; when he slipped his tongue inside, it changed from a so-glad-to-see-you-made-it-through-the-night kiss into a let's-stay-in-bed-for-hours kind of enticement.

Ripping her mouth away from his plundering, she groaned when he panted into the crook of her neck. "Drake, please. My morning breath has to be killing you. It's bad enough when you just forget to brush your teeth the night before, but morning breath after almost being poisoned to death and throwing up for hours, has to be torture."

"Do you normally almost get poisoned to death?"

"No," she chuckled. The question was muffled and mangled due to his face still being buried, but there was just enough of this scrumptious man to still make her toes curl and heat up her core like a microwave. "It means we're not doing any more kissing until I've brushed my teeth a few dozen times."

Drake picked his head up to stare at her. His Sally's hair was a mangled mess around her face, she had dark circles under her eyes and her pallor was of a cloud. Still, her eyes were filled with desire and her body was moving under him as if already anticipating his possession. No female had ever looked as desirable as the one spread beneath him with such trust. And he knew without a doubt, as soon as she caught sight of her face, she was going to send him away to protect him from her ugliness. *If she looked any frigging better than she already did, he would die of frustrated desire.*

"I don't suppose you'd give at all about this?"

"No," she set her mouth in such an adorable pout Drake could not resist brushing another kiss to the corner of her lips.

"Woman, you will be the death of me yet."

Standing up, he gathered Sally into his arms with the sheet and lifted her. "Drake," she screeched. "You don't have to carry me. You'll hurt your back."

He shook his head. If she knew just what kind of weights he was accustomed to lifting, she would be horrified. "Sally-mine, you are nothing at all for my superior strength. You've chosen to mate with a dragon, love; there is no mightier being in two universes. Have a little faith in your man's ability ... please?"

She dropped her head against his shoulder and sighed. "You know I can't resist you when you say please." He stopped in the middle of the bathroom and slid her down his body, keeping his arms circled around her to make sure she was steady on her feet. Drake began to nibble at her neck and her fingers clenched on his shoulders. "Not that I can't try," she teased as she used her grip to push him one pace back. Sally knew he allowed her to move him, but she still felt a small feeling of triumph.

"I will wait right outside the door," he informed her with severity.

Sally made a shooing motion with her hands and gave him her best smile. "I promise not to disappear."

When he shut the door behind him, Sally closed her eyes and turned to the mirror. She suspected what she was about to see was going to be horrible, and she was determined to be braced before she did. Her fingers were tight around the countertop, the cold marble giving a pleasing bite to her hot and sticky skin. Opening her eyes, she gasped, and turned away just as fast. "I've decided to take a shower," she called out to him. Looking at the mirror again, Sally bit back her cry of horror.

It was far worse than she imagined.

She looked like she'd stuck her finger in an electrical socket, let her body get dragged behind a galloping horse, lived indoors for most of her life, and had been beaten by all of the residents in the asylum. *He kissed this?* Her whimpers inside her mind were acerbic against her weak self-esteem.

The door slammed open and she was forced to face an infuriated male. Drake stepped into the room, and without speaking, he put toothpaste on a brush, turned on the water, and handed it to her.

"Drake," she started to speak but her man just guided the toothbrush to her face.

She did what she was told. When she finished rinsing out her mouth, Drake wiped her glistening lips and picked her up once more. "Drake, I need to take a shower. And put on some make-up. And blow-dry my hair."

He settled her back in the bed, which seemed to have fresh bedding. His jaw was so tight, she was sure he was grinding his teeth. "Drake?"

"You almost died yesterday, baby. You are to rest today."

"Drake I'll feel better with a good shower."

"No," he sat next to her and caged her inside his arms.

"Please?"

He scowled at her and put a kiss on the edge of her jaw. "No," he repeated with a hard look. "But it flatters me you strive to manipulate with your magic word."

Sally managed to pull her hands out from the bedding and cover her face. "You're impossible." The smile he gave her was so unrepentant and charming, Sally could not help the groan that escaped her lips. "Completely impossible."

"His nickname," Aquos announced before entering the room.

Stealth, Turbo and Mach followed close behind; each carrying a different item. Turbo placed his large tray of food on the small table. Mach brought a crystal vase of fresh flowers filling the room with all the smells of the outdoors. Stealth brought a small pot of tea and cup, which he left by the bed; and Aquos had a mirror.

"They brought gifts," Drake pointed out with his dry sense of humor.

Stealth chuckled, "Blade stood over the elementals who prepared all of this with his largest sword to ensure its safety."

"I figured you wouldn't want to leave her to order food," Turbo explained.

Mach beamed, "I know women like flowers."

Stealth gestured to the tea, "This should help you feel better. The side effects of the poison and the antidote can both be brutal."

"My gift is a great deal harder to explain."

Sally looked to the man of blue and felt her heart clench. He looked so lonely. Forlorn. It made her insides ache. "If that is really a mirror, I'd rather take a pass."

"It is not a normal mirror," he confessed.

All of the men turned to stare at Aquos. Drake was the only one who seemed to know what was going on. "You do not have to do this, brother."

"She needs it."

"Once again, guys, I've already seen what I look like, and if there was a bag handy I'd have it over my head right now."

Aquos handed Sally the gift. "This mirror will let you look at yourself through someone you love's eyes." When she refused to hold the glass up,

Aquos moved closer and positioned it so she could see her reflection. "See what you are when Drake looks at you, Sally Eversham."

"Why do you guys keep using my last name? You can call me …"

Mach joked, "She wants us to call her nothing? Won't that make it hard to get her to come for dinner?"

Sally's voice had trailed off when she caught sight of her appearance. She hadn't even looked this good when she had dressed up for prom night. Something within her somersaulted and turned, as she acknowledged the one thing she had never considered to be true in her world.

In Drake's eyes, she was beautiful.

The other guys exchanged smug looks. Stealth was the one who caught the gleam in Drake's gaze. "I think it's time we took our leave."

"How do you take leave," Mach began to tease when his friends pushed him out of the room and closed the door behind them.

Sally lay the mirror down with care as her brain continued to reel with what she had seen. It was magic. There was no way she had changed into the beauty she had just seen from the few steps between the bathroom and the bed. So somehow, what the mirror did, was magical. It made her feel uneasy with a good dose of unsure. How could you possibly deal with such a thing?

"You are not pleased?"

"No," she assured Drake, putting her hand on his bicep and giving it a squeeze. "I'm just a little surprised."

Drake poured her a cup of tea while she sat up in the bed. "Why?"

"I've never seen myself in that way."

"You see yourself through the eyes of the family that resents you," he nodded his head with understanding as he handed her the cup.

Sally took a sip and was happy to taste what seemed like green tea with mango sweetening it. "What is this?"

"Something to strengthen you."

Another sip, and Sally felt a buzz of electricity course through her body.

"Now let me discuss your schedule for the day."

She hid her roll of her eyes in the steam of the mug. "Let me guess. Bed rest?"

"And more bed rest."

"You're going to drive me nuts, aren't you?"

Drake chuckled as he leaned forward to brush a kiss against the tip of her nose. "It is probable. There is no way I will ever again survive watching you writhe on the floor as your life drains away."

"You'd rather see me writhe for other reasons?"

The lecherous look he gave her was so leering it was comical. "I'd be on the floor with you."

When she finished the tea, he refilled the mug and moved to the tray of food to select what he deemed suitable. As he agonized over the varied offerings, Sally could not help worrying about what had occurred. "The old man that handed us the goblets. What happened to him?"

"He died."

Her fingers clenched around the ceramic mug. "By your hand?"

The look he gave her was so fierce and piercing she swallowed with unease. Drake took the time required to finish filling her plate before answering her. "He died by his own hand, Sally-mine." He handed her breakfast before sitting next to her on the bed. Drake took control of the tea as she settled the plate on her lap and started to pick at the food. "I have killed, Sally. Often and many. The elemental who dared to try and end our lives would expect no less. One that almost took yours, deserves it."

"It's just he looked so conflicted when he handed out the drinks."

When she stopped eating and grimaced at the rest of the food, he growled low in his throat. "That was all for you."

"I can't eat anymore," she confessed, tears in her eyes.

Sighing, he took the plate back and pressed the cup into her hand. "Then you'll need to finish all of the tea." When she opened her mouth to argue, he used one finger to shut her lips. "Sally-mine, if I am going to consume all of the food to make Turbo feel good about going to the trouble to bring it, the least you can do is drink Stealth's tea. I hate tea."

"What do you like to have?"

Her smile was light and he felt the deepest recess of his heart fill with ease. "I love to drink your soda pop, ginger ale gives me a great buzz with no aftereffects; but as a rule I stick to water. Food doesn't matter to me as long as it's plentiful and made by someone else. But the one thing I truly love to have Sally-mine – is you."

She drank the tea.

CHAPTER FIFTEEN

Floating like a paper plate on a pool of oil the moon was full and heavy in the sky. Blade was moving past the front door to the walled-in side yard he used to practice his swordplay. It had been years since he had another of his kind to spar with, so each time he went to keep his skills fresh it felt like a small dagger ripping through his side. The honor of his blood demanded he keep going. No matter how much it wounded his heart.

He stopped when he saw Turbo standing near one of the brotherhood's many vehicles.

"I was under the illusion our leader demanded we lock down the borders."

Turbo shrugged to the accusation in his voice. "Mach has a date."

"What Mach does with those women is not dating."

"Well," the one they discussed appeared out of the main house. "We can't all be ascetics like the rest of our brothers."

"I shudder to imagine what you do to those women."

"Give them endless pleasure, my brother. Endless pleasure."

With a half smile, Blade shook his head over the young man's boasts. "Do you think it wise to go out under our current circumstances?"

"Luke said he wanted us to find other women like Drake's toy."

Blade resisted the urge to roll his eyes. Sure. Now they wanted to follow orders.

Turbo bit his lip with indecision. "Do you go to train?"

"As I always do this time of night."

Turbo shifted on his feet as he felt his heart tear. Never before had they felt close enough for him to even consider requesting what was in his soul, but he had hungered for it for so long he felt his need overwhelm his fear of rebuff. "Need you go alone?"

Both the other men recoiled at Turbo's question, making him feel even more like an ass. Blade stiffened with self-righteous outrage. "I need no women from you."

"That's not what I mean."

"What do you mean," Mach asked his amusement bubbling from his eyes.

"I wondered if you would train me."

Mach's eyebrows rose so high and fast they almost disappeared in the fall of his hair.

It was Blade's reaction that meant the most to him.

The older man recognized this moment for what it was ... a momentous, incredible sign. Perhaps if they began to learn more about their ancestral ways things would begin to change. He could not deny him. He also could not treat this decision with less than his clan's typical studious considerate due. "If you begin to train with me, you cannot stop. Once set on the warrior's path there is no turning back."

"U-turn is not in Blade's blood's language."

Turbo ignored his cousin's joke. "I am aware of it."

"Friend ..."

"Brother." Turbo's gentle alteration of Blade's sentence made all three of them smile.

"Why would you wish this?"

"We fight by using the wind and our quickness. I wish to know more."

"He's always reading," Mach drawled, as if the pursuit of knowledge was a ridiculous thing.

"Books are such a rarity in our world, all of us like to read."

"I'm more of a hands-on type of guy." Mach checked his watch and grimaced. "Speaking of hands on, my ladies are waiting."

"Ladies? As in more than one?"

"Of course," Mach shrugged.

"Have you not heard the saying it is quality over quantity?"

"Until I find someone like Godzilla has," Mach shrugged. "I'm going for everything I can get."

Blade shook his head. "Don't call Drake, Godzilla."

"Why not?"

"It pisses him off, and I'm the one who had to rebuild the hall the last time he exploded."

"Literally and figuratively," Turbo inserted as he chuckled at the memory.

"So what's it to be, my cousin?" Mach turned to his best friend and only family. "Hit the club for some fine-assed women?" He took a beat before he added, "Literally and figuratively. Or stay here with knife-boy, and practice your throwing skills."

"I would rather stay."

In his typical fashion, Mach bowed his head, not hurt by his cousin's defection from their plans. "More for me, then."

As he jumped in the Range Rover and drove into the night, his two friends stood side-by-side to watch the glow of his rear lights fade. "Is he always that ..." Blade tried to find a word to encompass the young man's ability to roll with any punches.

"Happy?"

Blade chuckled. "Yes."

"Basically ... yeah."

"How do you put up with it?"

"Alcohol."

The deadpan answer made Blade throw his head back and laugh deep from his core. "You two have certainly kept things interesting over the ages we've been stuck here. I am serious though, little brother. If you start to train in our way, you will not be able to stop. There is no failure in my kind. No lack of honor."

"I know that," Turbo swore. "It's why I wish to learn."

Blade held out his hand in friendship, brotherhood and as a sign of faith. "Then let us begin."

"I thought we already had."

CHAPTER SIXTEEN

When Sally woke next, she found her dragon draped over and around her, as he liked to do. Cherished. It hit her as if a bolt of lightning sent from the heavens. This was what it was like to be cherished. To have a man hold you as if you were the most precious thing on Earth, and could not stand the thought of even one moment without you by his side. She wondered if any of her siblings had ever known this pleasure.

And felt very sad when she doubted it.

As she tried to do her slither and slide move to go to the bathroom, the arm around her waist tightened, and she found her body wrenched back into the cradle Drake had made of his own. "Where are you going?"

"A girl needs some privacy."

"Sally-mine, your skin has been cleared of all remnants of illness and sweat. There is no need to shower."

"I just want to."

He could hear the pout in her voice, so for his own safety, chose not to look in her face. "Sally-mine, you need to rest."

Hope flourished in her breast with a speed that left her breathless. "So you want sex?"

"No," he roared.

Well, so much for a sudden self-esteem shot of adrenalin, she muttered in her heart. *If he wanted to have sex with her when she looked so horrible; it had to be a sign he loved her. Saw her as the mirror showed. Guess not, though.* "Then what," she snapped.

He turned her over with gentle hands, though tightened his grip when she sought to move her eyes away from his probing look. "Sally, you almost died."

"I'm fine now."

"I wish to make sure."

"Fine." She turned over once more and closed her eyes so he would not see her tears. "Great."

"Do you think you serve no purpose by my side but to appease a physical need?"

"Drake," she tried to speak but her voice cracked so much with one word, she stopped so she could take a deep breath. "If I am to rest you should leave."

"What?"

"Leave."

"No."

"Yes."

He felt as if she had just impaled him on a stake. The pain was so great he could see the glow of his crimson eyes as he gazed at her tense back. *She was ill*, he tried to remind himself. Rest was what was needed. He would leave her be. Go away. She just needed some time. Drake pulled his body from the bed feeling as if some part of his insides had been turned to stone. "I will go, and leave you to slumber."

There was no answer.

"I will return soon."

Silence.

At the door he paused to look back with longing and need. Her eyes were closed, and he guessed she'd already passed on to a healing rest. "Be well, Sally-mine."

Somehow, Sally managed to keep her sobs back until the thunder of his footsteps faded away. She had learned her lesson. The problem with painful lessons was they were so very hard to remember sometimes. Hope was so much more attractive.

It just was not real.

* * *

In the hallway, Drake bumped into Aquos. "What's wrong?"

"Nothing," Drake avoided his friend's eyes.

"Listen Godzilla, you know you'll tell me eventually."

He stopped in his tracks and stared down the cold blue stare of his best friend.

"Sorry. Once Mach started it, we just got used to using it."

"Please stop."

Aquos put a hand on Drake's shoulder. "Is it Sally?"

"Yes," Drake began walking once more. "And no."

"What is it?"

"She wants to be alone."

Aquos sighed. He wished he could help him. He wished even more he could go to Sally's side and teach her there was more wonder to be found in the ocean than there ever would be in the air. This made him wish he could help himself. "Give her some time. Perhaps this is just some odd homo sapiens female thing."

"I fear the greatest battle I shall ever fight will be with the demons inside my mate's mind."

"Come," Aquos strung his arm over his shoulder. "We'll get you some ginger ale."

* * *

Once Sally had showered and changed she felt far more ready to face the world. She was wearing a long skirt, with a tunic over it, and an additional sweater over that. Drake had not seen fit to provide her with shoes for some reason, so she was stuck pulling on two different pairs of his socks to leave the room. The doorway the brothers used was easy to find now she knew where the hidden portal was concealed within the wall.

In the hallway, she knew just where to head to get to the front door. Sally guessed it could not be hard to find a road, and from there she was determined to get herself to some kind of phone or taxi.

"Where are you going?"

Why did that question send a shaft of pure dread shooting through her? She sighed and turned to face the one she knew was called Stealth. He seemed to appear from the wall, as if he had been hiding within the wood wainscoting and deep green paint. "I'm leaving."

"Sally Eversham ... why would you wish to do that?"

"Please, Stealth." Sally took a step closer to him and placed her hand on his arm. "Let me go."

"Why?"

"If I stay any longer it won't be possible for me to handle it when he dumps me."

"Why would he dump you?"

Sally's head fell forward as her eyes turned liquid with her tears. "Just let me go."

For a moment Stealth considered it. Letting her free would strike a permanent and deep wound in the dragon's heart. If he destroyed him, perhaps his kind would be free. The nightmares would go. The guilt at letting his people down.

His honor as well.

That was the one thing he would not sacrifice . "I cannot."

"He'll ruin me."

"What do you mean?" Stealth gazed at her, trying to understand how the dragon might be hurting her. There were rumors of their cruelty, but over the ages, Stealth had never seen any woman leave Drake's arms with anything but a smile on her face.

"My heart," she gasped. "He'll destroy my heart."

"You give both of you little credit," he chided.

Her head fell forward as defeat settled over her shoulders like a cumbersome cloak from which she would not escape. "I just can't believe it."

"Sally Eversham …"

"Why do you do that?"

"What?"

"Call me by both of my names."

"It is a mark of honor."

"I don't understand."

"To use both your first and clan's name. It is our way of honoring you."

"Oh," she shrugged. "The truth is … Sally … is just my nickname."

"We like nicknames," he smiled thinking of the many words they used over the year to refer to one another. "What is your true name?"

"It's silly."

"As silly as running away?"

"You're not going to tell him are you?"

"Why should I not?"

"I gave him my word that I would stay."

"Then you had best scurry back to your lair where you belong."

Sally opened her mouth to protest the order, but Stealth just pointed back the way from where she had come. If he chuckled at each reluctant step she took, she felt it much wiser just to ignore it.

* * *

Stealth searched through the house until he found Aquos and Drake, sprawled on the couch in the arboretum. The fireplace roared with flames, explained by the empty soda bottles that riddled the floor around the dragon's chair. "I see you two have been busy."

"I thought it best he work out some stress."

He leaned against the wall and folded his arms over his chest. "And you felt it would work best by having him empty out the ginger ale stock throughout the Delaware valley? I would have thought you could come up with a better solution than that."

"What's up, my brothers?"

Stealth and Aquos smiled as Mach and Turbo sauntered in. "Seems Drake went on a bender."

"Whoa," Turbo kicked one of the green bottles out of the way.

"What's wrong with Godzilla?"

Drake snapped his mouth at Mach for using the hated nickname, making a sound like a large cat. "I hate that word."

"Did you find out what was wrong?"

"The remake sucked, " Drake muttered.

Aquos shrugged his shoulders. "Sally Eversham is giving him fits."

"Demons," Drake growled. "Her stupid family makes her act crazy."

"You know," Stealth tread with care, wanting to keep his promise to Sally and still assist a member of his planet. "If you share a little of your demons with her she might shed her own. It seems to me that the two of you are suited in more ways than you realize."

"I don't know what you're talking about."

Aquos stood and started to pull Drake's nerveless form from the couch. "Let's go, friend. Time to go to bed."

"You think this wise?"

He shrugged at Turbo's question. "He's not going to work it out here. Better she see him at his worst. Maybe they can find a way to talk."

"I think you are very blithe about this female's safety."

Aquos shrugged and almost lost the hold he had on his friend's form. "We know no more than he. Best do what we can to help."

"So in combined ignorance you feel we will find wisdom?"

"Would you three help me? He's heavier than the house."

They each took a side and began to muscle Drake's semi-conscious form back to his aerie. Turbo asked his question once more. "Are we sure that this is wise? We know little of women-"

"Other than the great pleasure to be found in their bodies."

Stealth and Aquos both shook their heads at Mach's statement.

"What if she's angered by his condition?"

Aquos shrugged at Turbo's query as they began the long walk up the stairs. "She made him want to get like this. She can figure out how to help him through it."

"If she starts asking why enough, maybe he'll tell her."

"And if he won't?"

"Then I'm guessing," Stealth cried out when Turbo dropped Drake's leg and it fell on his foot, "watch it," he snarled. "That we'll soon have to decide which of us is going to keep her. She was trying to escape earlier."

"She can't leave," Drake thundered.

"Oops," Mach joked.

"He's up."

Without another word Drake's wings exploded from his back, ripping his t-shirt into shreds. As the air current from his flight pushed them against the wall, all four of the men chuckled. "Well," Stealth drawled. "It seems they're going to talk now."

"They'll do something," Mach joked. "I just don't think it'll be talking."

As they returned to the main part of the house, Aquos lingered behind. *What will you do? Stand here, and should you hear her scream, rush to her aid? Destroying an alliance that goes back to your cradle? Or join your friends and spend the night's hours with them trying to ignore the call of your heart. Stay and jeopardize the Sanctuary compact or go and jeopardize the future of your heart?*

There was no choice.

He followed his brothers without a backward glance.

* * *

Drake exploded into the room and caused Sally to jump up from the bed as if lying on it were some kind of crime. She was examining almost seven feet of seething, hungry, infuriated male, with her heart thundering like a freight train. "You tried to leave me." He did one of those mind-blowing leaps, pushing her back onto the bedding, and landing to cage her with his body. "You were going to break your word."

"Drake," she gasped as he buried his face in the crook of her neck and took a small delicate bite of her skin. Sally punched him in his side. "That hurt."

"It is nothing compared to the pain you wished to cause me," he said.

His tongue began to soothe the bite, as he moved up her neck to her ear. The rumbling he made against her skin turned her body into a thriving pulse of need as she lost the ability to think. "Drake, what's gotten into you?"

"You sought to leave me."

Another bite, to her ear this time, made her squeak with a combination of terror and interest. This was a new side to him that she was not sure how to handle. "Drake, I just considered it. What's different about you?"

He moved his hips so that he could rub the solid piece of iron between his legs into her center. When she moaned at the feeling and her hips began to respond he shifted his body away to punish her. "I've been drinking," he confessed. "Why were you going to leave me? How could you do such a thing, Sally-mine?" An additional bite to her neck, the other side this time, made her hit him in the side once more.

"Ow," she complained. "I said, that hurts."

He placed small gentle kisses to the throbbing skin. "Good."

"Drake, I just got scared that's all. Leaving was a reaction to it."

He leapt off her once more, and she was left staring up at the ceiling, boneless with need. His breath was coming so fast, it sounded like a lumberjack's saw. "You blame me for being poisoned. I have sworn to you it will not happen again."

"No," her terror that he could think such a thing gave her limbs back some feeling. Sally rushed over to him, but Drake just jumped to the other side of the room. "That's not true."

"Then what?"

His eyes were rubies, filled with the turmoil of his fear that she would cast fault where there should be none. "Drake, I do not blame you for the poisoning."

"Then where was the hurt?"

When she tried to reach him he jumped once more. "Stop that," she demanded with a stamp of her foot. He crouched down with eyes so wary and afraid that it made her heart clench with agony. This time he allowed her to get within arm's reach, so she extended one hand as if trying to pet an injured animal. Looking deep into his face she understood he was injured. She also recognized he was a little bit drunk. Did she do this to him? This anger? Confusion? Need? Could all this truly be due to her actions? "Drake," she took a large swallow of her guilt as she prepared to leap off a very large cliff. "It was not you."

"Then who?"

The two words were wrenched from his lips as if he were trying to lock them in a deep prison cell. "Me. My family. My past. They all rise up and make me crazy sometimes, but you have my full and complete permission to do whatever you need to snap me out of it."

He wrenched her into his arms and catapulted the two of them back to the bed. She felt no pain as they landed, for his body kept hers from the impact. "I will hold you to it."

"Just no biting," she warned him with a mock growl.

As his teeth scraped against the beat of her wild pulse, he chuckled. "Only the kind you appreciate," he promised her.

Her response was to moan with her need.

* * *

When the brothers reached the main room, they found Luke waiting for them. Mach started their X-box, rubbing his hands together with eagerness. "What's up, oh fearless leader? We were planning on a marathon of Doom. Care to join us?"

"Have any of you seen Blade?"

A series of confused looks were exchanged which answered the question long before Aquos said, "No."

"He go out to the Underbelly?"

Luke shook his head to Mach's question. "He would be the last to break the lockdown."

"So what do you think happened?" Stealth's eyes glowed.

Luke clenched his teeth as he considered how to announce the manifestation of his greatest fears. "Is the mage still here?"

"I put him into the isolation cottage as you requested."

He nodded his head.

"Hold up," Turbo looked around at his friends shaking his head, "there is no way that Blade is the one betraying us. It doesn't make any sense."

"Then explain him disappearing."

"I don't care if Blade was frigging Houdini," Turbo sneered. "No way he killed us."

"He didn't kill us," Aquos pointed out with faked calm. "We're alive."

"Blade wouldn't have tried to hurt us," Turbo maintained, folding his arms over his chest.

Mach ached for his cousin, "It does seem strange."

"What?"

"The one man who is the biggest believer in the old ways and discipline, would mysteriously go poof right when we need to stick together the most."

Turbo made a point of taking a large step away from his friends. "Not Blade."

"He knew we opened the investigation. Why wouldn't he be here unless he has something to hide?"

"Maybe someone got the drop on him," Turbo offered.

The others all tried to hide their disbelief of Turbo's naiveté, but they failed. Even Mach turned to him with a gaping mouth and amusement bubbling in his eyes, "You're kidding … right? I mean, seriously? Blade has an arsenal on his body when he sleeps. Our brother likes to eat with a knife and a switchblade. This is not someone you want to take on in a dark alley without a serious death wish."

"I don't care what you say." Turbo turned away from his friends and began to stalk back to his own wing. "No way Blade betrays us."

Mach went chasing after him, "Turbo, brother – let's talk about this."

As the two youngest and most impetuous of their number disappeared, Luke collapsed on the couch. "I didn't intend to upset him. It seemed wiser to warn him, to warn all of us. At least we know what we are fighting now."

Aquos felt the world reeling at the premise that Blade had tried to kill them. "We are going to need to change all of the security protocols."

Stealth nodded his head, "And I'll need to take Altea through Blade's room. Maybe we can come up with what his grand plan is for all of this. All of us. Why someone who was normally so loyal would have decided to take us out."

"I don't know," Luke's jaw was so tense he didn't even move his lips when he spoke. "I just know he's gone."

Without another word, Stealth left to take on the confrontation with the mage. Aquos looked to Luke with an empty expression. "I thought things were going so well. This will be a hard hit to come back from."

"The elementals will have to be ordered to ignore all of Blade's requests."

Aquos chuckled, "Well, that would be your job."

"I take it that Drake and his toy are doing better?"

Aquos rose with murder in his eyes, his fists clenched. "You ever call her that again, oh fearless leader, and I will drown you in your sleep."

When the room was empty again, Luke let his head fall forward as he considered how long the journey had been to get to this point. It seemed as if no matter how many eons passed, he was still the same weeping child that had arrived on this planet. They called him fearless leader to remind him of just what a coward he truly was. It was his responsibility to announce to the people of Omnicom that they would have to leave their home.

Fleeing for their lives.

It was his choice to move Sanctuary to the beta site in this country when the Inquisition had begun to sweep closer to their home. Again it was his choice to separate the more violent clans in a vain attempt to protect the few men that were building some kind of bond. The riddles that the Oracle had given them were the excuse, but the truth was that he just could not stand the thought of losing the handful of souls he called friend.

Some kind of leader he made.

Pausing by the hallway to the dragon clan's people he smiled with a great deal of wistfulness. "I wish you well, Drake. You and your mate. One of us deserves some kind of pleasure."

* * *

When Sally woke up the next time it felt like her lucky day. Drake was fast asleep, making the cutest little panting noises. While she could, she managed to slip into the bathroom and start a shower. There was no way he was getting in the way of her taking a moment to do a complete change of her appearance. Aquos's mirror was great, but there was no way it was enough.

She was blow-drying her hair when he confronted her. The fierce look in his eyes did little to scare her. "What?"

"You were supposed to be resting."

"I'm resting better knowing I'm clean and my hair's pretty."

"Your hair is always pretty," he snapped at her. Without a word, he snatched the dryer out of her hands and turned it off. Picking her up, Sally wrapped her arms around his neck with a small sigh. "I wasn't done yet."

"Be grateful I didn't break in on your shower."

"Why not?"

He froze and looked at her with disbelief. "You would not have minded?"

Her smile was so seductive it made his balls ache. "I am sure," Sally pressed a gentle kiss to his cheek. "You'd have made sure I didn't mind for long."

Drake shook his head as he was once again hit by a wave of sensual images that was so beguiling it felt like his eyes were crossing. It was bad enough that for the last twenty minutes he had been racked with the torture of imagining what she looked like in the large steam shower, scented suds running down her body, dripping from her nipples. Now she was making it worse by revealing he could have come in without a problem, even though their one real night together was done in pitch dark.

This woman was going to be the death of him yet. Or the making of him.

"No," he set her down on the bed with a pout. "You're resting."

"We didn't do a lot of resting when you came back last night."

"I was drunk."

"You are very interesting when you're drunk," she confessed while her features grew bright red. "And may I add, devastatingly handsome when you're so imaginative."

His scowl at her teasing made her brush a kiss to the side of his mouth.

"You are very beautiful all the time."

Sally pulled him down before he could withdraw to brush another kiss against his jaw. "I think you are very sweet."

He snarled. She couldn't help herself; Sally brushed another kiss against the same spot.

"You are teasing me."

"I am," she giggled.

"You do realize I'm a fierce dragon who sends hardened warriors running home, crying for their mommies?"

"Ooh," she gave a mock shiver. "I'm shaking in my towel."

Drake bared his teeth at her and she burst out with giggles. "Women, entire cultures have worshipped me. They would give me offerings, hoping I would protect them and not go through the night roasting them in their beds."

She shook her head and giggled more.

"Find me funny do you?" Drake delved his fingers into the folds of the towel to find the curve of her waist. He began to tickle her, which sent out a round of laughter that soon had tears streaming from her eyes. "Woman, you will learn to respect me."

"Mercy," she cried. "Mercy."

Aquos entered the room without knocking to chortle at the sight that greeted him. It did his heart good to see one of them feeling happy. At least Sally was with someone who made her laugh. He said nothing when Drake moved the covers to shroud Sally up to her neck, and looked liked he'd have liked to pull them over her head. "In an act as miraculous as the creation of this planet, our fearless leader has decreed that we have a little party in honor of your guest."

"She can't come," Drake turned to Aquos, glowering. "She's resting."

"Drake," Sally turned him back to her so that she could kiss his cheek again. "Please?"

He sighed, as his head fell forward to rest against her shoulder. "I really hate when you do that."

"I know, honey," she patted his back trying to console him. "But you're a big bad dragon. Try and grin and bear it for now, okay?" When he gave her a hard stare she tried to ignore it. She tried not to laugh.

Just because she failed, didn't mean she didn't try.

"Good to see you're keeping your mate in her place," Aquos drawled.

"Clearly her place is beside me so that she can wrap me around her little finger," Drake snapped. "Where is this party to take place?"

"Luke thought she might enjoy a picnic since you've kept her locked up."

"Her has a name," Sally's voice was acerbic from her frustration of being discussed as if she were not present.

Aquos bowed, "My apologies, Sally. It is considered rude to speak with a dragon's mate before obtaining permission. Drake is tame at the moment, but his fierceness and temper are legendary in our world."

"You have a temper?"

Drake groaned at Aquos' laughter to Sally's question. "Why do you think there are so many fireplaces in the room?"

She looked around and shrugged. "I just thought you get cold easy."

"Sally-mine, I can regulate my body temperature at all times. I would not get cold walking naked through Antarctica."

"Which, might I add, he did once on a dare."

Her smile was slow, but the light in her eyes had such hunger in it Drake came close to purring in response. "I would have liked to have witnessed that," she admitted.

"Well, your friend was so busy regulating his temperature to do it, he managed to melt an iceberg the size of Connecticut in the process."

Sally glowed at him. She actually glowed. "So you're responsible for global warming. The Republicans will want to have a word with you." When the two men gave each other confused looks and shrugged, she could not resist chuckling. "Never mind. So let's go to the party."

"Resting, Sally-mine."

"Party," she folded her arms over her chest and pouted at him for good measure.

"Resting."

"Party first and then resting," she offered, hopefully.

Aquos laughed at his friend, uncaring that he was being seared with a brutal glare. "What? She is so stubborn, I cannot think of another woman more perfect for you."

A fireball erupted from Drake's eyes and would have singed Aquos where he stood but he was fast enough to dart out of the way before it hit. As he laughed, Aquos sent a small flood of water from his hands to put the flames out before they had a chance to catch. Sally looked between the two of them with clear amazement. "Wait. Are you telling me that the guy who shoots fire is best friends with the one who controls water?"

"It is not a surprise to you that I control water?"

"Just a lucky guess."

Drake felt an overwhelming sense of pride at his female's acceptance. "How did you guess?"

"He's blue," Sally shrugged, "Plus the cold. And when he told me he was sick, all of the servants had to go and clean up a flood. It just seemed natural to chalk his affiliation with water."

Aquos took a few half steps to the side of the bed. Drake saw his hand reaching out to touch her, and he quickly withdrew it, shoving them deep into his pockets. "Sally," he shuffled back, needing to keep some distance so he did not forget himself. He smiled when he saw Drake relax. "How are you taking to all of this so easily? You're with a dragon. You know I have some kind of weird relationship with water. I would think you would be running around pulling out your hair."

"I have always believed that, though some things are improbable, nothing is impossible."

Drake wished he could throw Aquos out on his ass right now. He'd never wanted to make love to a woman more. Oh wait, she was supposed to be resting. All he could really do is tell her how much he wanted her. Restraint not being his strong point, maybe it was a good thing Aquos was still in the room. "That's it? That's all you need?"

"If Carl Sagan could admit there has to be life on other planets, who am I to argue?"

"But Sally," Aquos shook his head. "Dragons? Water people?"

"Wait," she sat up, pushing past Drake's light restraint. "Are you like a mermaid?"

Drake burst into laughter. A small glimpse of Aquos' face was enough to turn him into a cackling hyena. "I keep imagining you with one of those seashell bras and a long fishy tale."

"I've decided I need to kill Drake, Sally. You don't really mind, do you?"

Sally bit her lip as she gazed at her man rolling around the floor as he shook with laughter. He was getting so bad the bed was beginning to move. "I have to admit you might be justified."

"At the very least you should let me carry you down to the party in your towel."

"How do you know I'm wearing a towel?"

"X-ray vision," Aquos teased. When she dove under the down coverlet he held up his hands. "Just a guess, Sally."

"Better be," Drake growled.

Sally peeked over the edge of the blanket, not quite sure if Aquos was telling the truth or not. Either way, she was horrified.

"Go downstairs Aquos, and assure them we are coming."

After Aquos was gone, Sally started to emerge from the bedding only to watch all of the color drain from Drake's face. Looking down she realized that the towel had slipped and most of her breasts were hanging out for him to see. He made some kind of mumbled excuse and slipped inside the bath.

Taking this as a cue she needed to be clothed before he returned, she staggered to the armoire to retrieve an outfit. At first she was going to reach for pants and a shirt, but all the talk about a party indicated something nicer might be required.

The other cabinet had some very slinky dresses by designers she had only seen on television. There were also a few skirts and tops that seemed appropriate for the event. A long purple cotton knit skirt that was so well made it bordered on silk, with a light green cap-sleeved top suited her taste. She dropped the towel and pulled it on without any time to spare for under things, just as she zipped up the skirt, Drake came out of the bathroom. He had also changed, she noticed, and was now sporting a pair of blue dress pants and a light blue button down shirt that had pale white stripes. "I didn't know what to wear."

"Luke prefers we dress for dinner," Drake confessed. "It keeps us reasonably civilized. I didn't think it'd be too fancy since Aquos said it's a picnic."

Sally brightened at this news, "Great. Let me just get my shoes."

He grabbed a black shawl that was made out of wool so fine it slithered as it moved. Swirling it around her shoulders, he picked her up. "You are still resting. There is no way I am letting you have shoes. You walk over me enough as it is."

She sighed. "I am going to use those stairs sooner or later."

"At least you're not threatening to take the dumb waiter again."

Drake was the one to walk the hidden passage, taking two and three treads at a time through the pitch black without a problem. He liked that the daringness of his path inspired her to cling tighter to him and close her eyes with a small sigh. "Sally, whatever happens, no matter what anyone says, know that we belong to each other. It is a miracle that we found each other, and I will never let you go easily."

Her arms tightening around him were her only response.

When they reached the outside, Sally leaned away from him. "Drake, please let me walk. I want to feel the grass between my toes."

He put her down, but kept his arms around her as if she were some kind of accident victim on the first round of physical therapy. Ten yards away, Sally could see a gathering of men, that in any other circumstances would have terrified her. They were each dressed in a different definition of casual elegance, but looking like Delta Force warriors. Mach and Turbo were dressed in blue jeans with colorful silk shirts and leather jackets that they were hanging on the backs of their chairs. Aquos was in a cobalt blue suit and Stealth was in linen. She guessed that the one guy in a pair of black silk pants and a crisp white shirt was the leader, Luke.

Who happened to be the one who had decided to throw this little picnic.

Sally had envisioned a red-checkered blanket laid out and a big basket with Yogi Bear and Booboo trying to steal it. What she found was a setting that made her feel like someone had stolen a set-up from a five star French restaurant and transported it to a magical grove. There was a floor-length bone colored tablecloth, silver candlesticks with long white tapers, Waterford crystal, chairs draped in white and bone brocade covers, and china that looked like if it were held up to the candle flames, you could see right through it. Someone had threaded Christmas lights with small white twinkling bulbs through the surrounding trees to finish off the magical feeling.

When the men saw Sally and Drake approaching, they bowed low from the waist to welcome her. "Greetings, Sally Eversham," Luke intoned.

"Hello," Sally whispered digging her toes into the soft grass.

The appreciation and interest that flared in all their eyes when they looked at her made her shift partially behind Drake. When their stares turned hungry she moved so he was a complete shield. He reached behind him so he could embrace her, even if all he could reach was her elbows. Glaring at his friends until they looked away, he gave Sally a moment before turning to embrace her against him. "Sally-mine, there is nothing to fear here," he murmured against her hair.

"I'm just not accustomed to so much attention," she whispered.

Drake gritted his teeth so he did not mutter a promise to kill her family again. "You should be," was all he could think to offer.

When he felt her square her shoulders, Drake guided her to the table to sit at one of the sides. Normally there would have been more people in attendance, but he could see someone would not be attending. "Where's Blade?"

Aquos shook his head at him and the subject was dropped - fast. He'd tell him the answers later, the expression cried.

As they sat down, Sally noticed that each of the brothers seemed to have a different way of praying over the plates of food. The men that served the food either wore long blue or green robes, and they communicated with silent hand gestures. It was so quiet in the glade she felt as if you could hear a pin drop, on cotton. Leaning over to Drake's side she murmured, "Is talking not allowed?"

"It is."

Looking around she felt a little assured when the men began to speak among themselves as soon as their prayers were over. Mach and Turbo made such an effort to turn away from each other, she guessed they were fighting. She also took note of the tense looks and set of everyone's shoulders. Something was wrong.

"Do you do this often?"

"It was the way of the Omega high clans to have ceremonial meals." Luke gestured to the formal table and the forks that indicated multiple courses. "This is a sad replica of those occasions, but the best we can do."

"So you come from another planet," Sally was shocked that she was even trying to make conversation but she didn't know what else to do at a large gathering where she hadn't made the food and everyone seemed to be locked in their own concerns. "I mean, that's right? Isn't it? No way I'm buying that you are from another country."

"It seems the dragon has loose lips."

Drake felt insulted Luke had assumed it was he. He was also tied from saying anything. The dragon clan had received an invitation to the ceremonial dinners Luke was speaking of only during the last decade before they had left. It seemed humorous to him that, just when their civilization was officially dying, they were asked to be a part of things.

"I was the one who told her," Aquos winked at Sally when he took the blame.

"What's wrong with my knowing? I mean seriously, who do you think I would tell?"

"You have family don't you?"

Stealth glowed at his friends, "Seems to me her family is right here."

Her gaze dropped when she tried to hide how much Stealth's statement meant to her. Drake covered her hand on the table and hid it within the folds of the cloth, keeping it close to his leg. She gave him a small smile that always made his heart flip over. "Luke, you are going to have to get over this prejudice, my friend. Sally is here to stay, and you are the only one who seems to have a problem with that fact."

"Only until she's better," Luke reminded him.

Mach grabbed a bottle of Jack Daniels from the elemental's hands. "Let's lighten up, brother."

"This is supposed to be a party," Turbo added lifting a bottle of Tequila Patron.

"I thought you get drunk on ginger ale," Sally murmured to Drake.

Drake laughed at her concern, "I do. The lightning boys have their own kinds of poison."

"Speaking of poison," Sally's forehead creased with her concern. "What are you doing about the person trying to kill you?"

Luke sat back with shock, his mouth hanging open. "Excuse me?"

"I'm not allowed to ask?"

"No," Luke snapped.

She released a deep breath and dropped her eyes to her plate. There was a salad that was arranged to be artful and yet have a delicious balance. Even the dressing looked like it was painted on.

Drake stood up, sending the chair shuttling backwards. Holding out his hand he waited for Sally to give her fingers to him so that he could draw her up from the table with old world manners. "It would seem the party is over," his words rolled over her like a soothing caress. "You would forgive me, Luke, but I find your disrespect to my mate to be the height of rudeness and incivility. We will dine elsewhere."

"No," Luke stood as well, his eyes narrowing. "I'll go. Forgive me, Sally. I should not have spoke with such harshness. The day has been trying for us all and I allowed it to get the worst of me."

She leaned back against Drake, trembling with indecision. "It's fine."

"I beg to differ."

As he turned to leave, Sally felt her heart do a funny little flip. Drake guided her back to her seat and she gazed around with dawning realization. "You are each so different, but at heart, the same. Each lonely in your own way."

The men's faces colored slightly as most of them turned away from her or down to their plates.

"No way, honey," Mach drawled, giving her a teasing look, "Anytime I lack company all I need to do is hit the nearest bar and crook my finger. Before I can say 'I'll have a double' I have ten girls running over - each pulling up their skirts, ready to go."

Turbo grabbed his bottle of alcohol, stood up, and left.

The silence that gripped the table was uncomfortable and surprising. Sally reached over to grip Drake's hand and gave Mach a pointed look. "Listen, brother," Drake cleared his throat. "Maybe you can hang with us tonight?"

Mach shrugged, his eyes following Turbo's egress as if he were jealous.

A flash of light blinded Sally as she began to pick up her salad fork with her free hand. When she looked up, she was shocked to see a new man standing by the table. This one was tall with a military brush cut and was wearing enough leather to give a motorcycle club a run for its money. In fact, he could easily be heading for his Harley at any minute. The only odd thing other than the method of his arrival was the fact that a blue incandescence seemed cast by his appearance. All of the occupants at the table rose and bowed low from the waist, except for Sally.

"Be seated, Lords of Omega," the newcomer directed. "You called for me?"

Drake stepped forward pulling Sally behind him. "I did, Raphael. My mate is of your people and needs to be healed."

"No, I don't," Sally scoffed.

Stealth turned to Mach and Aquos, rolling his eyes. "No, she doesn't."

Raphael looked Sally up and down and turned back to Drake, "Your mate is fine. How is it that you would take one of our own as a mate?" He looked at Sally again and blanched. Shaking his head, he began to back away from her. "This is most unfortunate," he muttered. "I shall have to let them know."

When he disappeared without an additional word, Sally felt her mouth fall open. "What just happened?"

"I don't know."

She looked to the three guys sitting at the table. "Do any of you?"

"As a rule, we try to avoid the guardians of this world. I've never seen any of them get so, I don't know what the word is, uncomfortable?"

Mach's laughter stopped Drake from trying to answer Aquos's comment. "I would say terrified. What are you, Sally Eversham?"

"I'm nothing special," she sputtered.

The others all laughed, though Drake drew her into his arms as he did so. "We know better."

"Who was that?" she asked.

Drake began to sit them both down at the table, "Archangel Raphael. He heals people."

"You can just call on an angel?"

"So can you," Aquos began to eat his salad. "You just don't always have the ability to see them when they come."

Sally pushed her salad around on the plate, her appetite flown. "I wish I could have talked to him. There are a lot of questions I have. You have no idea how hard I prayed when my mom got sick. It would be nice to know why no one came."

"Sometimes it is your path to grow ill and die," Drake tried consoling her.

Aquos scowled at him when he saw how much his words had hurt her, "Or it could be how you worded the prayers."

"What?"

Mach tossed his glass aside and began to just drink from his bottle of Jack. "Fun stuff, huh? If you use the wrong words or screw up your sentence structure – poof goes your answer. Or you do use the right words and then happen to state something that goes against your original request and once again – poof. It is a hard road that faith built, and it has little forgiveness for wrong turns."

"I don't think it's that bad," Sally spoke with a soft voice, feeling as if the wrong word would send the other brother stalking from the table. "I guess it's really about how much you believe and trust in them."

All of the men got involved with their food, and Sally looked around the clearing once more. She noticed the men in blue and green who were standing in the shadows. Smiling at one in forest green, she said, "Hello. I am so sorry that we have not met yet. My name is Sally, and you are?"

Drake looked at her with a blank stare, "That's an elemental."

"And?"

"We don't normally call them by name," Aquos explained.

Stealth chuckled, "We don't bother knowing their names."

"You let these people serve you and don't even know their names?"

Mach took a long pull from his bottle, "They're elementals."

Sally rose and strode over to the one man in blue and another in green. "Hello, I'm Sally. What's your name?"

The man in blue bowed to her, "I am Kel."

"And what's your friend's name?"

"I am not his friend," the emerald green stated.

"Why not?"

Drake came to stand next to her, "The elementals don't mix."

"Why not?" she asked again.

Kel smiled at her, "We each have a different function. There is no reason to mingle."

"But think what you might be missing by not getting to know each other. I also think, you have so few of your people left, you can't be so picky."

"We don't," Kel acknowledged. "There is still no reason to mingle."

"Why," she challenged. "What is your purpose?"

"My people are artists," Kel boasted. "We cook; create images and music."

Sally drew the emerald man into the circle, "What about you?"

"I am Tana, my Lady. My people clean and are caretakers."

Her smile was so broad that Drake felt like sunshine had just warmed his heart. "So Kel, please tell me, when you cook – who cleans?"

"Tana."

"And Tana, what would you do if Kel didn't cook?"

He blinked his eyes several times as his mouth opened and closed. "I don't know, my Lady."

"That's my point," Sally beamed at them. "You may not have the same tasks but that doesn't mean you don't need one another. We are all interconnected on some level. It's just like when I plant a garden. I always have to be aware of what I am planting and where I am putting it. Each thing will affect the other."

Kel and Tana gave each other small smiles. They began to speak in low voices as Drake guided Sally back to the table. "Would you please eat your dinner?"

"I can't believe you guys never thought of that."

Aquos looked at the elementals, who all seemed to be conferring and introducing themselves. "I'm not sure you just did us any real favors."

"Nonsense," Sally waved her hands. "Now that they are getting to know each other, you guys need to start talking to them."

Mach raised his bottle to her in a toast, "You are one of a kind, Sally Eversham."

"Yes, she is," Drake murmured, his eyes hot as they locked with hers. She felt a shiver of desire snake down her spine in response and the answering flare in his eyes stated that he was well aware of it.

Kel came over with a platter of small savory vegetarian pastries. "Lady Sally, perhaps some of these will interest you more. They are almost as rare as you."

"And apparently everyone is beginning to realize that."

Sally shifted with unease at Aquos' penetrating eyes. As the brothers began to regale her with different facts about their history, she tried to put all thoughts aside of her future in this place that was starting to mean much more to her than home. All concerns over the archangel and his mysterious reaction to her presence, and all fears over what her family was doing, went into the same basket she planned to sort out later.

Right now, all she wanted to feel, was pleasure.

The night was beautiful, she was in the company of a group of gorgeous men, the hottest of whom was running his hand over her thigh and sending her libido soaring, and she was happy.

What more could one woman want?

CHAPTER SEVENTEEN

The Architect stood at the summit, watching over the gathering that was building below him. He had never imagined that his few hits to the community would bring about these kinds of results. They were bonding. For the first time in the history of two worlds, the Omega clans were intermixing with no thought or concern to their histories or agenda.

He didn't know if he should laugh until he cried or just cry.

With the first rays of dawn's light the scouts had begun to arrive. The family that excelled at finding things was coming home. The scouts had been sent out decades before by the Light Leader in response to the growing problem of fights between the families. It was Luke's brilliant decision to send them away.

Now he brought them back, and the Architect faced having to walk a gauntlet of beings that lived for identifying problems and eradicating them.

Death by disembowelment was one of their favorites.

He crouched down when he saw some of the men turn toward his position on the side of the mountain. This was the end of his plans, he fumed. The elementals were sharing information and orders. All of the clans had reassembled in one place where they were bound to start sharing information. Even the Clan Lords had begun to let go of ancient feuds and talk. If this continued, he was not going to succeed.

Something he would never have even considered.

* * *

The Gold elementals were trying to deal with the sudden need for finding campsites for fifty hardened warriors who were accustomed to spending days on end by themselves. Each one needed a campsite that was isolated in some way, and yet centrally located around the greater spoke that the main encampment was so that messages could be passed between them with freedom. The blues and greens were going nuts trying to figure out how to bring in the additional supplies and materials the scouts would require.

It was for this reason that morning Sally found herself standing in the main kitchen faced off with five very hungry men.

Drake scowled, "We'll order food in."

"I don't mind cooking," Sally assured him.

"You shouldn't have to serve us," Drake folded his arms over his chest.

Sally chuckled at his obstinate belief that she found cooking to be a chore. "I don't mind, Drake. Why don't you all go and help the elementals finish what they are doing while I work on breakfast."

Aquos began to usher everyone out of the room, "Let's go before she changes her mind."

When Turbo and Mach went to step through the door at the same time, Turbo shoved his friend back and scowled at him. "Mach," Sally called seeing the naked pain in the young man's face, "could you stay?"

Drake whirled around, "I'll stay."

She laughed at his hopeful expression, "No. Go with the others."

"Dude," Stealth opined. "Your toy is harsh."

"She's just mad at him for babying her so much," Luke quipped.

Mach closed the door after his friends and rested his head against the panel with a heavy sigh. "I wanted him to forgive me."

"He will."

"How can you tell?"

"You two have a friendship that goes deeper than blood ties," she promised him. "He'll forgive you if you give him some time."

Mach gave her a teasing grin, "You promise?"

"What did you fight about?"

He shifted back and forth giving her quick side-glances.

Sally sighed, "Let me guess. The big lunk-head who treats me like a piece of china told you not to tell me."

Mach nodded his head eager to see what she would say next.

"Does it have something to do with the guy that's missing?"

Another nod.

"Are you worried about him?"

"I'm worried about us," Mach admitted.

She sighed and turned to the refrigerator to start pulling out foods and pile them on the counter. The kitchen was organized so well it felt like she had lived here for years, it was so easy to find the items she required. Sally wondered who was responsible, for she doubted it was either the blues or the greens. "Turbo is worried about the guy that's missing ... what is his name?"

"Blade."

"You're worried about what he's doing."

"Yes."

Sally turned to him and positioned the brother in front of a pile of mushrooms, onions, green peppers and left over baked potatoes. Handing him a knife she gestured, "Cut, please."

"You were serious about me helping?"

She laughed at his stunned astonishment. "Of course."

"I thought you were kidding," he grumbled.

"Nope." She showed him how to cut the ingredients and began to heat up the pans. "I was just wondering something, though. If you are worried about what Blade is doing or if he's planning on hurting you, and Turbo is concerned over what's happening to him ... doesn't that mean that you both want to find him?"

A wave of noise erupted and Sally turned from the stove to witness something that defied her imagination. And she had just gone on a ride on a dragon a few days ago.

Mach had managed to cut everything she handed him, exactly the way she demonstrated, in a few seconds. He caught her stunned expression and gave her a flirty wink. "I'm the one who does everything real fast," he joked.

"Fast isn't always a good idea."

Her suggestive look explained what she was trying to say and she was pleased when his face colored a deep red color. "I don't do everything fast," he grumbled.

"Just checking."

Mach turned to her with a lightened expression. "So you mean I should agree with Turbo to find Blade?"

"How else will you uncover what he's up to?"

"But Turbo doesn't think he's up to anything."

Sally hid her exasperation. *Apparently men were just as obtuse on other planets as they were here.* Still, it was fun to talk this out with him. She'd always wanted to be able to have a conversation with a true exchange of ideas with her brothers. This was just as much fun as she'd always dreamt. She started to crack eggs into a bowl and whip them up for omelets. "I'm not telling you any different. I just think you need to go to Turbo and offer to help him hunt for Blade. Tell him you still have doubts over Blade's innocence, but you are willing to put that aside to find him."

"I don't think Turbo will be happy."

"He will if you listen to his reasons why he believes in Blade's innocence. He will if you promise to apologize if you're wrong."

"I'm not," he barked.

Drake came in from the other side of the door with a dark look on his face. "Do not talk to her in that tone of voice."

"Calm down, Drake," Sally moved toward him.

He grabbed her arm and shoved her behind his body. "Apologize," he snarled.

Mach moved around the room to the large fireplace that had a wood oven on top of it. "No."

"Now," he thundered.

Sally rubbed her hand over the expanse of his back. He was trembling from head to toe and was so stiff she was concerned he would crack in two. "Drake," she whispered resting her cheek against the center. "Relax."

"Apologize," he snarled one more time.

Mach stiffened with umbrage, "I did nothing wrong."

A flash of light heralded the arrival of Luke, looking bored and strangely amused. "You spoke with a harsh tone to a female taken by a dragon Lord. The fact that he hasn't roasted you where you stand is a bloody miracle."

Turbo, Stealth and Aquos came running in. "What did we miss?" Aquos asked.

"Is breakfast ready yet?"

Sally laughed at Stealth's hopeful question.

"Apologize to my woman," Drake leaned forward as if he were readying his body to attack.

The female in question was busy trying to grasp Drake's belt to make sure he couldn't go far if he lunged. Stealth gave Mach a look of disbelief. "Do you have some kind of death wish?"

Turbo moved to stand with his cousin. "You should apologize. We like Sally."

"She cooks."

"And as a rule," Luke added. "She keeps Drake pretty tame."

"I do not," Sally was horrified he would even hint at such a thing.

Drake gave a curt shake of his head, "No, she doesn't."

"Anyone else believe that," Stealth inquired.

"Not really," Aquos answered.

"You should apologize," Turbo muttered to his friend.

Mach was so happy at a chink in Turbo's icy façade he would have jumped through hoops if asked. "I apologize."

"Now here's the deal," Sally's eyes narrowed at the array of men crowding the room. "Anyone still here in thirty seconds is going to be put to work cooking breakfast or cleaning dishes."

She'd barely gotten the words out of her mouth before half the men dashed for the door and the other half disappeared in small bursts of light. "The disappearing and appearing thing is truly fascinating," she muttered. Seeing Drake was still here, she looked at him with interest. "Can you do that?"

"No," he explained, regretfully. He pulled her into his arms and drew her close to his body, "I can just take you sailing over land and sea, manipulate fire, and call out all the wealth from the earth."

"Those are pretty good, too."

He chuckled at her begrudging assessment as he started to brush small kisses from the corner of her eye to her ear. "You know, good dragon wives don't usually spend time with other men. You know … ever."

"Good thing I'm not a dragon wife."

"You don't complain when my friends call you my mate."

"I thought that meant girlfriend." When Drake's eyebrows rose, almost disappearing into his hairline, she guessed she said the wrong thing. "I guess not. I don't suppose you have a translation book somewhere?"

"You are my mate, Sally-mine."

She pushed the idea that this strange and unusual, beautiful man would want to keep her forever. "We'll talk about it."

"In truth, we are doing that now."

"Why were you eavesdropping?"

Drake shrugged, "I didn't like the thought of you alone with Mach."

The idea that he might have been jealous was so unreal to her it took a few moments for her to gather her thought process again. "You know he really wasn't all that harsh when he spoke to me. You didn't have to insist that he apologize."

"Yes, I did."

"Why?"

"It was clear Mach and Turbo's feud was troubling you. The fastest way to get Mach to see his cousin still loved him was to have Mach be threatened."

"So you did it for me?"

A nod earned him a searing kiss that made him forget all his good intentions to help his friends make the newcomers more comfortable. Sally ran her hands over his back and gave him a sultry look, which made his eyes cross. "You now have a choice," her voice lowered as she pressed her lips to the side of his neck. "Either leave now … or help me cook."

He fisted his hands in her hair to position her head for a searing kiss designed to heat her up faster than a kernel of corn over a fire. She was soon panting with obvious wanting, her toes curled. He moved them to a free area of the counter and deposited his woman on the surface. He was no longer hungry for food. Drake's mouth began to wander down to the vee of her shirt, as his hands positioned her hips.

Sally dug her heels into his ass and pulled him tight against her core. Two could play at this game of heating up their partner until they couldn't walk straight.

Drake moved his mouth to place open-mouthed wet endearments over her jaw to the sweet spot in the back of her ear that he knew made her go liquid. They should have called in for food. If they had, he could have had Sally in several positions before it even got here. He was just considering how to pick her up without her noticing the change in venue, when she wrenched her face away from him. "Drake, I have to cook."

"Baby, we're cooking with a vengeance. Now how about going upstairs?" He repositioned her head so that he could capture her lips once more. "Or of course, there's always the option of right where we are."

"Cooking," she purred, ripping her head away.

Drake groaned with dismay when he caught the militant look in her eyes. "Are you sure?"

"Positive," she hopped off of the counter and side stepped away from his reaching arms before he could capture her once more. There was only so much seduction she could refuse. "Do you want to wash or dry?"

Her laughter as he fled from the room followed him for the rest of the day.

CHAPTER EIGHTEEN

Aquos found her later in the day, cleaning up from the lunch she had served them. "You know," he started with a light conversational tone. "You are one amazing cook. I don't understand why you didn't do anything with such talent."

"Obviously I like food," she looked down at her body, chagrined.

"It seems to me that the only one preoccupied with your weight and how you look," his eyes blazed like priceless sapphires, "is you."

Sally sighed, "I'm beginning to realize that."

"The elementals don't know how to thank you enough for all the help today."

"Where are they?"

"They have been trying to get the scouts settled." When Sally gave him a bewildered look he decided to explain in full. "With the danger getting so serious, Luke asked all of the tribes to convene here. He separated us to cut down on the wars and the fighting. This is the first time that all of the Omega have joined together in many centuries - a planetary reunion, as it were."

"What is the Omega?"

He hopped up so that he could sit on the counter. "The Omega is what we are."

She decided not to tell him that was the exact spot where Drake had tried to seduce her earlier. "So, it's like I'm a homo sapiens?"

"Well, technically we're kind of both of those."

She picked up a pan to dry before returning it to the pot rack. "I don't get it."

"The way it was explained to us is simple. God made the planet. When the universal influence, or whatever you want to call it, was finished, it realized that in making this place another was formed as well. That was that Omegicon."

"You mean in another place?"

"No," he shook his head. "Another dimension."

Sally smiled, "That makes sense. I touched upon some of Einstein's theories in college about dimensions and the concept of balance. So what happened next?"

"Think of us as sort of the testing ground for God. Life was started and experimented within our dimension. When things were perfected, here God came to create its final manifestations. So when we realized our world was close to dying, we found a dimensional bridge, what some here might call a tesseract, and sent some of our people through to try and save our world."

"So what are you doing to save your planet? Do you have scientists working on it?"

"No," Aquos gave a bark of laughter that sounded like the surge of a thunderstorm. "Our Oracle, who you should think of a high priestess with a direct link to the almighty, sent us with a riddle. Once we find what we need in the poem, we will be able to return home."

"How's it going?"

"We're still here, aren't we?"

Sally looked around with a deep sense of satisfaction as she hung up the final pot. The room was as clean as she could get it. "I think this will be fine until dinner," she murmured. "Though what I'll make is escaping me."

"The elementals said they would handle third meal. Why don't you come meet the scouts?"

"Explain the clans to me," Sally inquired as she gave Aquos her hand. Together they walked from the kitchen to the lush outside. She took in a deep breath of the rich, mossy smell of the woods that surrounded the main building. This was the first time she had been free to walk outside for several days and she had missed it. "It's beautiful," she whispered, awed at the endless feeling of the trees towering over them.

Aquos looked around with distaste, "You don't find it kind of staid?"

"What do you mean?"

"It's all so," the sneer on his face expressed his distaste without needing words. "Stationary. Colorless."

Her smile was fond and understanding. "Let me see if I remember," she mused. "Your clan has something to do with water, so you're looking for waves."

"Well ... yes."

She shook her head and pointed to the trees they could see on the other side of the clearing. A strong breeze picked up and sent the leaves dancing. "Look," she encouraged. "You just have to look a little higher to see the motion. It's more subtle. The colors can be breathtaking."

"Not as soothing," he grumbled.

When they reached the top of a small hill that looked out over the valley, they found Mach and Stealth standing guard. "Hey guys," she smiled at them.

"What are you doing here?"

"Drake released your chains," Stealth sneered.

Choosing to answer the more polite question asked by Mach, Sally shrugged. "Aquos thought I would like meeting the scout clan."

"No," Aquos stood to her side positioning his body between her and the other men. "What I said was I thought you should see them. No way am I letting you get in breathing room of the scouts. They are brutal monsters and Drake would kill me."

"Who is also a brutal monster," Mach quipped.

Her jaw tensed and her eyes became mere slits with her anger. "Do not talk about him like that."

"Why not?"

Stealth grimaced for his obtuse friend, "Mach, you're being an ass."

"He went out of his way to help you and Turbo get back together," she pointed out repressively. "You should be grateful."

Mach shook his head, "You don't get me. I'm supposed to be the immature jerk."

"Well, you're doing a very good job of it," she snapped.

"Calm down, honey," Aquos pus his hand on her shoulder and tried to ease the knotted muscles. "Everyone takes Mach with a grain of sand."

"They should try a two-by-four."

All three men began to laugh so hard, she folded her arms over her chest and glared at them. "Don't be mad," Aquos gasped out.

"It's just that we really like you," Stealth added.

"Yup, you fit in perfectly."

Mach's compliment was enough to make her look down, shocked at how much satisfaction she felt at his words. They were all gifting her with such smiles of camaraderie, she began to blink back her tears in response. "Oh no," Mach's eyes widened with his fear. "We made her cry."

"No," she was fast to assure them. "I'm just touched."

Glancing down into the valley again, and in a sheer desperate grab to get the subject changed, Sally commented on what they were gazing at. Or at least, what she thought they were looking at, for she could not see anything at all. "Where are the scouts?"

"They're down there," Aquos pointed.

She looked between the empty expanse of heavy woods and the men around her. "Where?"

"The scouts are experts at blending in. They have to be since they are so often sent out to walk through enemy's camps and untouched societies.

They are experts at absorbing languages and cultures within a few seconds." Mach put a bent arm on Stealth's shoulder and leaned against him. "Basically they are incredible pains in the ass."

Sally kept looking down into the trees not comprehending what they were seeing. "Where are they?"

"Look not for the movement of people but for the ones that do not move at all."

She scowled at Stealth, "What do you mean?"

He moved behind her and wrapped his arms around her so that when he pointed she could gaze right down the line of his arm. "Look there … in that one strand of trees. She how the branches on the side are moving and yet on the other they're not? Now keep watching. The problem with the scouts is sooner or later they will always betray their hand. They will blink or breathe too heavily. If you wait them out, there will always be some kind of 'tell' to see them, no matter how well they're camouflaged."

Sally kept trying to see what Stealth was promising her. It was so odd to be in the circle of his arms. No matter how close you get to someone there was always some kind of odor - even if the person doesn't use perfume or cologne. There is always a smell of soap, food, or sweat. With Stealth, no matter how close he stood to her; she still only sensed her own body. It was as if her eyes could see him, but none of her other senses were able to detect him. At all. Just then, Sally spotted a movement in the trees of something fluttering; some difference that did not blend in harmony with the surroundings. It jumped out at her for its difference. "Wait," she whispered. "What was that?"

"That was the scouts."

"It is said that the scouts stole their abilities from my people," he whispered in her ear.

Sally tried to step away from Stealth but his arms tightened for a moment and she chose not to fight him. "Apparently, not very well," she drawled.

"You're not surprised?"

"Aquos was explaining about the clans," she explained. "Anyone who takes the name Stealth must have something to do with disappearing."

He nuzzled his nose in her hair and she could feel by his chest's movement that he was taking in a deep breath. He's smelling my hair, she thought to herself with horror. Good thing I shampooed and conditioned today. Otherwise all he might smell is my vomit from drinking the poison.

"You are a very unusual woman."

"She is also taken," Aquos snapped before wrenching her away from Stealth.

Mach looked down, feeling guilty that he had not done anything to help Sally get free of Stealth's hold. "There is a great deal of uncomfortable truths about the clans. Our tendency to take from others is the first rule. Thou shall always covet, appears to be our first commandment."

"You should learn better," Sally stepped away from them.

"You see, Sally Eversham," Stealth's voice was modulated to be smoother than the finest red wine and it made every hair on her body stand on end. "You smell like our home. The one thing in the entire world that none of us has been able to get near is anything that reminds us of home. Why do you think Luke had forbidden all of our friends to set foot on the main property?"

"I don't know."

Mach stepped in before Stealth answered, worried that she was about to get attacked. "It is in concern for you. If they are in the house they might catch a whiff of you and then we would be faced with a clan war. Everyone would want to get a piece of you."

Sally started to swallow as her heart pounded out her fear. "What is so important about how I smell?"

"It's physics," Aquos tried to explain. "When we came here, we did not know how the physical laws of this universe would affect us. The longer we stay here, shut off from our home, the more apart we become. Our atoms are literally breaking down because we do not belong in this world. This dimension."

Mach tried to give her a friendly smile but it came out as a wavering grin. "Anything that might change the balance, give us enough of what we need from both, is something we would fight and kill for."

"This is why our friends are sent into exile."

"They aren't in exile," Mach groused. "They're in the valley. Stop trying to make her feel bad," he threatened Stealth. "Sally has done nothing wrong."

"She saved our lives," Aquos reminded him.

Mach beamed, "And she fed us."

Stealth shook himself as if a dog dispelling water was the same as a man releasing a building rage. "I apologize," he ground out through his clenched teeth. "I do not know what's coming over me."

"Drake said your potion saved my life."

"It did," Stealth's eyes closed and he seemed to fade before her eyes. "With it I showed my gratitude for your actions that day. It is just that it goes against everything in me to see a member of the dragon clan so happy." His eyes blazed like mercury when he opened them, "and you make him very happy indeed."

Sally smiled and thought about squeezing his arm in understanding but she guessed that getting near him would not be wise. "Why do you hate him?"

"I don't."

"So why can't you be happy for him?"

Aquos stepped in, hoping he could explain the truth behind the complexities of their history. "The clan history says that the Stealth learned their abilities to disappear, as a defense mechanism to protect their people from the dragon clan."

"His people used to gorge on mine."

"Drake did this?"

"No," Stealth shook his head. "His people did."

"People Drake knew?"

"No," Mach was smiling as he explained. "His ancestors."

Sally smiled, "Isn't that kind of silly?"

When the wind turned and began to come from behind her, blowing her smell directly at the three men, she noticed they each changed their breathing patterns. They were noticeably taking in deep lungs-full of her smell. That's just gross, she thought to herself. *I think I'll start to shower twice a day*, she swore inside her mind.

Aquos looked at his friends, "She has a point."

"Time to let it go," Sally stated. "Don't you think?"

The roar of a large predator split the mood, and Drake came leaping into the clearing to land directly in front of her. He unfolded his body to his full height, and with one hand tucked her behind him as if the three men were coming at her with a knife. Sally changed from being amused at the friends' clinging to ancient prejudices to being terrified.

Of the man who called her his mate.

"Drake," she put her hand on his back wishing she had the guts to move around to his front. "Drake, what's wrong?"

With a flash of light Luke appeared to stand between Drake and the rest of the men. "These idiots took the mate of a dragon out of its lair without asking permission."

"Permission," Sally screeched. "You expect them to ask your permission before taking me for a walk?" She smacked at his back when he roared again at her reminder of why he was blazing with a red-hot rage. "Cut that out!"

He turned to her with a flashing look.

"I said," she smacked him against his sternum. "Cut it out." When his eyes opened to almost regular pupils, rather than the mere slits they were, she continued. "Let's get one thing straight. If I want to go for a walk with someone, I'm going to do it without having to ask you for permission. I am not a child."

Drake's hands closed around her upper arms as he tried to calm down. "What you are ... is mine."

She ignored the flare of sensual heat his growl sent coursing through her. "What I am is a free and independent woman. You had better not forget that I am from the twenty-first century, not the first."

His head fell forward to her shoulder and then popped back up. "You smell of Stealth."

In horror, the other witnesses watched as Stealth called a sword into his hand that wavered with a silver liquidity. Luke yelled, "No killing," before the two men could reach each other.

Sally caught at the back of Drake's shirt before he could do another of those jaw-dropping leaps. "Drake, if you hurt him, I will never talk to you again."

The look he turned on her made her stomach clench into a tiny ball, her heart took on a whole new cadence of terror, and her body heated with desire. *Great, she still had a small amount of mental power; now he turns me on when he's in a rage? Is there anything this guy does that wouldn't turn me into a nympho? There goes the rest of my self-esteem*, she mocked in her heart.

"This is not how a dragon mate should act."

"Well this is how this dragon's mate acts," she gave him a confident nod that she was shocked she could accomplish.

Drake pulled her into his arms and covered her mouth with a kiss so searing she was sure it left the ends of hair smoldering. He bent her back so far she felt as if she would snap in two, and covered her body with such complete ownership that all thought of anyone else watching fled from her mind. Without speaking to his friends, he bent over and put his shoulder into her stomach and rose with her draped over his body like some kind of mighty hunter's triumphant kill. Her screech was stopped when he jostled her on purpose to cut off enough of the supply of air she needed to speak, but not enough to hurt her.

His hand clasped one of her butt cheeks to steady her as, with two steps, he took off from the ground with the flurried beat of his wings.

Sally could see the astonished and jealous faces of his friends before she let her head fall forward to mask the view. Whatever was about to happen she knew she was in no danger. She just wasn't sure if she'd survive it.

CHAPTER NINETEEN

Sally figured out fast she was far wiser to keep her silence. Any time she tried to speak, Drake would just bounce her on his shoulders to take the air from her lungs. The halls of Sanctuary were constructed to take his wing span into account, with many well stocked fireplaces in consistent spacing so his anger could be released before he put them into their confrontation. His mate needed to learn some rules.

At home, women were kept in their caves at all times. They left the confines of the enclosure on only the rarest of occasions. Their duty was to allow their mate to tend them. Bring new life into the world.

Be available for the continual worship by their male.

His female needed to understand just how many concessions he had already made for her ignorance for his kind's ways.

He kept them moving until they arrived in one of the deepest recesses of the Sanctuary hall. The bathing pool had been gouged out from the earth before the mansion had been constructed, for his dragon form to have peace when despair and homesickness swamped his spirit. As he landed, he set Sally down and wandered over to the edge of the water, transforming into his natural state before diving beneath the surface of the lake.

Sally looked around with her mouth hanging open. The space was a large, natural cave with five-foot crystals bursting out of the walls and ceilings. Light seemed to come from the glass ceiling to fill the cave with a moving, living source of multi-colored illumination. It was as if she were inside a breathing rainbow. There was a small hot spring to her far right, but most of the space was a gigantic pool of water where her man, well, right now her dragon, was swimming around. "What is this?"

"Dragons adore water," a voice rumbled in her mind.

"Why did you bring me here?"

"It is where I am most at home. Where my powers are the strongest."

Sally had a sudden thought that sent a frisson of terror through her heart. "Drake, you can't keep me down here forever."

"Just until you understand," the voice answered.

"Understand what?"

His dragon form stepped from the water and shook off the liquid as if he were a dog. As he began to saunter to her, his body transformed into that of the man she knew so well. When he was close enough to reach her, he was pleased to note that her eyes were dilating with need, as her open mouth tried to catch her runaway breath. "That you are Sally-mine."

"I am Sally Eversham," she teased him.

He said nothing.

"Drake?"

As a response to her unasked question and the doubt shining in her eyes, he pushed her up against the wall and kissed her. Hard. His tongue thrust into her mouth as a sign of possession and a taste of what he had in store for her. It was time for her to understand. His possession was absolute, for she had just as much power over him. They were one. Sally tried to hide her response, but she could not help it. Drake, in this mood, made her knees go weak, her body pliant, and her center molten liquid. As if of their own volition, her arms went around his neck and her fingers tangled in the silk of his hair. A moan welled in her throat and spilled over to echo through the chamber.

"I love you, Sally-mine. And will you, nil you, we belong together."

Sally's head fell back as her mind turned blank. She could hear her body as it desperately searched for enough oxygen to make her faculties work. "Drake, I was just talking with them. There is no need for you to have such a tantrum."

"Which tells me there is every need," he whispered against her lips.

He whirled Sally around to face the cavern wall, and leaned her forward so her hands were firmly braced against the side of one of the crystals. The surface almost reminded her of fingernails, smooth and yet still retaining a trace of pliancy. Drake ran his palm over her back, chuckling at the feeling of the trembles shaking her from head to toe. "You are not cold, Sally-mine. I can feel your need of me."

She gasped as his hand cupped her between her legs, his burning skin easily capturing the truth of her soaked center. "You are wet for me."

"I am always that way with you."

"Good."

He tore her clothes from her body. Each time she tried to move from the walls, he used his superior weight to keep her where he wanted. Looking down, she was amazed he had managed to shred her garments without once marring her skin. When he once more cupped her between her legs, Sally tried to rise to face him. "No, Sally-mine," his shirt abraded her skin as his fingers entered her body. Her gasp sent a seductive rumbling through her that took her right over the edge. As her orgasm made her buck, he kept a tight hold on her wrists to keep her bent over as he wished.

When she settled, he used his thumb to begin to circle the pearl of her pleasure until she was once more writhing against his fingers. "Drake," she gasped out. "Stop this. I'd rather you be inside me."

"No," he said. "This is what you must learn. It is my right and responsibility to tend your body's needs."

"You'd be tending them from inside of me," she pleaded.

His teeth scraped against her neck and he chuckled as she let out small cries for mercy. "A dragon's mate does not give orders, unless they are ... More. Don't stop. Harder. Faster. Or just, please."

"How about ... inside of me?"

His hand raked the fall of her curling hair to the side as he positioned his body behind her. "You are beginning to learn, Sally-mine." She could not keep her moans of ecstasy and pain from escaping her lips as his hard hands positioned her body for his entry again. Teeth scraped and bit at her skin. Hands bruised as they moved her hips, arched her back, and turned her face to the side for his kiss. When his cock entered her from behind, his tongue was so deep inside her that all her mind could do was scream with release.

Drake knew he was being too rough. He could not care at the moment. Her third orgasm as he entered his woman made his male body take on the beast's brain. Her velvet sheath clung to him as if it knew that the one that belonged in its walls had come home. His thrusts were without mercy as his blood pooled in his cock, his balls tight until they felt as if he would explode. When the top of his shaft went off, it felt as if his entire being was deposited into the treasure of a cradle that this woman was, just where it belonged.

The fact that she joined him made him chuckle with exultation.

"You are mine, baby."

The eyes that she turned up to him were fluid with her satisfaction. "As you are mine," she whispered before slipping into unconsciousness.

* * *

When she came to, Drake was holding her. They were sleeping on what felt like a cloud, though it seemed to be a pile of down mattresses. Silk sheets surrounded her and sent her nerve endings roaring to life with need. As she looked into the eyes of the man she adored, she was surprised to see his golden orbs brimming with guilt. Her hand cupped his cheek, "What is it?"

He looked over her body and winced. She was covered with bruises and bites, the claiming a brutal one, as the beast's mind had taken over his body. "I am so sorry."

"For what?"

Drake traced the string of purple marks that went from her neck down to the crook of her shoulder. "All of this."

"For more pleasure than I could ever have imagined?"

He winced again as he placed a butterfly kiss against one of the darker purple marks on the creamy skin of her hip. "This does not look good."

"Or for thinking I would cheat on you?"

Words meant nothing to him. All that this female had paid was written across her face and body for him to witness on his own. He had not meant to turn their gentle wooing into this act of brutal subjugation. She was a weak mortal. He knew he was supposed to be more careful. "Sally-mine," he took a moment as he tried to swallow back his bile. "I am so sorry."

"For thinking I would cheat on you … I accept."

"No," he thundered as he jumped from the bed.

She watched as he began to stalk around the cave, shimmering between man and dragon. Sally knew deep inside her heart that neither of them would ever harm a hair on her head. Without fear she went to him and caught his hand so he would stop. "Drake," she stepped into his embrace and wrapped as much of her body around his. "I'm not upset about what just happened. I didn't even know a woman could come that many times."

"You didn't know anything about sex before we met."

"You mean making love."

When she began to brush kisses from his cheek to his ear, his chest rumbled with waking desire. What the hell was she thinking? She should be crying and running from him for her very life. Didn't she realize how close what just happened between them came to turning into something vile and despicable? Cherishing females was written into his genetic code. How could he forget for a moment that she was not one of his kind? "Sally-mine," he groaned when she began to nibble at his ear with her clever mouth. "I will return you to your world."

Once those words would have cut her in two.

Now they just made her chuckle.

"Drake," she spoke staring straight into his eyes so that he could see every inch of her spirited resolve. "If you think we're going anywhere before we make love again, then you really have lost your mind."

"But I hurt you …"

"You gave me far more pleasure than pain."

"You're all marked up."

Sally shrugged. "Your strength is ten thousand times more than mine. It's bound to happen from time to time."

He scowled at her. "I will not hurt you more."

She looked around with exasperation as she tried to determine the best course to get around his misgivings and back to the one place she had ever felt like she truly belonged. Under this man, with him so far inside her she felt as if he were touching her womb. The bubble of the smaller pool reached out to her as if it were calling her name. "You know, humans find the feeling of hot water very soothing."

His eyes turned to rubies, and his chest rumbled at the direction of her thoughts. "Baby," he gasped when her hand circled his hardness and she licked at her dry lips. "Are you sure about this?"

Her chuckles went dancing over his flesh as if a caress from her tongue. Together they discovered just how inventive one-half dragon and one full female could be in the heat of the water; after they figured out a way to be equally as productive in the colder water of the larger pool. The cavern was filled with the sounds of a dragon well sated, and his mate, who was familiar, for the first time, with how much power she could have.

CHAPTER TWENTY

Luke sat in the portal room gazing at the swirling rainbow colors with longing. Home. Now it was becoming little more than a faded memory for him. A dream he had nearly forgotten and could only grab small snatches in the most lax moments of his day. This woman, who had invaded their Sanctuary, albeit against her will, was like an abrasion against a healing wound. There was no ending of his need, and no respite from the pain. A small chorus of notes heralded the arrival of an interloper to his brooding time.

"It's funny," he mused. "I wonder what humans would think if they found out that some angels had ring tones to mark their entrance."

Gabrielle chuckled, "Who do you think inspired them?"

"What do you want, Archangel?"

She sighed and the smell of flowers filled the air. That was the thing about angels. They affected, in some way, everything around them. Smells. Lights. Sounds. If mortals could not see, all they really needed was to look harder. There were always signs, one just needed to know how to read them. "To what do I owe this dubious pleasure? Last I checked none of my people have time traveled, killed or destroyed anything in quite a few years. We strive to make the smallest impact possible on the world around us."

Gabrielle breezed in and perched on the side of his chair. She hid her smile. *How like this Emperor.* His throne was a twentieth century easy chair, with patched plaid fabric. Even his clothing displayed his dichotomy. Faded jeans with a mail shirt. "You had a visit from Raphael."

"Drake was concerned about a woman staying with him. She was caught in a plan to kill us."

"So I heard," Gabrielle took a moment to broach the next subject that she was concerned over his reaction. "I take it you are all well?"

"What do you care?" he sneered.

She reached out a hand for a moment, wanting to touch him, but knowing it was the one thing she was not allowed. "Luke, son of the light clan … why this animosity?"

"I am just tired," he grumbled.

"No. You are not."

Luke shook his head and stood. He had no desire for her comfort. The one thing the Guardians had made clear was they were not welcome, and would have to leave as soon as possible. It was the battle over their presence over the centuries that had been warped and altered over the course of time to become the immortal fight between heaven and hell. This would make him Lucifer. How humorous is that? The uneasy truce they existed in was like a knife that swung above their heads all the time. Living on the precipice was not a place to rest. "What is this visit about, Gabrielle? Raphael had a very unusual reaction to the sight of Sally in our midst."

"Who is Sally?"

"The girl," Luke waved his hand at her. "The girl with Drake."

"Is that what she calls herself?" Gabrielle's voice was part question and part wonder.

Luke scowled, "What else would she call herself but her name?"

"I know people by many names."

His bark of laughter was as grating as the rusty hinge on a door. "Yes, the mysterious ambiguity that you love so well. Play no games with me, female archangel. There must be some greater reason for this visit than just checking in."

"Why did you break the compact?"

He winced. This was just what he had feared when Mach and Turbo had arrived with the girl in the first place. They had agreed to certain restrictions when they had arrived. Taking an Earth woman out of the stream of her life was the break of their first commandment. "They were trying to save their friend's life. I had no knowledge or control of their plans."

"And yet you sanctioned it."

"I did what I had to."

Gabrielle shook her head, "You did what you wanted."

He tried to be conciliatory but it was just not his nature. "I made him promise to send her back. She has been poisoned and needs some time to heal."

"She would not have been poisoned had she not been here."

"But she was," Luke's jaw tensed. "And now she needs to be tended by us. Our poison requires our method of healing."

Gabrielle frowned, "We both know that she's fine now."

"Drake is so happy." His voice was softened with his longing.

"This is not about Drake. It is about Sal-" Gabrielle cut off her voice. "It is about the girl."

"What do you want?"

"Send her back."

His stare-down with the Archangel did little. He was not sure if she had eyelids or even had to blink. "Drake gave me his word. By Sanctuary law, he will hold true to it."

"Well, that is something." She shrugged, "I guess."

Luke turned back to her with a piercing stare, "Why does this girl merit such attention?"

"What do you mean?"

"Come on, Gabrielle," he put the emphasis on the last syllable of her name so that it was as drawn out as a lover's caress.

"This girl is special," her confession was begrudging. "Unique."

"She smells like our home," his voice snapped at her.

Gabrielle measured each word as if it were a perfectly cut diamond, "Sally is unique. She is special for this world. I do not care what she smells like. What matters is that her destiny be decided by the rules of free will."

"What if it is her free will to stay here?" He had to try. Drake was one of his people, and this female was their first sign of hope since the great devastation.

"You already decreed, by the law of Sanctuary, she must be returned."

"Gabrielle," Luke begged. "Talk to me. You have my word, on Sanctuary ground, I will not repeat what I am told. Surely you can see how much I need to know what is going on with this female, so the appropriate actions may be taken."

"Return her to the world," she ordered. "And there will be no question about appropriateness."

Luke rose to his full height and tried to remember who he was. What he was. It was so easy to forget in the deluge of banality they lived in. "Why does she get so much special attention, Gabrielle? I will not give in to your wishes unless you explain."

"She is one of my own," her voice had changed to have all the fury of a hurricane. "Sally is a soul I watch over. She is an artist. A genius with plants and flowers. When she finally chooses to accept her destiny, she has the ability to change a world. Would you deny her that future? It must be her free and clear choice to stay or to go. That opportunity will be forever out of her reach until you return her to her blood family and see which way fate propels her down her path."

"What if she chooses to return here?"

Gabrielle grimaced at the idea of all the problems that would bring about. "As long as she makes that choice, free and clear from influence, I will have no argument. I will even cover you with the others."

He gave her a curt nod of his head. "Very well."

"I will have your word."

Luke glared, "Perhaps you are aware of the true nature of the dragon clan? They do not take orders well. I can only suggest to Drake the importance of leaving Sally in her world, until she has chosen without question, to leave it."

Gabrielle shook her head while chuckling, "Perhaps you are right."

"I am," he shared in her laughter. "I don't want to be, but I usually am."

"Then we are agreed."

Luke reached out a hand to stop her and felt his fingers turn glacial as they passed through her arm. It was like submerging your body into ice water; pins and needles that bordered on pain, with a sense of exhilaration. "Gabrielle, explain to me about her ... please. Why does she smell like our home?"

"I am permitted to discuss little where she is concerned. She is a hybrid. A gift that was given to me, to protect from all dangers. Her destiny is a great one, but it must be one she chooses to embrace. She is not to be forced or manipulated into this path. I know Drake's nature. I understand what calls him to Sally with such force. I also know she thinks she is so much less than she truly is, even a smile from your dragon could send her head reeling as if she were drunk. This soul deserves my protection, Luke. She needs to be free to walk her path, no matter what the outcome."

"You do realize that if he loses her it will devastate him."

"How much worse will it be for him, knowing his interference kept her from being all she could?"

Without an additional word she disappeared.

CHAPTER TWENTY-ONE

He found Drake sitting on top of the balcony of his aerie gazing out at the valley stretched below them. Luke paused for a moment before he broke the dragon's reverie. Out of all the brothers, it was Drake he understood the best. They were both the only ones of their kind. Irreplaceable. The idea of anyone, especially the one person who understood his loneliness, taking away someone who was willing to share all aspects of the truth of his soul was inconceivable to him. In a humorous way, Sally Eversham had done more to bring the brothers of the Omegicon together than all of his best efforts over the years, and he now suspected her leaving would be the one thing that would rip them all apart.

It hurt him more than he could bear.

The face Drake turned to Luke was one that glowed. When their eyes locked, they both sighed. "You are here to tell me to send her back, aren't you?"

"Gabrielle came. She assures me that Sally has a great destiny ahead of her."

How could his body feel so replete and exhausted, while his soul felt ripped in two? Drake shuddered so hard with his pain and longing that he almost fell from the perch where he crouched. "Just not one with us."

"This woman was born here-"

"Then why does she reek of everything that is home?" When Luke opened his mouth to fight the statement, Drake hopped down from the banister. "You know I am right, Luke. You are so troubled by it, you sent the scouts into the woods to keep them from getting close to her. Why does she smell like home? How can she be of this planet when her presence here has lessened the pull on our atoms? I spoke to the others. I know everyone's symptoms have lessened since she came – even yours."

Luke made a point of shaking his head as if to try to regain his hearing. One of the many things you could say about dragons, they knew how to roar. "Gabrielle is absolute in her decision. Sally must be returned."

"It will kill me."

"You gave your word."

Drake shook his head. "My plan was to bring her back and then take her again."

"So why fight me?"

"The thought of spending even a second away from her is like a sword through my heart," Drake's voice was hoarse as his eyes swam with tears.

Luke swallowed hard, "I am sorry for this pain."

"What did she tell you about her?"

"Gabrielle?"

Drake nodded.

"The Archangel says that your Sally is an artist. She has a great destiny, one she must be free of all influences, if she is to accept. Gabrielle was understanding of your connection." Luke looked off to the twinkling wonder that was Harrisburg in the distance, the large swaths of green fields and forest like a priceless carpet in the moonlight. "She says Sally has the ability to change the world."

Drake's chuckle was grating and did little to dissipate the grief in his eyes. "I believe that; she has certainly changed mine."

"What will you do?"

Drake's head fell forward as his shoulders slumped. "I will take her back."

"For how long," Luke tried to smile but his strength was gone as his heart bled.

"Forever," Drake choked out.

Luke reached out and managed to grasp Drake's shoulder. "Take her back and give it a few days. Maybe you'll change your mind."

"I love her."

"I know."

Drake smiled as tears flowed from his eyes. Luke was impressed that not once did the dragon flinch away from his pain. Or show shame for crying. Such was the depth of the agony he was experiencing and the pride of this man. "How could I love her and keep her from being everything she is meant to be? She's been overlooked and underappreciated all of her life. I won't be another person who takes everything from her and gives nothing."

He nodded, and clasped his friend's shoulder once more. "We'll be there for you."

"Will you?"

"Of course," Luke swore.

"It is funny to me you could even say that," Drake's voice was scornful.

"I am not one of your trusted advisors."

Luke shook his head, "You really don't know, do you?" When Drake continued to glare at him Luke continued. "This world has no honor in it. No sense of dignity. Loyalty and morality are dead. I don't rely on your counsel in meetings because you are not that kind of man. You are a being of the most noble attributes of any world, especially this one. How can I ask a man who can only be good to fight evil? How could I drag you into that world? Expose you to that kind of pain?"

"It doesn't make me feel any better."

The two men stood staring at each other, trying to resolve a list of such insurmountable hurt and misunderstanding they might as well have been trying to bridge the Grand Canyon with a toothpick.

Drake was the one who broke first. "Respect, considering all the times I chose the compact over my own kind, is just as vital to me."

Luke stepped back as if he had been punched. It would have hurt less if he had.

"I don't rely on your counsel because I am ashamed of the type of man I have become to survive in this world."

"You don't get it do you? The only way to make a difference is to be the change you want to see in the world, Luke. Gandhi knew that. So have most of the ascended masters of this planet. How can you, as the son of the Oracle, not?"

* * *

Drake waited until the tears had dried from his face. They would never leave his soul. Walking back into the room he found his woman fast asleep on her stomach, the sheets a ribbon of white satin that was low on her ass and draped the tops of her thighs. There was so much more he wanted to do with her. To show her. Experience with her. In her. She sighed a small breathy sound that made his gut tighten. He wanted her again, even now. He would want her every day for the rest of his life.

Using some of his dragon will, he forced the tears away.

What purpose could they serve?

He ran the back of his hand down her spine, enjoying the chance to caress the globes of her ass. She was sweet. He could exist off her for centuries before he would ever get close to getting bored. Even then, he doubted it was possible.

She woke up and stretched like a cat under his embrace. Sally's legs fell open and she moaned when his hand slid down to cup her, enjoying the rush of heated nectar that coated his palm. It was rare to find a woman so responsive, rarer to find one that could match his own drive. She did so with plenty of room to spare. Putting aside what he was about to do, Drake decided they both deserved one more time. Dropping his jeans, he crawled over her body, placing licks on key response points as he sought the cradle for which he would dream the rest of his life.

Sally found that casting off sleep with her usual ease was impossible when her body was exhausted from making love with her dragon all night. He had flown them from the pool back to their room where he had spent the evening explaining the many different moods in which sex could happen. Drake's hands had chased the fog of sleep into the haze of desire.

He slid into her with a conquering push that felt as if it went straight to her womb.

Drake caught her hands and braided their fingers together. When she turned her head as if to breathe better he caught her lips for a searing kiss. Mouths sealed, he kept pumping her body, sliding in and out, letting the tight heat of her sheath be the magic that pushed them both over the edge and into pure heaven.

When she was able to move and think once more, she found Drake had repositioned them so that she was draped over his chest. "That's one heck of a way to wake a girl up in the morning," she purred.

"I am glad you liked it."

She scowled at the strange detached tone in his voice. When she tried to lean up to look in his face his arms held her in place. "Drake," she tried to move away again but he kept her still. "What's wrong?"

"I need to take you home today."

His words were said with such quiet, lethal precision she felt as if he'd just whipped her with each syllable he uttered. "Oh," her head was reeling. "I guess that's it then." This was just like every time her brothers and sisters had pushed her away, talking about her as if she were a burden. He was bored with her. Now he wanted her gone. When she tried to leave his arms he tightened his hold again. "Drake," she swallowed praying with fervor she had not experienced since she was five years old and her father had announced her mother's death. "Let me go." *Don't let me break down in front of him*, she thought to herself. *Don't let me cry. I will not be that weak, weeping imbecile that sobs to her boyfriend not to let her go. I deserve better than that.*

"It's not time yet," his voice came out strangled as if he were the one hurting and not the one plunging the dagger in her heart.

Sally clenched her jaw, longing to scream at him. She would not hold on much longer. "I would like to take a shower before I have to leave," she tried to explain with a gathered dignity that would do a queen proud.

His arms slid from her, keeping constant contact with her skin as if they longed to continue to hold her, but could not. He watched as she dashed into the bathroom and slammed the door, the noise echoing through the room. Drake sat back and listened, using his hearing that was more sensitive than a human. The water went on in the shower and a few seconds later he heard them.

She was crying.

Sobbing as if the world was ending.

He moved to the door and rested his head against it. Looking down, he realized water droplets were falling at his feet. He was crying as well. Silently and alone. Knowing that this was going to be the one battle from which he would find it impossible to walk away whole.

Why would he want to?

Who wants to live without his heart?

CHAPTER TWENTY-TWO

When she came out of the shower, Sally found the room empty and was grateful for it. Going to the closet and dressers, she searched for the clothing she had worn to this place, but there was no sign. Her skirt and sweater were gone.

Along with her will to live.

She dressed in a pair of jeans and a t-shirt, guessing that they were the least valuable items in the wardrobe Drake had secured for her. Why did he bother? She'd barely been there for a week before he dumped her. What was the purpose? For the lingerie she chose the stuff with the La Perla labels, hoping they were the most expensive. If she were going to hide her pain, she deserved to hide some beauty as well. The green lace bra and panty set would be something she could wear and remember the beautiful man, who, for a little while, had made her feel like a goddess.

It might make living like the troll a tad easier to cope with.

A knock on the door made her bite her lip. Time was flying so fast, and all she wanted was to stretch out each moment as far as she could. Opening up the hidden portal that Drake had tried to keep from her she glared at Luke. "I was just finishing," she explained. Returning to the bed she sat down so that she could pull on her socks and sneakers.

Luke cleared his throat until she looked at him. She looked so delicate. Her eyes were glass crystals that shone with all the torment he sensed in Drake.

"I'll be done in a moment," she repeated, her brain sluggish with shock.

"This is an official visit," he explained.

Sally's blank stare was all that she could manage given the circumstance. "Okay."

"I am Luke, the leader of the light clan. It is my responsibility to rule Sanctuary and safeguard the compact that allows us to stay here."

She turned her head back to her task, finding it easier to understand than this strange angelic-looking male. What did it matter who he was? His responsibilities? She was dying inside.

Luke smiled at the woman who was focusing on her laces, trying to tie them into neat bows. "As such, I have the right to offer my protection to any of my people. Once it is extended, especially given the rules of this place, it can never be taken away by anyone else. Humans. Omega. Elementals. Even the angels are prohibited from interference."

The sneakers tied, she stood, burying her hands in her pockets to hide their tremors.

"My point here, Sally Eversham, is I am now extending that protection to you. Should you have need, any need at all, just call out the word Sanctuary and we will come for you."

"Why would you do that?"

Luke shrugged, "You are one of us now."

"He doesn't want me," she gasped.

"You don't believe that in your heart."

"My heart hurts too much right now to know what to believe."

He laughed and reached out to clasp her arms in his hands and hold her steady. "I ask you to look deep inside; into the place we call your secret heart. The hidden part of your soul that few people ever see or experience. It is rare for an earth human to have the courage to search out that place, but we both know you have plenty to spare. Look into your secret heart and ask that same question."

"I don't know how."

Luke brought her into his embrace and rested her shaking body against his chest. "Yes, you do, Sally. Look there and you will see he loves you. He does not want to do this, but his honor demands he comply."

"That doesn't make me feel any better."

"It should," Luke laughed. "There is no creature with more integrity than the final dragon."

"Why is he the last one?"

"The wars were hard on our world. They destroyed our ecosystem, almost all our women, and most of our advancements. The dragons were deeply rooted to both the planet and its balance. Our blithe wasting of the world made them angry and sick. Without us even realizing it, they began to disappear. When the Oracle made her prophecy--"

"The what?"

"The prophecy," he repeated. "For the dragon it shall salvation be--"

"What?"

He smiled at her shock and eager interruption. "That's how it starts. For the dragon it shall salvation be. Why? Does that mean something to you? "

Sally shook her head. "It doesn't matter. What else does it say? "

"Happiness is found in three. Clearest sight is found below, what was gone, must start to show. Your armor will have to break, the last will cause the big mistake. Lay down your inherited power, Do not stop in the final hour. Your lives will grow again here, when the Jewels provide the key to fear. For the one who is my very own, your greatest destiny is alone."

"What's it mean?"

"No clue. It's the riddle the Oracle, or our God, gave us. A guide on how to return our world to greatness again. Anyway, the Oracle declared we should send the clan leaders and the healthiest of our remnant through the dimensional portal, it was going to be a dragon that would open and tend it. They refused."

"So how did you go through?"

"Drake came to me and offered to do it. He was so young, and so sure we deserved a second chance."

Sally smiled, her eyes shining like stars as tears filled them. Luke was floored by her sense of generosity. She was not willing to show her tears for her own hurt, but felt no problem at letting others see her pain for her mate's. It was humbling. "How like him," she whispered. "He wouldn't let his friends die."

"We were enemies then. What he would not do was give up hope. Even when hope was a mere memory."

"That makes sense," she nodded.

Luke squeezed her arms. "So do you accept my extension of protection?"

"Won't he be mad?"

"It is not his choice," he smiled. "I have my own powers. He can do little to hurt me."

Sally shook her head, "You guys really know how to play dirty."

"It is what we excel at."

"Your offer of protection is accepted," she bowed to him not knowing why she would do so but that it just felt appropriate. "I am grateful."

An electric current moved through her and seemed to weave into her soul.

Luke raised her up and kissed her hand. "You are enchanting."

"You keep mauling her and Drake will have your guts for curtain ropes," Mach joked as he and Turbo entered the room.

"I was only saying my good-byes," Luke explained with cool civility.

Turbo smiled, "That's why we're here, too."

"Nah," Mach drawled. "We're here so we can get to hug her without Drake promising to kill us later."

"If Drake had any right to be angry at either of you, he would not be sending me away."

They all gave her looks with such pity she had to mentally slap her own face. This was no way to go. She would face this as she had everything else in her life. Alone. *Give them a smile; show them her brave face.* She would see about looking into her secret heart and tending her soul when she was alone. "Sorry," Sally released a deep sigh. "I am glad you guys came."

Giving each of them a hug, she pressed her face into their necks so she could blink away her tears. "Remember to consider his side of things," she advised Mach.

To Turbo she whispered, "He loves you. Don't let anything stand in the way of that."

"We won't be missing you," Mach boasted. "We're going to look for Blade."

"Glad to hear it," Sally gifted him with a wink.

Turning to the room, Sally sighed again. She wouldn't need anything to remember the last few days. It was embedded in her memory for all time. It would have to be. "I'm ready."

"Aren't you taking your clothes?"

"No," Sally answered Turbo without looking around her. "They're not mine."

"Drake bought them for you," Mach pointed out.

"You should take them," Turbo insisted.

"No," she repeated. "I'm only wearing this, because he got rid of the ones I was wearing when you found me."

"You mean kidnapped you."

"To me it was finding." She closed her eyes as a wave of torment ripped through her. "I'd been alone for so long," her voice came from so deep in her soul it sounded as if it were echoing from a well. "Bringing me here was finding me."

Sally turned and walked down the stairway from the secret door, not giving them a chance to stop her and make her reconsider. It would hurt too much. She could hear them behind her, scrambling to keep up. When she reached the hallway that led to the main room, she kept moving. Somehow she had to get through this, and the only way she would keep from falling apart, was if she kept moving.

Which was when she found Stealth.

He was waiting for her.

"I wish you weren't leaving," he whispered as he hugged her hard.

"As do I," she confessed.

Stealth's smile was mischievous, "I could keep you."

"You would never do that," she chided him with a gentle look. "He'd kill you."

"He'd try," Stealth shrugged. "It's a lot harder to do than you think."

"No," she shook her head. "It's not."

"Be well, Sally Eversham. You have the thanks of the clan that is not seen."

"That's a terrible name for a family," she grimaced. "You should change it."

"For you, I will consider it," he promised.

Aquos appeared in the doorway and his eyes blazed at her like twin sapphires. "I refuse to say good-bye."

"I have to leave," she locked her muscles to keep from throwing her body into his arms.

He shook his head.

"Don't do this, Aquos."

"You are not leaving," he gritted out.

Sally wished he would stop with all of her heart. She had no idea how much longer she would be able to hang on, and breaking down in front of these good men would shame her like nothing else. "I have to go."

He clasped her shoulders and stared with a heated intensity deep inside his eyes, "Stay with me. I'll keep you."

"I am not a pet. Or a belonging. You can't pass me around."

"You know that's not it," he swore at her.

"I do," she nodded. "I also know I would always think of him. I would want to be with him. We both deserve better than that. You deserve someone who has you as her first priority. Not a substitute."

Aquos buried his head in her neck and took a deep breath of her hair. "I would find a way to make you happy."

"I have never doubted that."

He let her go, and taking one final look at the five men who had come to mean more to her than her own brothers, she continued.

Back to her nightmare.

Sally forced her feet to keep moving. She found if she kept swallowing, and held her eyes really wide and still, never once blinking, she could hold her emotions at bay. Her mind made idle note of the lushness of the building that these men took for granted. It was a pity when you thought about it. The place was beautiful, but it was cold and antiseptic. No one had ever made it into a home.

She would have liked to have tried.

Drake was waiting for her by a long black limousine. There were three men in shades of black and gold waiting nearby. He held open the door in silence, while the elementals got in front.

As a measure of insurance she refused to look back again as she slid into the dark leather interior.

When he got in he refused to let her hold her body away from him. Drake captured her hiding hand and wrapped both of his around her to keep it on his lap. If he had thought she would allow it he would have wrapped his body around her like a coat and protected her from all harm. That would help him alone though, not her.

It felt like they reached her home in seconds.

She sat in the car, immobilized by the thought this was truly happening.

She was about to say good-bye to the only thing really wonderful that had happened to her since her mother had died.

How could she still breathe when it hurt so much?

Why was she still alive?

"I want you to know," he paused as he tried to squeeze some air into lungs that felt as if they were being compressed into pancakes. "I want you to know I will always be there for you. If you need anything, anything at all, just call me."

"You don't have a phone."

"I made the elementals get us each one. They have the number preprogrammed so that all you need to do is press a button."

Sally shuddered from head to toe. "No."

"What?"

"No."

"Why not?"

"If you're sending me away, make it for real. Make it forever. I'm an all or nothing kind of girl. I've seen my brothers and sisters promise former lovers for years they would stay friends. Keep in touch. All that will do is make me keep hoping there's still a chance for us, and I cannot live that way."

The eyes he turned on her were wide with hurt. "Why not? Hope is everything to my people."

"Hope will keep me from moving on. Accepting what is rather than dreaming about what could be. I will die under that kind of burden." She turned to him, appealing with naked raw desperation. "Drake, you gave me a week of every dream come true I have ever had. This is my reality and I can't live in both worlds."

"So what," he shook his head. "You'll forget me?"

"No," she swore. "I'll go back to who I was before, so I can survive living without you."

Drake ran his hand through his hair as he tried to decide the best course.

She caught his hands and grasped them in hers. "Thank you, Drake. I will never forget one moment of the last week."

"Even the vomiting?"

"Even that," she confessed with a wince. "I will cherish every moment of it."

He fisted his hands in her hair and dragged her across the supple leather seat to give her a kiss that would seal every passionate moment they shared into her soul. She had no idea what it was to cherish every moment. He would have an eternity to ache for her. And he was the only one who knew it. When he released her, they were both panting, their bodies ready for a coupling that would shock anyone else in any different situation, and they knew it was the last thing they could do.

"It's time," she insisted.

They got out of the car together and walked to her front door in silence. The old Victorian was pleasing to Drake's eye. It was almost enough of a palace to be appropriate for his woman, and no matter what, she would always be his. What really set it apart in the neighborhood was the lush greenery that filled the front yard. If this was Sally's work she was more than an artist, she is a genius. She opened the door and walked inside, stopping short when she found all of her siblings assembled in the living room.

"Where have you been," Austin roared as he charged from his chair.

Drake shoved Sally behind him as he faced off with her siblings. When Austin got close he put one hand on his forehead and sent him flying backwards. "You will not touch her," he snarled at the sprawled man. Spearing Mitch with his stare he added for good measure, "If either of you go near her, I will come back and rip you apart with my bare hands. Laughing."

Robin and Dawn stood up, hissing at him, their backs arched like ticked-off cats.

"Listen well, your sister has returned but she is no longer the person you knew. If you put one more wound on her soul, one bruise, I will return and your life will end in that moment. I swear it."

"Drake," Sally's voice was authoritative as she moved to stand between him and her family. "It's time for you to go."

His mouth fell open with shock. "I am not leaving until I know you are safe."

Mitch lunged to knock him down, and Drake caught him around the throat slamming him into a wall. He continued to look at Sally, his face showing no indication of his efforts as he lifted her sibling slowly until he was standing on his toes.

She sighed. "Please go."

"As soon as I know they will give you respect."

Her stare was unwavering. "That is not your concern."

"We're her family," Dawn scathed.

Robin's lip lifted with her sneer, "Not some stranger."

"I am not a stranger," Drake drawled. "To her."

"Drake," Sally hollered. "Go away."

He stared at her with mute appeal as his mouth open and closed while he tried to phrase some kind of retort. The resolve in her eyes was an impossible barrier for him to bridge, and he knew it. Releasing Mitch he took no small satisfaction in the way he fell limp to the floor. Without another sound, he turned and walked away.

The sound of the door closing behind him was the beginning of the crack in the façade she was using to get through this moment.

Facing the room of astounded and confused dark stares she raised her chin.

"Do you know how late you are on the Pullwater Lane house?"

She shrugged away Austin's question. "You said you wanted it done by the end of the month. I still have a few days."

"You can't landscape that entire yard in a few days," Robin spat.

Sally looked her in the eyes, her expression neutral. Not letting her see any reaction made her sister back down as if she had been Drake about to spit fire at her. Ouch. That was a reminder that hurt. "It'll be done in time."

Turning away from them she began to walk to her room.

"Where are you going?"

She didn't care which one of them yelled. "To my room."

"We need to talk about some things."

"Later," Sally made it to the head of the stairs and turned to go up the next set to the third floor.

"What are we going to have for dinner?"

"I'm not hungry," she called down before she reached the haven of her room and slammed the door shut. Their squeals of outrage would have made her laugh in any other situation. She turned her music up loud so that they would not hear her sobs, and she wouldn't have to listen to them.

 # CHAPTER TWENTY-THREE

Luke walked into the living room, to find everyone sprawled on the couches looking glum. "Anyone tried to talk to him?"

All of them shook their heads while wiping their heavily perspiring faces.

"Anyone see about updating the central air," he added while taking his favorite chair and putting his feet up.

Stealth grimaced, "There is no way it can manage this heat. I didn't want to burn out the system over something I hoped was only a temporary problem. If you think he's going to do much more of this I might want to consider putting it on line again."

"That's not a bad idea," Mach had an entire bath sheet to wipe his flushed face.

"It's November," Aquos shrugged. "Who knew we'd need central air?"

Luke gritted his teeth as he decided to state the obvious, "When a dragon is in a bad mood he breathes fire and puts out heat. Clearly our dragon is having a few issues."

"He's grieving," Aquos snapped.

"We all are," Stealth reminded him.

Luke shook his head, "We lost a friend." He rose from his chair determined to prove to his friend he was not alone. "Drake lost far more."

"What?"

Stealth swallowed past the lump in his throat, "His heart."

"No," Aquos stood as well, needing to return to his pools where he would at least be cool. "Drake lost his soul."

***

Drake was sitting in the center of his bedroom. The furniture had been reduced to bare timbers in his rage at Sally's loss. All four fireplaces had blazes roaring in them. The flames were running so hot they made Luke think of the old days when it was fires that were the only things they had to keep their homes warm. God had done well with this planet when he gave humans a finite lifespan. Immortality was a real bitch on the memory.

He was crouched down, his arms wrapped around his body as if he feared being ripped apart by the waves of pain.

"You are not alone."

The eyes that the great dragon turned to him were haunting with their devastation. This was an emotional storm the size of a hurricane and he could not imagine any of them getting out of it unscathed. "She is gone."

"We are still here."

He turned away from Luke and allowed his head to fall forward once more. "I do not care."

"Yes, you do," Luke crouched next to him and clasped his shoulder. "We are still here. Our mission is still here. Our people are still waiting for us, hoping that we will return and save them. There is much for you to live for."

His head flew back and a stream of fire came out of his mouth. Drake directed his aim at the fireplace, but he still managed to scorch most of the wall.

His body shaking, he fell forward and lay on the floor in the fetal position.

Luke sat next to him, and tried to channel some energy into his friend's shaking body. His aura was a cloud of smoke and pollution, the negativity and pain deep black bands tight around his friend's heart and lungs. It was a legend in their clans that the dragons were dying not from the actual devastation to their ecosystem, but rather due to the pain of seeing what had been done. He had suspected they willed themselves into illness. Now he knew without a doubt it was true.

Luke was watching his friend do the same thing.

* * *

The Architect slipped through the back halls of the building, intent on getting outside before he was discovered. He grimaced at the overwhelming heat. Though they had been wise in the planning of the structure, putting the dragon at the top so that any heat generated would be funneled outside, his grief was coming close to setting the very air on fire. Someone should explain the concept of global warming to Drake before the floods hit the middle of the country, and not just the coastline. The last thing he needed was for any of the remnant to find him now. It would destroy all of his plans. When he got outside, he moved as fast as he could to the tree line. From there he could blend into the woods that protected the privacy of the building.

He had known the hardest one to take out would be the mighty dragon.

Drake's ability to open the portal between the dimensions was the one weakness in his plan. The only real way to discard these interlopers, this filth that remained of their world, was to make sure that they understood they would never go home. They would never find the redemption that was their sole reason for life. Taking out that final thread of hope was the key point of his plan.

The problem had always been that the dragon was protected in more ways than he could attack. This world still had enough people that believed in dragons so Drake was empowered with the strength of those people's sense of worship. They were seen as loyal and honorable, guardians of the earth spirits that people, especially the Asian people, venerated. He sneered. What did he need with such entities? His world was dead. This one was well on its way to the same end.

Self-destruction through the rampaging curse of over consumption.

A roar shook the building and the heat went up once more. Drake was not taking the loss of his mate well. In fact, he doubted that the dragon's heart would survive the separation. They get bonded so fast. All his plans and it was one little, well not so little, earth woman who took the dragon down.

Little did he expect, that in the end, it would be love that killed the beast.

He finally understood the moral of King Kong.

# CHAPTER TWENTY-FOUR

The buzzing of the alarm was the last thing she needed to break her out of her dreams. It's not like she had slept. Anymore. Sally opened up her eyes to glare at the ceiling above her head. The room was her haven. It was still painted with the flower-filled landscape her mother had created a few months before she died. The tiny rose buds and Gerber daisies stretching out over the fields had been a beautiful way to begin the day when she was growing up. Now it was only a sad reminder of everything she felt she had lost from her life.

Beauty. Grace. Love.

Her body felt like a yearning maw of hunger. She hadn't eaten much since Drake had gone. Food held no interest. The desire he had wakened in her body was the only need she wished to feed, and she had no ability to do so. Masturbation just seemed so lonely, and after reaching ecstasy in her dragon's arms, it was even less appealing.

She felt so different now.

Sally grimaced at the fact staring her in the face. This was more than heartache. She was tired all of the time, even when she spent the entire day in bed. She couldn't eat anything, but kept thinking about great huge slabs of rare steak, when she hadn't eaten meat in years. Her skin was glowing, her breasts sore, and she was on a constant roller coaster of emotions that left her reeling in hysterical laughter or sobbing her heart out. At this rate she was going to have to go to the doctor soon. Even her brothers commented she was acting odd.

If Mitch and Austin noticed something was up, she must be sick.

It was Monday, though, and there was still work to do. She had survived the last month by taking each moment as it came. Each second, with a grain of salt. If she kept herself grounded by what was happening right now, right this instant, and did not think about tomorrow, or next week, or anything else for that matter, she could keep the pain away, the tears inside. It was a soulless way to live, but the only option she seemed to have available.

She pulled on an ancient pair of jeans and a t-shirt. Flip-flops were the most evident pair of shoes so she went with those rather than something she would have to hunt down. Starting a new garden was supposed to be fun for her.

Nothing was fun, now.

Sally jumped when she entered the kitchen. All her siblings were assembled. In the morning. Before dawn. Apparently pigs really can fly.

"What's going on," she asked them.

Dawn tittered. She really needed to stop doing that. It was cute when she was little, passable when she was in her teens, but just plain annoying now that she'd left forty long behind. "Now she asks."

"We knew she'd break out of that bubble sooner or later."

She hid her face when she rolled her eyes at Austin's sarcasm. Someone woke up on the wrong side of the bed this morning, or the wrong girl.

Mitch banged his hand against the table. "Are you sure the banks won't help?"

"We used up our credit on the fairy tale village."

Sally bent down to look through the cereals on the bottom shelf of the pantry. Fairy Tale Village. What a lame name for a housing complex built with spit and balsa wood. She'd told them it was a mistake. At least the flora and fauna were gorgeous. She had filled the gardens with exotic plants in free flowing beds that mimicked a natural growing pattern, so it looked like you were in the middle of an enchanted glade.

Unfortunately the houses were finished right when the housing industry imploded.

"So what do we have left?"

"Nothing," Austin answered Robin.

All of them groaned, which Sally took as a sign to step in. "If you guys need a loan, I would be happy to help," she offered. "I've got Mom's inheritance and just about all of my salary from the last few years."

No answer.

Giving up on the dreams of a healthy and nutritious breakfast, Sally decided she would just grab something on the way to the job site. At least it would be more fun than the processed cardboard waiting for her here. Looking at her family, she scowled, "What? Isn't it enough?"

They shifted and avoided her eyes.

"What's going on guys?"

"We had to use your money to maintain the interest payments on the property."

Her knees sagged and she had to catch herself on the counter to keep her body from collapsing. "How much is left?"

"None of it," Austin informed her with a sneer.

She shook her head. "There was over two hundred thousand dollars in that account," she gasped. "It was all the money I had in the world."

Austin shrugged.

"We also pawned your mom's jewelry."

Sally felt her stomach convulse at this fact delivered with such calm by her sister, Dawn. Who were these people? What were they? How was it humanly possible that they shared half their genes in common?

"So," she looked down and saw her knuckles were turning as white as she felt. "You took all of my money, and everything I had left of my mom, and threw it away on a housing project that isn't worth the paper the deeds are written on. In the mean time, I am curious … have you stopped gambling Austin? Mitch, exactly how much money have you spent on prostitutes in the last month alone? Dawn, are those new Prada shoes on your feet or are you just happy to see us? Can you even understand what's happening or are you too busy thinking about how to score your next cocaine hit?"

"What," Robin's eyes narrowed. "Nothing you want to say to me?"

She shook her head. "I am sure anything you have on was given to you from some guy you picked up in some bar. The one thing I can accuse you of is never once giving a damn about me or sticking up for anyone that isn't sitting next to you."

The door slammed behind her before she could give them the satisfaction of seeing her cry. Austin looked at his siblings and shrugged. "That's it then."

"Are you sure they'll make it fast?"

He nodded in answer to Mitch's question. "They promised. She'll be dead and the insurance should take care of most of our problems."

"We have no choice."

Robin and Dawn exchanged a silent look and shrugged. "We knew we put up with her for something."

The brothers nodded. "Her insurance was the one thing we made sure to keep paying."

"And now she can pay us," Robin purred as she rose from the table.

* * *

Sally kept driving, trying to unravel everything crowding her head and make sense of it. Her breath came in gasps as she tried to deal with this harsh reality. The money they had taken was all she had. She had saved for years, hoping to open up her own landscaping office one day. It was a dream she had kept hidden so deep inside, terrified that someone would try and take it from her, and she had never realized how important it was to her soul. The work she did for the company did little to assuage her artistic impulse. She had so many plans and hopes.

They were as gone as Drake.

Skipping her plan for breakfast, she headed to the house. Walking through soil, free from any interference of her siblings was the best medicine for her right now.

Sally tried to decide what she should do. It wasn't like she had any real friends. She had tried her best to be invisible most of her life; it meant that no one would pass judgment on you that way. The trends of her childhood had held steady through most of her adulthood. Don't be seen. Don't be known. Then you get left alone.

Reaching the house she grimaced. It was a quick flip, but it still looked like hell. Lots of tall bushy trees she noted. Anything to mask the stench of poverty.

Using her key she let herself in. There were tumbled marble tiles lining the hall, which seemed like a waste of money. Linoleum everywhere else, which meant they had run out of budget in the middle of construction. No wonder she only had a few hundred to complete the outside. This would take a miracle.

With a heavy sigh she entered the kitchen.

Once again, Mitch had created a kitchen that was designed for people who hated food. The tile countertops would be hell to keep clean, and erode in a few months. There was no backsplash. The sinks were so small you'd be hard pressed to fit in a dinner plate, and the stovetop only had two burners. The poor family that moved in here. She hoped they liked eating out.

Sally smiled as she opened one of the cabinets. Eating out sounded good. She's do anything for a piece of strawberry shortcake right now.

She blinked when she found it. Inside the cabinet, sitting on a white china plate with drizzled chocolate and coconut as if a waitress had just delivered it from her favorite diner. Slamming the door, she began to pant. "Well," she announced with false cheer to the empty house. "That was shocking. Next thing I know, I'll open up one of these cabinets and find a stock of rubies to solve our money problems."

Shaking her head she opened up the same cabinet and an avalanche of shining red gems fell out.

Holding one up to the light she began to shake.

It was a ruby. Cut and shining, it caught the light to refract it back in scarlet rainbows as if she were looking into Drake's eyes. She was holding an actual ruby, with a pile of them around her feet. Sally crouched and began to shove the rest of them back into the cabinet, shaking with a combination of excitement and fear. What the heck? Her laughter began to burst out of her mouth in short staccato rounds. This was crazy, right?

"Yeah, Sally, and getting snatched by some refugees from another dimension and falling in love with a dragon is the height of sanity."

Recognizing suddenly appearing with a fortune in gems would cause her more problems than good, Sally knew she had to get rid of them. Some of them resembled Drake's eyes so she made sure to tuck them in her pocket. When the rest were back inside, she closed her eyes and wished them gone with all her heart. Opening the door she released her breath when she saw they had disappeared.

Going outside she ditched her shoes and began to walk through the backyard in bare feet. Sally tried to corral her head and focus on the job at hand. Purples, gold and blue flowers filled her mind. A collage of color and scent with no discernible path or other features. A garden that was a feast for the eyes, one that was almost intimidating because you would be so appreciative of the effect you would never dare to step foot over its boundaries. Her head reeling with the smells of the flowers she was imagining, she opened her eyes.

The garden was done.

A path of flowers extended out behind her, just as she had envisioned them.

Perfect in each detail. It would have taken her weeks to accomplish by hand.

She decided she'd better go home.

At this rate, she might have one idle thought and find the entire house remade. It was such a piece of crap it should be blown up. That might be difficult to explain to her siblings. Or the neighborhood. Or the police. Driving away she began to shake. "What do I do?" Her gasped question was met by the silence of the car. There was no one to turn to.

No help to be found.

She had never before felt so completely alone.

When she caught sight of her favorite diner she pulled in with relief. This was an idea. She would sit in here and eat. Food was a good thing. She needed to eat something and maybe she would start to feel better. This was the actual location that made the delectable strawberry shortcake. Eating one that she knew for a fact had been cooked, and not conjured out of the air, was a good plan.

The best thing about this place was it also had a great many booths that were set up so that you had privacy.

She had no intention of being bothered or seen by anyone.

Waiting for the hostess to seat her, she noticed two of the men at the counter were checking her out. They must be sailors, she counseled herself. On leave. For the first time in six months.

Or ex-cons.

She heard the explosion when she sat down. The waitress passed her the news. A house nearby had just exploded. Sally was glad she was sitting down when she received the confirmation because it was the location she had just fled from. Pushing away her cake, she understood it was time to recognize the truth.

Her problems were a great deal bigger than she'd realized.

.

CHAPTER TWENTY-FIVE

"We've had it."

The announcement from Mach was said in such a hard and uncompromising voice, everyone looked up. They were assembled in the gateway room, each sprawled in their thrones, gazing into the kaleidoscope. "Excuse me," Luke queried.

"We've had it with waiting. We've had it with life without Sally, and not having any kind of evidence of what happened to Blade."

The others looked to Turbo. How could the motion clan suddenly have found accord in the middle of such dark days? Drake shook his head. *It had to be Sally's continued influence.* They sat in the main room, every one of them stripped down to their boxer shorts and Speedos in consideration for his ongoing affliction. He had begun to get some better control; at least fire was no longer bursting from his mouth every five minutes. Good Lord, he needed to look into some new kind of breath mints. Sulfur was not an appetizing taste to walk around with in your mouth.

"Drake refuses to get Sally."

"Fine," Stealth interrupted before Aquos could speak. "I'll take her."

Drake launched out of the chair where he was sprawled and aimed to take Stealth down with a chokehold on his neck. His adversary blinked out of the room and across the chamber before he even got close. The idea of anyone, especially the man who hated him the most, getting close to Sally was making his dragon nature want to burst free. He turned to go after Stealth again, when Luke threw up his hand to freeze him in place. "He dares," Drake growled. "He dares to think he is worthy of breathing her air? Much less touching her?"

Luke wanted to bang his head against something hard. Really hard. For days. "Would you two cut the shit? Sally is not up for auction. Stop fighting over her."

"She's worth fighting for," Stealth pointed out, doing little to calm Drake.

Mach ripped through the room at top speed, causing a shock wave that sent everyone toppling back into their seats. When he was done he panted, resting his hands against his knees. Turbo gazed at the clan masters with a smug sense of triumph. "This is not meant to be a chance for us to go after each other's throats. We are here to focus on the real and concrete concerns facing us right now."

"What do you want?" Aquos earned disbelieving looks with his query.

"We want to use the mage to find Blade."

"His name is Altea," Stealth hissed.

"What he is, Stealth, is terrifying."

"He's my friend."

The others couldn't believe Stealth's staunch defense of the mage clan. No one denied the mage his friendship or place with their kind. They were just wigged out by the intensity of the clan. They never laughed. Never showed any kind of emotion or response to the world around them. It was freaky. They were each the cover men of the freaky society, but the mages moved into a whole new orbit.

"We know that," Luke tried to be conciliatory; "I do not think using the mage is a bad idea."

"What about Sally?" Turbo pounced.

Drake threw up his hands. "Gabrielle told Luke that Sally has a great destiny. She is unique for this world. I cannot take her away from that … none of us have the right. Sally needs to have the freedom and time to make her own choice. She cannot do that with all of us holding onto her like some life preserver to remind us of home."

They grew silent as Drake's words scathed them. Shamed them.

"We didn't know," Aquos reminded him.

Luke looked to Drake and longed to do something to ease his friend's pain. "He knows."

"A great destiny," Stealth mused.

"Way to go Sally," Turbo and Mach spoke as one in a whisper.

"There is still Blade to consider."

Luke flinched at Mach's reminder of their lost friend. "The plan to ask Altea for assistance is not bad. If he has some clue, then by all means proceed."

"Will you help us?" Mach asked Stealth.

"No one works those guys like you do," Turbo pointed out.

Mach shrugged, "You were the one who just reminded us that he's your friend."

"I'll do it," Stealth sighed.

Drake nodded. "If you'll excuse me, I will return to my room and try to ease the heat in the house."

As he stood to leave the others rose as well. Luke turned to Drake. "We could help," he offered him. The look that the dragon turned to him was so hot it was as if he had just received third degree burns. Luke was flattered when all the other Lords joined him to stand shoulder to shoulder. "It would be our honor to stand with you," Stealth added with quiet dignity.

"We all mourn the loss of Sally," Aquos provided him.

"You don't understand," Drake laughed. "I will never stop missing her."

As Drake left, Aquos cursed. "He knows what kind of hell he sent her back to. Mourning her loss is one thing. Knowing you have condemned the love of your life to an existence with people who treat you like dirt is torturous."

Luke smiled ready to announce his secret. "She has another option."

"What do you mean?"

He shrugged to Stealth's question. "Before she left I offered Sally protection."

"Did she accept it," they all asked with eagerness.

"She did."

The looks they gave him were a combination of awe and respect. It made him feel like a true leader for the first time in a very long period of dismal days. "And before she left, I cast a tracer on her. Should Sally call out for help, she will receive it. Should she need us, we will know. There is no way to break the hold of light that I gave her."

"You know," Mach beamed, rocking back and forth.

Turbo finished, "You got some chops, boss man."

"Must be why he is our fearless leader."

For the first time Luke did not feel denigrated by the title that Stealth used. For the first time he felt as if he might just deserve it.

* * *

Austin and Mitch walked into the office, closing the door behind them with a quick glance to insure that they were alone. Robin and Dawn were waiting inside with boutique bags piled around them. "She isn't even dead yet and you're already shopping?"

Dawn shrugged, "We needed something to wear for the funeral."

"Speaking of that," Robin interrupted. "What happened?"

"I guess the bomb went off too fast," Mitch shrugged.

"Doesn't really matter," Austin's smile was chilling. "They'll get her tomorrow."

CHAPTER TWENTY-SIX

Sally sat back on her heels and wiped her brow. She hadn't been able to close her eyes for a week, terrified of what would dance through her brain and happen. It had become of such vital importance for her to keep her mind blank, she was starting to think it was changing her eye color.

It had been almost eight days since the house had blown up. No one had said anything to her about it, and she was feeling so guilty that she had started to avoid her family the easiest way she knew how. Skipping meals. Her body felt like someone had fried her internal wiring. She swung back and forth between being hot and cold, weak and strong, hungry and full. It was bewildering, and the number of times she had to catch herself from falling by grabbing onto a wall was starting to equal every other minute. "Oh, Sally," she was hit by a series of shivers that rocked her entire body. "You are in so much trouble."

She might as well face it. She was sick. And she seemed to be getting sicker.

What on earth was she supposed to do about it?

A doctor seemed out of the question. How could she explain to a physician she had been living with a group of aliens, and fell in love with a man that was half dragon? She would be on an express train to the psych ward before she finished filling out the insurance information on the form.

If she still had an insurance policy.

There was so much going on now with the family and their shaky future she couldn't even begin to process. No other weird things had happened for a week, but she had worked very hard to make sure that they didn't happen. What was she going to have to face when she did let down her guard?

Emus dancing in the garden?

Whirling around she crossed her fingers, hoping that did not happen. There was little consolation when she saw she was alone, but, still, that was her point. She needed to make sure she didn't have those kinds of moments. It was a sad way to live but at least she wasn't wearing any kind of white jacket that had buckles in the back.

Picking up her tools she stretched out her lower back and looked over the progress. One more day, a good rain, and the house would be done. Sally wondered where Austin was finding the capital to keep them going. The others had always made it clear to her that the financial aspect of their company was none of her business. She was just a hired hand to them. No different from any of the other subcontractors they used on a daily basis. Except that those people actually got paid. The only reason why they used subcontractors was because they were cheaper – no need to pay for health insurance or worry about benefits - but she guessed that was not her business either.

Letting herself inside the house, she went to the kitchen to clean up.

This house was bigger than usual. It was over six thousand square feet, and was overabundant with marble and carved wood. Someone with a brain had chosen this place. And with good taste. No way was it one of her siblings. The rooms were beautifully apportioned and the architectural features would sell well with a quality market.

Sally stopped short when she saw there was already a man inside the building. The ski mask and dark clothes stated what he was there for as well as if he had worn a neon sign. She threw her tools at him and whirled around to run back the way she had come but went full-speed into another assailant. Recognizing she was outnumbered and out gunned, she opened her mouth and let out a scream of pure terror.

The men began to circle her.

She looked around her, trying to come up with some other plan. They were facing off in the living room. There was a smaller archway into the kitchen, and a larger one for the foyer. The windows were covered with protective film and there was no way she would manage to get through it before she was dragged back. Also, the street was a quiet one. There would be no saving her outside.

Sally began to pant like a wounded animal, making little mewls of terror. "What do you want?"

"Sorry, lady," one of the men spoke with a broken Spanish accent.

"You have to die."

"Make it easy for us and we promise to keep it painless."

Sally shook her head as she started to edge her way to the windows. It was her only hope.

"Your brothers didn't say you'd be so hot."

The bad guy near the kitchen smiled through the hole in his mask and she shuddered with revulsion at his look of sexual interest. "Maybe we have some fun first, ay?"

"Stay away from me," she gasped before diving for the window.

One of the men took her down with a flying leap. The other dragged her away from his friend and dived onto her bucking body. She began to shake, scratch, and writhe to try to escape the two men who were fighting each other to get on top of her and her own efforts to get free. One of the men managed to mash his mouth over her lips. She wanted to puke. The other pulled her hair and grabbed at her breasts.

Wrenching her lips away she let out one scream. One word that was the only thing that saved her from loneliness, despair and pain. "Draaaaaaaaaake."

The syllable was drawn out with her pain and then cut off when one of the men managed to land a punch to the side of her chest, making all the air in her lungs disappear. Her tears streamed from her eyes, falling into her mouth and ears. This was it. After everything she had gone through, could this be how she died? "Sanctuary," she managed to whisper as everything started to grow dim.

A burst of light exploded in the room with the force of a supernova.

The two men looked up with shock to see six men standing before them in different states of battle readiness. Drake launched his body from where he stood in a single leap and sent both of them flying into the wall. He saw Sally pull herself up and back into the corner of the room. Mach and Turbo moved to stand in front of her, an impenetrable wall of warriors who would let no harm come close to his woman.

Stealth and Aquos stood on either side of him as the two villains drew themselves up to their feet.

One pulled out a switchblade as he eyed the three men looking at him.

"What's that?" Stealth asked.

"That's a knife," Aquos drawled.

"That's not a knife," Drake joked, pulling his sword from his sheath. He held the five foot length of razor sharp steel to glisten in the sunlight that came through the windows. "Now that's a knife."

Mach shook his head, "We really need to work on your choice of movies."

"He has sadly neglected Clint Eastwood."

Mach turned to Turbo with raised eyebrows, "What about some classic Mel?"

"No way," Aquos inserted. "Hands down he needs some Russell Crowe."

"If you guys are done," Luke smiled. "I think it's time we let Drake kill these idiots."

"Ask them why they're here."

Sally's question made them turn and look at her, though Stealth kept his eyes glued on the two men who still wore their black ski caps. "Why are you here?" Drake shook with the need to tear them limb from limb.

"Madre de dios," one muttered making the sign of the cross over his chest.

"Now, now," Mach mocked.

"Don't be bringing her in," Turbo added.

"She's his mom," Aquos pointed to Luke.

The two assailants dropped to their knees and lowered their heads.

Stealth rolled his eyes, "Now they get righteous."

"That's only because they feel the brush of death coming closer," Mach joked.

"Closer? I thought he was already here."

Stealth shrugged, "I thought we were death."

"They deserve no less for touching Sally," Aquos hissed at all of them.

"Why are they here," Sally asked again, wishing like crazy that the brothers would stop with the Improv routines and focus on the two guys who wanted to rape her and then kill her.

"Her brothers hired us," one of them supplied.

"They need her insurance money."

Sally flinched as if they had struck her and Drake felt the animal inside him wanting to break loose again. "Okay."

Drake strode over to her, knowing his friends would keep the two men from leaving or hurting anyone else. Mach and Turbo parted without words and he was standing in front of her. His eyes feasted on the bounty of her face; taking note of the changes that had happened over the last two months of their separation. She had dropped a great deal of weight. There were dark shadows beneath her eyes, and though he knew she spent most of the days in the sun, her pallor was a shade above fine bone china. When he absorbed everything on the outside, he tried to guess what was going on within her.

"Are you really here," she whispered.

"I am."

Her eyes fell closed and her knees turned to jelly. Drake caught her against his chest before she could fall far and held her for a moment, taking in a deep breath of her delicate scent. "I will not leave you again."

She opened her eyes and looked up into his, knowing that the sentence he just uttered was a vow from his soul. "Luke?"

"Yes, Sally Eversham."

"Is your offer of protection still open?" She stepped away from Drake and straightened.

"You are one of the family, sweetheart. Nothing has changed."

"How do you think we all got here so fast," Aquos asked.

Stealth smiled, though he never withdrew his gaze from the two cowering men at his feet, "When you call upon one of us, you reach us all."

"I accept your offer," Sally informed him.

Luke beamed at her, "Good to hear it."

"What do you want us to do with them?"

She looked to the two men and winced. "Can you make sure that they never do anything like this again, without killing them?"

The men all looked at each other and shrugged with remorse. "Probably."

Stealth gifted her with a wink, "I'll do it."

He grabbed each of the men by their upper arms and blinked out of the room. Sally turned to Luke, "Can you please get my brothers here?"

Mach seemed to glow with hope, "Do we get to kill them?"

"No," Sally ordered.

All of the remaining men's faces fell. "You really know how to take all the fun out of our day," Turbo shared.

Luke did not have to go anywhere. He simply nodded his head and both Austin and Mitch appeared in the room. All of the men drew their swords and aimed them straight for the brother's throats. Austin sputtered, "What the hell is going on here?"

"Tell me something," Sally's voice was smooth with false control. "When you were ordering my death, did you ever once consider it might not work?"

Mitch looked around sensing his possible death, "We didn't think we had a choice."

"Fine," she sighed and her eyes closed again as a shudder rocked her frame.

Drake moved instantly and surrounded her with his arms. "Let me take you home."

"She won't have a home when we lose everything," Austin thundered.

All the blades that were pointed at their throats moved closer, nicking their skin and sending small streams of blood trickling down to their collars. "What are you," he continued to bellow, not recognizing the gleam of death in the eyes staring into his.

"We're Sally's friends." Aquos purred.

Stealth arrived in a flash of light and bowed low to Sally. "It is done."

"Thank you, Stealth."

"Sally doesn't have any friends," Mitch muttered.

Luke threw out his hand and sent the brother flying into the ceiling, then tumbling to the floor. "Not only does she have friends, but we're also her family."

"Good," Austin hissed. "Take the fat bitch."

Drake drew his sword back to spear Austin through his middle. It was

Sally who kept him from letting it loose. "No."

"Please let us kill them," Mach pleaded.

Turbo brightened, "We promise to make it painful."

Sally pulled out the handful of rubies that were still in her pocket from the previous week. "These should end your problems with money. As of this moment we are done. I will disappear from your lives, and you are to never say my name again." She hurled them at their heads, enjoying their looks of pain when they were struck in the face, since the swords at their throats prohibited movement.

The two men grabbed at the stones, never once looking her in the eye.

For some reason, that hurt more than she could say.

Drake's jaw clenched as he longed once again to carve all the reasons why he loved their sister into their skin. "They are not getting out of this so easily, Sally-mine."

She looked at him, her eyes containing a strange detachment, "They have to live with each other. You have no idea how much they will be punished with themselves for company. I am done with them, Drake. Just please make them go away."

Luke looked to Drake, and he gave a nod. With a wave her brothers disappeared.

"Thank you," she whispered, before giving into her exhaustion and emotional devastation and passing into the darkness of unconsciousness.

She knew that Drake would catch her, and he did.

Just as she knew that these good men, each with their burdensome demons, would guard her now as if she were their own.

For she was.

 CHAPTER TWENTY SEVEN

It was barely past dawn when he went to the gateway room. Luke clung to the memories of his home, and it was only here that he could keep close to them. Sighing, he cast his body into a chair and closed his eyes. At least Sally's return meant the damned house was no longer melting. One more day of them all walking around in their boxers and they were going to have had some serious male testosterone issues.

"What ails the leader of the Omega," Gabrielle purred.

"I am sorry, Archangel. We took Sally from her world against your advice."

Gabrielle shook her head, "I never told you not to take her."

"I don't understand," he rubbed his hand over his face.

"Sally's great destiny always lay with your people."

"Why didn't you tell me?"

"It had to be her choice."

He could not help wincing. Luke suspected that by the ideals of the compact he might have circumvented the rules. Or at least, danced around them. "I offered her protection," he admitted.

"As I hoped you would."

"What?" His eyes were wide with shock.

Gabrielle shrugged and let loose a string of laughter that skipped through the room like flower petals on a breeze. "I never said you should not support her. No soul can reach its destiny without a team of people to help lift it into the light. What you did was just what Sally Eversham needed. I am proud of you, Omega leader."

"I need to speak with my mom."

"Yes, you do."

The look he gave her was as pleading and full of entreaty as any soul had tried. "I don't know how," he confessed.

She moved behind him and leaned forward to whisper in his right ear. "If you wish to speak with your mother, all you need do is what anyone does when seeking God's ear." She moved to his left, "Call her name, Leader of Light. She is always with you."

When he knew he was alone, he took a shaking breath in and scowled. How like the angels. Uriel said one thing. Gabriel said another. Which was he meant to follow? Whom should he obey? Call upon this place's son of God? Call upon his dam? He chuckled as he shook his head with chagrin.

Call her.

Great.

Sounded so easy.

Conversations with his mother were many things. Easy was not one of them.

* * *

It took hours for Sally to wake up. Naturally, Drake was sitting on the bed next to her. The intense stare he seared her with was not the best way to say good morning. "Hi," she whispered.

"You have been ill."

"A little," she confessed.

He scowled. "You will stay in bed until you are better."

Sally smiled and stretched under the covers. She was nearly naked, no surprise there. The only clothing left on her body was her panties. "I hope you are the one who put me to bed last night." She winced at the idea of any of the others seeing her body.

"Of course," he grimaced. "That is what you wanted ... wasn't it?"

"Yes," she began to sit up so that she could look him directly in the eyes, but he needed to help her. She was still so weak and achy. "What did you think?" When she realized he was still looking at her tentatively, uneasily, she knew that there was more going on than she realized. "Drake, what's wrong?"

"You asked Luke for protection."

"I did."

"Why did you need it? I swore I would never leave your side again."

She cupped his cheek and leaned forward to brush her lips against his mouth. "I know that and believe it."

"So why did you need to ask Luke?"

Her sigh feathered past his cheek. He felt a small surge of triumph when she rested her head against his shoulder. The flare turned into a wildfire when Sally nestled her body into his and her muscles relaxed. "I asked Luke for protection because I needed to know that everyone here accepted me. My entire life was spent feeling as if the people around me resented my presence. I needed to know that everyone here was happy that I was asking to be made into a permanent feature."

Drake was outraged at the idea. "I would kill anyone who denied you."

Her laughter felt like a sensual caress over his skin. "I know that, Drake," she assured him. "I just wanted to make sure all of the guys were okay with my being here. Please don't be insulted. If this is going to be a new life for me, I want it to be different as well."

He felt eased by her mirth. "Fine."

She smiled at his disgruntled acknowledgement. It seemed she would have some soothing to do. Her dragon's feathers were all ruffled by her sense of propriety and need to be accepted. "Drake, Luke told me you're the last dragon because you chose to open up the portal. What really happened to all of the others?"

"You can't leave me."

The stark terror in his voice was enough to give her the strength to open her eyes. "Why would I leave you?"

He started to get up from the bed but her arms caught him to her. She loved that, though she had not nearly enough strength to physically force him to do anything he didn't want to, he still gave in. "My past is unpleasant."

"Okay," she answered slowly as she tried to guess where this was going.

Drake turned his head so she could not see the fear in his eyes. "I do not want to discuss this," he confessed.

"Why not?"

"You will think less of me if you know the truth."

"Not possible."

"What do you mean?"

Sally smiled and made a point to look at their contorted bodies. "Drake, could we please lie back down? I feel like an acrobat here. The truth is that I am feeling ill, bed rest is a good idea, but there is no way in hell I'm able to handle this position."

"I have to get you a yoga teacher," he grumbled as he settled back into the bed and made a point of draping her on him. "Flexibility can be fun."

"Only if we're having sex."

"What else would I be referring to," he asked with a bewildered look.

Sally shook her head, "Of course."

The silence wrapped around them and they both just enjoyed holding each other, the comfort of their heartbeats, and the warmth of the room. Her sigh was descriptive and eloquent, and he knew his time was running out.

"Please talk to me."

Drake tensed though he didn't move away from her. "I was the one who could do it."

"Explain please."

"Sally."

"Drake."

He sighed and refused to speak. She looked up at him and gave him a small smile. "Nothing you can say will change how I feel."

"They were dying. Our planet was a step away from becoming an endless wasteland. The humans were ill; most of the women from all the clans were deceased. Dragon health is decided upon how our spirit feels. The destruction surrounding them was no different from a million slices into our skin. I was one of the few of my kind left in any kind of healthy shape. The Oracle came to me and told me about the plan of sending the remnant through the portal."

"Did she make you open it?"

"No," he shook his head. "Though we were not gifted with the same level of free will you have, she tries. The Oracle asked me to open the portal, though she left it up to me to decide. I went to Luke the next day to offer my services."

Sally nodded her head, enjoying the feel of his skin against her cheek. "I understand what you did. I just don't understand why."

"Do you know anything about dragons?"

"Not really," she admitted with a chuckle.

Drake sighed and began to run his hand over her back. "The other clans are solitary family groups. Our males work as one interwoven team. When one of us hurt, we all hurt. There is strength in the pooling of our resources and abilities."

"It sounds nice."

"It also doesn't leave a great deal of room for rebellion. If we all don't move together, we lose our protection. If we let our guard down, and don't stand together, the enemy can sneak in without a word or murmur."

"So when you said you would open the portal when no one else would …"

"I was running against the grain."

"They were upset," she guessed.

Drake snorted, "They felt betrayed."

"What did they do?"

He shrugged.

When there was nothing but silence she realized that he planned not to answer her question. Sally looked up at him. "Drake," she whispered. "Just tell me. I love you. It will not change the way I feel."

Her confession made his eyes close as his senses reeled. "I love you, as well."

"So talk."

"Please don't make me," he begged her.

"Why?"

Drake closed his eyes. "I betrayed them. I broke from the pod. They made me into an outcast. I was condemned as a betrayer of our world. They will never take me back. They refuse to even acknowledge my existence."

"They're idiots."

"They took away everything from me," he added. "All of my possessions, my friends and family are gone."

She shrugged. "I didn't have anything either before you came into my life."

"You're not ashamed to be with me?"

"I am ashamed of your clan," she broke to him.

He smiled at her sworn oath. "They are just clinging to who they are and what they know."

Sally leaned up to give him a kiss of such tender passion and adoration, hoping that it would calm the frayed sense of worth she guessed was bubbling under the surface like an infected wound. He did what he had done for the survival of their people. All of them. If the other dragons could not understand the greatness of his sacrifice, then they all deserved the death that had apparently taken their lives.

It was his choice to break the contact. "Sally mine, if you keep this up, I will be inside you. We both know that you still require rest."

"Drake," she didn't care how close to a whine her voice sounded.

"No," he barked.

She growled at him. He gave her such a shocked look that she did it again. "I'll sleep after we have sex."

"Make love," he reminded her.

"I don't care what you call it," she purred as she ran her foot up his calf. "I just want to do it."

Drake moaned inside as he let her entice him into doing something that he knew they probably should not. The point was that she was here, in his bed and in his arms. She had heard how he had betrayed his entire bloodline and she didn't care. She knew he was an outcast, without home or family, and she tried to seduce him.

They decided to celebrate their reunion in the one way they both enjoyed.

* * *

In the main part of the house they had no way of knowing that one of their friends was mourning the homecoming being celebrated. Aquos sat on the couch with his feet up, a football game on the television he wasn't watching. His expression held such grief and torment, most people would have stayed as far away from him as possible.

Fortunately, his friends were not most people.

"You okay?" Mach asked as he joined him on the couch.

Turbo eyed him, "No way he's okay. He's surviving, though."

"I'm in love with Sally."

Aquos' confession was met with an understanding silence from his friends.

"We know," Stealth explained.

"I do not know what to do about it."

Luke's smile was grim, "Take it one day at a time."

"Lean on your friends," Stealth filled in.

"Which would be us," Mach supplied.

"And pray it will all work out," Turbo finished.

"I hate this feeling," Aquos shuddered.

"We know, brother," Luke's soft acknowledgements made him close his eyes to hide his tears.

"And we are here."

Aquos looked at Stealth with surprise.

The others all nodded with Stealth as he confirmed his support.

"You aren't alone, brother. We all stand with you."

The next time Aquos closed his eyes it was with a slight smile on his face. They were together and they cared. It was something. A few moments ago he'd felt as if he hadn't a single strand of hope on the horizon, and now he knew he had an entire roomful of it.

 # CHAPTER TWENTY-EIGHT

He walked into the bar feeling as if he owned it. Soon everything and everyone would be his. The Underbelly would be a miniscule part of his new empire, but there would be an extraordinary amount of satisfaction in taking over the preferred recreation spot for the Clan Lords. The mercenary waited for him in the corner booth, just as he had directed. He eyed the man with a small feeling of accomplishment. His research was comprehensive. Green Berets and Special Forces, the male's teams were known for operations throughout South America and Africa.

They were just the type of human he needed.

Slipping into the red leather seat he eyed him. "You got the money?"

"The wire transfer went through," the man nodded.

As the band went wild and the music blared, the people rushed to fill the dance floor. A waitress started to come over to wait on them, but he gave her a curt shake of his head to dissuade her. He'd been here often enough to ensure that his service was top shelf. She knew he'd take care of her at some other time.

Of course, that might mean an unfortunate accident on her way home.

The Architect handed over the plans and an envelope that had the pass codes for the security system. "This is all you need."

"Got it."

"Make sure you blow up the gate room. There can be no way for them to get in again or use it. All traces must be gone."

The commando shrugged. "No problem."

"Got any questions?"

"Any reason why we're destroying these men?"

"That would be my business."

His mercenary shrugged, "I don't really care, but I just wondered. It isn't often that we're hired to kill on our home soil."

"If that is a problem, tell me now or I leave."

"No," the man's eyes became narrowed slits. "We'll do it."

"Just make sure you have as many men as possible," the Architect sneered.

"We'll get the job done. Guaranteed."

The Architect stood and slid through the dancing crowds toward the exit, and then paused. He nodded his head as he moved to the waitress instead. He decided he'd take her out now rather than later. After all … why put off until tomorrow what you can kill today?

* * *

Drake was carrying Sally down the stairs, grumbling every step of the way. She giggled at his fussing, "I've been sleeping for five days."

"You need more rest."

"Drake," she turned his head to hers and smiled. "I need to get out every once in a while."

He scowled.

She laughed and shook her head.

When they reached the end of the hallway she noted that all the brothers were sitting around, some playing a video game that looked like Grand Theft Auto and the rest were trying to read. "Hello."

They turned with smiles when she was carried in. "This is a surprise."

"We thought Drake was going to keep you locked up forever," Turbo finished for Mach.

Sally shook her head, "He tried."

"She isn't well," he explained to the rest of them. "She needs rest."

Luke's smile was rueful. "How much sleep could she be getting with you in there with her? I doubt all you're doing is catching z's."

When she colored a bright red they all laughed at her discomfort.

This is what it's like, Sally realized. Having brothers. Being a part of a family. They teased and it didn't hurt. It didn't take anything away from you. Drake eyed her and put her in the armchair, immediately piling blankets on top of her. When she saw one of the elementals coming in with an electric blanket and a down comforter she had to stop him. "Drake, you're going to roast me."

"You need to be warm."

"It looks like you want her to broil," Mach joked.

Drake turned on him, but she caught his arm to keep him from attacking his brother. "I was just going to dent him a little bit."

"No fighting," she admonished.

When Drake slid in and wrapped his arms around her the others laughed. "Looks like someone tamed the dragon," Stealth said.

"I am," his smile was smug. "And loving every moment of it."

They brothers all laughed, the feeling of camaraderie a silken cloth that wrapped them with comfort. "So tell me what's been going on? I haven't seen any of you in so long. How are things?"

When no one answered her, she jabbed Drake with her elbow.

"What?" he exclaimed, scowling.

"Tell them they can talk to me."

Drake's lower lip went out. "Are you pouting?" Sally asked.

"I don't want you worrying yourself about things. Especially not Omega business."

"I'm sorry," Sally withdrew her body from his arms. "Am I not a part of this family?"

The others beamed. When all of them nodded, she gifted them with a thankful smile. Drake's jaw tensed as he realized he was outvoted. "Fine," he snapped. "Blade is still missing. Mach and Turbo had the mage clan go through his things and he says there is no way that Blade is a traitor."

"No luck in finding him, then?"

"No," Turbo snapped.

"How are you all feeling? No more physics ripping you apart?"

Luke smiled at her, "Your presence seems to eradicate the problem."

"What about attempts on your lives?"

They all shrugged. "Not a one."

"So," she observed. "Some good news. Yay."

"Yeah," Stealth provided, though he looked reluctant about it.

"What's wrong?"

All the brothers shrugged their shoulders. Luke was the one who felt he should answer, "We have no leads. Nothing to go on. No way to proceed."

"It's frustrating for us."

Sally laughed. "I don't understand you guys. You have so many resources. Why don't you try using some of them?"

"Like what?" Aquos asked.

"How about the small army that's camped around your walls?"

They all scowled. "We don't like them," Drake explained.

"You don't like the scouts?"

"Not really," Turbo answered.

"They're freaky."

"Would you guys just chill," Sally grimaced at the pile of coverings that felt like they were parboiling her skin. She started to push them off, "Drake this is crazy. I still need to breathe, you know."

"You need to stay warm."

"What I need is a fruit smoothie," she groused.

No sooner had she said the words that a tall Styrofoam cup appeared in her hand. Sally shrugged and took a long pull from the straw. "That will work." She went back to drinking from it, ignoring the other men and their stunned expressions.

"What?" she asked with feigned innocence. "Oh, right. We were discussing your refusal to use your resources. Why don't you meet with the leader of the scouts? There has to be one person that guides them." As soon as she finished saying the words a tall amber haired woman appeared in the room, her eyes flashing with green fire. "That must be you?"

All the men jumped away from her, staring with shock.

"What?" Sally looked around with discomfort. She thought they would see her newfound abilities as par for the course. Their unease was beginning to scare her in a very deep way. "Is something wrong?"

"What the hell did you guys do to me?"

Luke turned to the leader of the scouts with a conciliatory expression. "Keva, I apologize. Please feel free to return to your camp."

The woman disappeared without another word.

Drake approached Sally with soft eyes. "Sally, when did this begin?"

"Just a few days ago. Can't you all do this kind of thing?"

"No, baby, we can't."

"Oh," her head fell forward and her face colored with shame.

He pulled her out of the chair and sat down with her on his lap. "It's not something to feel bad about."

The others all sat as well, trying to understand what was going on.

"Does it hurt?"

"No," she shook her head. "It just happens. What hurts is when I don't use it."

Luke's eyebrows rose. "That is unique."

"Could it be due to the healing potion you gave her?"

Stealth shook his head to Aquos' question. "Not that I know of."

"So why is it happening?"

Her soft question made Drake feel pulled across a rack. "We don't know sweet, but we will figure it out."

"We will help you," Aquos swore to her with more fervor than even he felt was required.

The others gave him a sympathetic look.

"I thought you all had super powers," she grumbled.

"What do you think we are ... the Justice League?"

Mach slapped himself in the head. "Luke man, we need to work on your recreational viewing, my brother. Justice League was from like the nineteen seventies."

"Cartoons were classic back then."

"We are forced into an intervention here, my friend," Turbo instructed as he rose.

Mach stood, "You get the DVD's, I'll have the elementals start the popcorn."

The others looked to Sally, hoping for some saving. Once the cousins got started, there was little they could do to stop them. The two could demand that they stay up all night watching cartoons, drinking Red Bull, and eating Kettle Korn.

Sally leaned forward to yell after them, "If there isn't any real Japanese anime in there I'm calling the two of you out."

The cousins' laughter almost drowned out the groans from their friends.

 CHAPTER TWENTY-NINE

"You need to party, my brother."

Luke's eyes rolled at Turbo's explanation, for this enforced trip seemed pointless. He was content to stay at Sanctuary, haunting the halls and trying to keep the scouts from leaving the grounds and possibly offsetting the balance in the world around them. That was definitely a full time job.

Stepping into the bar, it was the smell that hit him first. Spilled drinks. Sweat. Perfume. And sheer sexual desperation.

He watched the women dancing near him.

Apparently there were some attractions for the trip.

The cousins took the corner booth and ordered their usual from the scantily clad waitress. She gave Luke the onceover several times and he realized that there was more on the menu than just alcoholic drinks. Mach caught his interest and gave him a smug smile. "I see you may come around to our way of thinking."

"There are definitely some finer things here."

"He means," Turbo took the drinks from the girl's tray with a wink. "Foiiiine."

Luke leaned back and stretched out his arms. "So how does this work?"

"Has it seriously been that long since you got some?"

Luke shrugged. "I believe that there was a tavern and a friendly wench involved."

The other two chuckled. "Colonial times were good to us."

"Those blouses that went off the shoulder," Mach added with a dreamy smile.

"Like I said," Turbo interrupted. "Colonial times were good."

Luke shifted uncomfortably. He looked around the packed bar.

"What is it?" Turbo asked.

"I don't know," he confessed.

Mach downed his whiskey and motioned to the waitress for more. "You're just nervous from being locked up at Sanctuary for so long."

"No," Luke denied. "It's more than that."

"What?"

"I don't know," he allowed.

A sudden flash of light, and he caught sight of Gabrielle smiling at him from across the room. He stood and moved to follow her, but she disappeared. Of course there was no reason why the archangel couldn't disappear, but she had to have come here for some reason more than that. The exit door closed and he moved to open it, but Mach waylaid him. "What's up, my brother?"

"I saw Gabrielle," he hissed in his ear. The music where they stood was deafening.

Mach motioned to Turbo and they joined Luke to make their way outside. Luke still felt that odd tingling in his stomach. A tight itch in his scalp. He looked around as he tried to fathom what pulled at him.

Something was about to happen.

He just had no idea what.

A small form came around the corner, running straight at them. Luke caught her to his body, shocked to realize it was a woman. She looked up with eyes as blue as a summer's night, silver flecks twirling in their centers. "Sanctuary," she gasped before she fell unconscious in his arms.

Luke felt something unstable in his heart slide into place.

The world made sense. His heart's barriers were shattered.

"Granted," he blinked away from the bar and back to his home.

Mach looked at Turbo, his eyebrows so far up they were disappearing into the thatch of black hair that eternally fell in his eyes. "Well," he sucked in a deep breath. "That was new."

"Ever seen her before?"

"Not once," Mach assured him.

Turbo pointed to the spot where Luke and the girl had stood. "Ever see Luke respond to a female like that?"

Mach shook his head. "I wasn't even sure he liked girls."

"Well," he shrugged. "Small comfort there."

"True, that."

"We gonna stand in this alley jabbing about Luke all night, or go inside and have some fun?"

Mach smiled, "If we were responsible, we would go back to Sanctuary to see what's up."

The two of them burst into laughter.

"If they need us they know how to find us."

Gabrielle watched from the shadows as the two cousins went back inside. Their time would come. Sooner than either of them realized, they would be ripped apart, heated in a crucible and reformed into something much greater than they were now. She hoped they had a good time this night.

There would not be that many after.

* * *

Luke blinked straight to his guest room. The woman in his arms was quite small. She reminded him of a doll he had seen once in a toyshop window. Definitely a woman, but still formed on a tiny scale. He didn't know if he should make a pass at her or wrap her up in colored paper with a shiny bow. The room was decorated in a Japanese style; the minimalist design suited his personality, the mattress of the finest quality. He placed her on the bed and covered her. The girl's long black hair was falling over her face so he used the back of his hand to wipe it out of her way.

He wondered if this was how Drake had felt when he first saw Sally.

A combination of sure overwhelming confusion, sexual heat, and absolute terror.

❧ CHAPTER THIRTY ❧

Sally walked through the Sanctuary house, Stealth dragging her on another one of his missions. He had taken to appearing in her area, eager to sneak her away from Drake, whenever he wasn't looking. She didn't know if he was trying to get her in trouble or get himself killed. The attraction for her was she greatly enjoyed it when Drake showed his possessive side. She found she could enjoy that for hours.

Her body still hummed from the last time he was compelled to take her to his dragon's bathing chamber and remind her of the proper attitude of a mate.

"Where are we going?"

Stealth smiled, "I thought you would like to see the gate room."

"You mean the place where you guys came through?"

"The very one."

Her smile was radiant. "Cool. Why don't you guys use it?"

"It imploded when we arrived. Our best theory is if we try, we will be ripped apart in the process. The gravitational forces will destroy any living things."

"I can see the wisdom in not using it."

Just then a series of sirens went off and the hallway filled with a flashing red light. Stealth's jaw tensed and he put his shoulder into Sally's midsection to lift her before tearing down the hall. "What are you doing?" she screeched.

"Sanctuary is under attack. I need to get you to a safe room."

"Take me to Drake," she begged.

He shook his head, "Drake will be busy protecting this place. Don't split his focus now."

"Shouldn't the scouts help?"

"They choose to fight when they want."

He flashed them direct to the portal room and dumped Sally into a chair. "Stay."

Her comedic barking was done in vain, for Stealth was gone faster than she could blink. She looked around the room inquisitively, recognizing that she might be stuck there for a while. The chamber was large and seemed to be rough-cut from the bedrock. Light glowed from niches in the walls, though she could not detect any electricity or features. Different kinds of chairs sat at equal distances around the room.. Apparently the Lords of the Clans love their comfort. They also seemed to love La-Z-Boy.

Sally guessed that the chair Stealth deposited her in was Drake's. She smiled as she saw hand-held video games lying by two of the chairs. Had to be Mach and Turbo's. A pitcher of water had to belong to Aquos. She guessed that Luke's was the one with the books piled next to it. That was one brother who always seemed to be near them, in one way or another.

When an explosion rocked the building and she felt it in the room located so deep in the earth, it dawned on her for the first time just how serious this must be.

She stood and began to pace around the chamber. She thought about the different brothers and how much they meant to her. Looking down she saw that the center of the space had a portal embedded in the floor. The glowing illumination it gave off was like looking into the heart of a diamond on fire. As the colors danced over her face her thoughts kept turning to what was happening above.

Who was attacking? And why?

How much danger were they in?

Sally tensed her jaw. She had just got a family, she would be damned if she lost them now. Closing her eyes, she summoned a mental picture of the woman she'd caught sight of for a few seconds the other day.

"I am happy to have a meeting with the leader of the scouts."

A flash of light and the woman from the other day appeared before her. "What the hell are you?"

"My name is Sally, I'm a friend of Drake's."

"The dragon? I'm shocked you're still alive."

"Your name, please."

"Keva," she spat. "I'm leaving."

"No," Sally spat back. "You're not. Or I'll just bring you back."

Keva examined the Earth girl trying to understand what she was seeing. "What are you?" She looked innocuous enough. Long red curling hair, pale green eyes, and skin the shade of parchment. She smelled like a combination of earth and home. There was also a shimmer of magic around her like rainbow sprinkles scattered over a frosted cupcake. Keva had no idea what this Sally was, but she knew that she wasn't ordinary.

"I want your clan to help the brothers."

"We seek," Keva tossed her head, "we do not find."

In that instant Sally could see Keva for the first time. She was well over six feet tall; her auburn hair pulled back tight to her skull so that she appeared almost androgynous, her eyes were blacker than midnight. "What do you seek?"

"What do you mean?"

"What is it you are searching for?" she repeated for the bristling woman.

Keva threw up her hands, "It is our job to find the answers to the Oracle's prophecy."

She closed her eyes, for she knew that this was her moment. Either she was going to accept the truth or live with the consequences. Those consequences could easily be Drake's painful and needless death. Or injury to any of the other men she cared so much about. None of those were acceptable.

"My full name is Salvation Eversham," she smiled at Keva. "So an answer has been found."

"What is it you want me to do?"

Sally smiled, "Protect Sanctuary."

Just then the door flew open and six commandos dressed all in black and carrying large guns came running down the stairs. Keva blinked out before Sally could say anything. "Great," she sneered as she began to back up. "Now she does something."

When the men reached the bottom of the stairs they stopped short at seeing her. One of the mercenaries lifted his gun and seemed to ready it to shoot.

* * *

Luke transported Drake as they followed Stealth to the portal room. Altea had already communicated that the mercenaries were there to take out their gate room, so it needed to be protected. When they blinked in, he was alarmed to see one of the men drawing a bead on Sally. She had nowhere to run or escape.

He screamed as he saw her close her eyes and leap into the portal.

Without speaking, Drake ran to jump in after her. He started his transformation as he moved, knowing that the best bet to save her was in his base form.

Luke and Stealth made fast work of destroying the men that had dared to enter their domain.

Sally wanted to scream as the pain hit but it hurt too much. It felt as if she were being pulled apart from the inside. The scouring of her internal organs was an agony beyond her worst nightmares. Suddenly something surrounded her. When she opened her eyes she saw the comforting red glow of Drake's.

He wrapped his wings around her and kept his head close to hers.

For the first time Drake cursed the fact that he was not able to speak on a telepathic link when in the other realm. His eyes pulsed reassurance and adoration. *I'm here*, he tried to communicate to her. *We are together. That is all that counts.*

I. Am. With. You.

She closed her eyes and nestled as close to his protective bulk as she could.

Whatever happened she would be fine.

CHAPTER THIRTY-ONE

They landed with a thump. Drake groaned and rolled away from Sally, changing back into a man as he did so. She stayed very still as she tried to understand what had happened. Where she was. What she was. It felt as if the computer that was her brain was coming back on-line after a complete electrical surge. Her muscles were not responding. Her mind began to send messages to her nerves as it searched for pain first. Next it tried to make some of her appendages work. Fingers and toes wiggling her eyelids gained the courage to pop open.

And quickly closed again.

The sky was purple. Not an eggplant purple like you might see at twilight during a summer weather anomaly. More neon purple teenage-girl room that she'd painted while her parents were out of town.

Sitting up, she looked around felt more disquiet. As if she thought that was possible. There was no ground. Well, there was a type of ground; I mean she was sitting on something. It's just that the ground was more of a fluffy white cloud kind of thing. She put her hand into the mist and watched as it stuck to her fingers and trailed around like cotton candy. Weird. Cool. But still definitely weird.

Moving over to Drake, she picked up his head and put it on her leg. Otherwise he was under the cloud line and she wasn't sure there was enough oxygen in it to keep him alive. No way was she losing him now.

When he opened his eyes she gave him a tremulous smile. "Hi."

"Are you okay?"

"I think we're dead," she confessed to him. "This isn't exactly my idea of heaven but there are some frightening similarities."

Drake leaned up, peered around, and fell back to her lap with a groan.

"What is it?" She looked around with a clenched stomach. "Is this hell?"

"Worse," he groaned again. "We're in dragon limbo."

Sally looked around curiously. "What's that?"

"The place all the dragons went to when our world got sick."

"Shouldn't you turn into a dragon when we're stuck in dragon limbo?"

He shook his head. "I can't."

"What do you mean?"

Drake sat up and avoided her eyes. "I was banished. I am not allowed to take dragon form when I am here."

She folded her arms over her chest. "They suck."

"Yes, they do," he pressed a gentle kiss against her cheek.

"What happened with the battle?"

"They hit us with a small army," he replied. "The rules of the Compact declare we are not allowed to end a human life. We cannot kill the people that are working so hard to kill us."

"What does that mean?"

"We are losing it, Sally-mine. We are losing it all."

"Why are we here?"

"I don't know," Drake shrugged. "We should have been killed in the trip."

"Why didn't we land on the Omegicon?"

He pressed his lips together and gathered her close to his body. "I don't know, sweet."

Giant footsteps sounded; they turned to see a shape coming out of the mist. A dragon, in different shades of silver, with a long muzzle the color of moonlight. His coloring and the ancient weariness in his eyes indicated that this was a creature that must predate the origin of time. They stood, and when Drake felt Sally's trembling, he tightened his embrace around her.

The dragon lowered his body into a bowed position with one mighty taloned leg extended.

Sally looked to Drake, who shrugged.

"We, who guard the passage of time, give greetings to the One."

Drake stepped forward and then quickly back after the dragon growled at him. Sally comprehended that the dragon must have not been speaking to him, but to her. "Hello," she offered, nervous and unsure. "I am Sally. This is Drake, my friend."

"Mate," he stated.

She hid her smile, "This is my mate, Drake. You are?"

"I am Tamarind, my Queen."

Drake held up one finger, "Uhm ... Queen?"

The corner of Tamarind's lip lifted in a dragon sneer that was so close to sinister it was unnerving. "I prefer not to speak with the traitor."

"If you speak with me," Sally drew her body up to her full height and tried her best to act regal – not an easy task for an American woman, certainly not her – and sneered back at their welcoming committee. "You speak with him."

"This is your final statement?"

"It is."

Tamarind turned to bow low to Drake, his eyes now filled with friendship. "Greetings, my Lord. I am Tamarind, guardian of the portal and these dragon lands. As mate to the Queen you are to be known as the Consort."

Drake shrugged. "Fine. Why is Sally the Queen?"

"I shall show you," he offered.

They followed the dragon, holding hands, their fingers braided together so tightly their knuckles were white. Neither was willing to speak, both their heads reeling with the implications of what had transpired. It was difficult to see around them to tell where they were going or to discern what the portal guardian was so determined to show them. The mist obscured everything.

Tamarind stopped and turned to look at them with what seemed like a smug smile. "This is the marker that declares you our Queen."

When he moved aside, Sally's knees almost gave out and she would have fallen if Drake had not caught her. He buried his head in her neck and kissed her. Whispering into her ear, he assured her, "You are going to be fine, sweet. This is no surprise to me. I knew you were special; this is only confirmation."

Sally stared up into a replica of her own face. The statue had the look of her body and face if she were at her ideal weight. Carved from what looked like pearl, the purple lights made it shimmer. She reached out a hand to cup her own face. "It must be my mother," she whispered, awestruck. "Or my grandmother."

"It is you, my Lady."

"It can't be," she denied.

"Long have your people waited, your Majesty, for your return. Our hearts sickened and began to die so we lay down and became like stones until you could come for us. We have dreamt and we have hungered. Please, your Majesty. We have been alone for so long. We wish to come back to life now."

Some deep knowing prompted her to move her hands and match her palms up with the statue. A surge of electricity threw her head back and filled her, making her hair crackle in the wind.

Drake lunged to pull her away, but Tamarind held him back. "Let me help her," he roared.

"This is what must be."

"She is just an Earth woman."

"She is our savior, Consort Drake. She cannot be stopped from helping

186

us."

The electricity broke off and Sally slowly crumpled to the floor. Drake burst free of Tamarind's hold and caught her. He pushed her hair out of her eyes and studied her face, concern pinching his face. "Sally-mine," he whispered. "Sally-mine ... wake up. Sweet, please, wake up for me. Come back."

When her eyes opened they were pure white. She gave him a smile of such confidence and seductive power he almost dropped her. This was not his woman. She stood up and regarded Tamarind. "Where are they?"

Tamarind bowed and pointed.

Sally moved quickly through the mist, her strides long and confident. They entered an area where there was no mist. Just an endless carpet of dragons, all shapes, colors and sizes, stretched out as far as the eye could see. Sally went to the first and placed her palms over the dragon's holes in his snout. She sent one puff of air from her lungs into her patient and smiled. "It is time to wake," she whispered.

When she stepped away, the dragon's eyes fluttered.

Drake watched, astonished, as the creature's lids opened and he lifted his head.

Next, Sally moved to a small amber colored dragon that, based on its proximity to the first, must be mated. She repeated her same ritual, and it, too, opened its eyes. He moved back to give his woman room to be who she was. What she was. Her ministrations to each of the dragons took only moments, but they woke fully healed. Even the ones with sores or wounds that had been left to fester and erode, were healed - inside and out.

In that moment he understood why he loved her. She was incandescent.

No dragon could resist someone who glowed with the fire of the rarest jewel.

It took some few moments for her to heal all the creatures in the field. He kept pace with her, every step of the way. When she had finished, all the dragons turned to her and bowed, as Tamarind had. With a smile she gave them a haughty look that made his heart swell with pride. "The Clan Lords of Sanctuary are under attack. If you come through the portal and turn the battle, our world could rise once more."

A great roaring began, making the ground beneath them shake and buckle.

"You grew ill when you lost your pride. Your hope. Turn away from these mistakes of the past and embrace the future before us all."

Again the dragons roared. Drake moved to stand by his mate's side and face the hoard with his woman.

"Retake your hope. Stand with your brethren. Stand together and nothing will ever take us apart again." As she delivered these words the dragons, one by one, lowered their bodies into another one of those low bows that Tamarind had given them as soon as they had arrived. Drake was transformed into a dragon; he quickly lowered his body like the others. Sally climbed onto his back and gazed out at her clan with pride. "Follow us, and take back your position as guardians of all the clans, of justice and right. No longer should any of us stand in the shadows. No longer will we hide."

With a great pulsing of wings they rose from the mist together and flew to use the portal once more.

CHAPTER THIRTY-TWO

Luke had no idea where the girl he had given Sanctuary to had gone. Their world was falling apart, and right at this moment all their lives concerned him, not just female's. Still, he longed to find the woman who had haunted his dreams, even if she had been unconscious since the moment he'd found her.

They were losing.

None of the brothers would violate the Compact and the people that had invaded his home were endless in their fervor to take them apart. They were all suffering from multiple wounds and he feared if the commandoes kept coming they would soon be dead.

Sanctuary was falling and there wasn't anything he could do about it.

With Mach and Turbo's help they had managed to push most of the men clad all in black out of the confines of their home. When they drew up two battle lines, the commandoes were hungry for triumph and the Omega weary, Luke was jolted to see that the scout clan had joined the battle to stand in front of the Clan Lords. He looked at their leader with a sarcastic grin, "Really? Now you seek solidarity?"

Keva shrugged her shoulders, "Some chick inside suggested it would be a good idea."

"Having Drake with us would be wise right about now," Stealth said.

"He did what he had to for Sally's survival," Aquos reminded him. "We cannot fault his choice." When Stealth snorted, his brother stared him down. "If she were your woman would you have done anything different?"

"Good point."

It took the men in black a few moments to realize that the Omega remnant was not attacking them. When they realized that all the Omega could do was fight defensively, a sick type of satisfaction appeared to grip them. They put aside their guns and drew long hunting knives, advancing on their ranks with the intent of carving them into little pieces. "Any last words?" Mach asked his friends.

"Yeah," Turbo sneered. "Lah di dooh dah day."

"What the hell is that?"

Turbo shrugged, "It seemed appropriate."

"Wouldn't something like don't fire until you see the whites of their eyes be better?" Luke suggested.

"So when you said you really miss those colonial times you weren't kidding?"

"Not a bit."

As the mercenaries came to within a few feet of them there came a sudden explosive cracking noise. Everyone turned and looked up to witness a stream of dragons bursting from the Sanctuary roof to fly straight at them. The mercenaries were each picked up in the beasts' claws and carried away, the creatures' mighty roars echoed over the valley. As the temperature plummeted, Stealth scowled at Luke. "Why is it getting so cold?"

"The dragons are taking the heat from the air to do their magic. Pennsylvania is about to get an ice storm for the first time in decades."

"That's what you want to know?"

Stealth shrugged in answer to Mach's question. "I don't like the cold."

"Dude," Mach pointed up. "An army of dragons, whom we believed were all dead, just burst out of our home and took out a rampaging army. Shouldn't asking about any of that have been your first priority?"

He gestured to the returning leader and they could see it was Drake, with Sally on his back.

"Oh," all the brothers cried, struck mute by the sight.

Keva strode over, "We shall return to the woods now."

"Our clan thanks you, friend."

"I am not, your friend," she sneered. "You may offer your thanks to the dragon's mate."

Mach and Turbo both scratched their heads, "What is it about that chick?"

"If you don't know," Stealth and Aquos answered together. "We're not going to tell you."

Drake and Sally landed in front of the others, while the remaining dragons returned to the Sanctuary home and disappeared the same way they had arrived. He let her off his back before switching back into his base form, his clothing only slightly singed. "Greetings, brother. I trust our return was seen with some relief?"

"Of course," Luke grasped Drake's forearm before giving Sally a hug. All the other Lords welcomed them back with the same enthusiasm.

"We dropped the mercenaries into the Atlantic Ocean. If they are lucky, a passing freighter will pick them up soon. In the meantime, they can focus on the error of their ways. The Compact is upheld; though some might say we bent it, a bit."

Mach picked Sally up and twirled her around, "Welcome home, little sister."

Drake extricated his woman from the young man's embrace. "Back off, fast boy."

"Good timing, guys," Turbo praised.

"One minute more and there would have been nothing to save," Luke admitted.

Sally started to say something but was hit by a wave of crushing pain that made her scream. Drake caught her close to him and looked at the brothers, incredulous. "I don't understand," he told them. "She wasn't harmed in the battle."

Tamarind landed next to them and gazed at his Queen with dismay. "You must return her to the limbo lands, your Majesty. The Queen is suffering from the healing."

Without a word Drake flashed into dragon form, holding Sally in his paws as he flew them back to the portal. Tamarind kept pace with him as if he knew he was neither worthy nor accomplished enough to claim this female as his mate. Drake swore he would give his own life with eagerness to know she would survive.

The world they left behind was immobilized into a frozen abyss.

***

"Uhm … Queen?"

The others laughed at Mach's drawled question. "Seems to me Drake and Sally will have quite a story to tell when they return," Aquos observed.

Luke looked at the ice and realized that he had never had the time to check on the girl in his room. "See what damage the dragons did to Sanctuary," he commanded the others. With a nod of his head he flashed out to his room. It was empty.

He caught the robes of one of the green elementals and snarled in the man's face, "Where is the girl?"

"I apologize, my Lord. The female fled during the battle."

The elemental ran for the first time in real fear when Luke dropped to his knees and began to cry. The tears were unwelcome and he suspected unwarranted. It was just that he felt as if something intrinsic to his survival had just slipped through his fingers. He had no idea how to find her again. How to explain why it had become so vital to him to know that she was close to his home.

He'd never even learned her name.

In truth, he had never had a chance to say one thing to her at all.

"You will find her again."

The sibilant whisper made the small hairs on the back of his neck stand up. Altea was here. Looking up into the fragmented pupils of the mage clan's leader, he gulped. "I don't know her name."

"She is the key to the gem warriors."

Luke recoiled. The gem warrior clan's death was the first sign of their world's destruction. "That's impossible."

"That is your future."

CHAPTER THIRTY-THREE

When Sally woke up she found herself ensconced in a four-poster bed hung with blood red curtains. There were more of those small-lit sconces along the perimeter and at the mouth of the cave she could see the fog-choked purple landscape that indicated the dragon's limbo lands. Somehow they had come home. Getting out of the bed without disturbing Drake was easy. Poor man was sleeping like the dead. She moved to the corner where she could see water dripping into a low basin.

There she found a full-length mirror.

Looking into the flat surface she could see a small part of her reflection. Her gasp was loud enough to wake the dead, but Drake did not move.

Running her hands over her body, a slow satisfied smile crossed her face. She was the image of the statue. Finally she had the body and look of the woman she had always longed to be. Tossing her hair over her shoulder, the feeling of it brushing the small of her back was as sensual as her lover's touch.

With a contemplating smile, Sally moved back to the bed. Summoning bonds to imprison Drake's arms and legs, a slow throaty laugh escaped her lips.

Time to have some fun.

He woke, feeling as if flames licked at every part of his skin. Moving down the inside of one leg, and up the other, never once straying to the one area that called out with every fiber of his being to this torturer. He could feel the silk that bound his wrists and ankles, and buried his fingers in the fabric, trying desperately to give his woman what she seemed to want the most.

Him at her mercy.

May the Oracle save him.

Or, you know … not any time soon.

Sally began to chuckle, sensing his wakefulness. She had made sure that the one part of him she was most interested in was up long before his mind sought consciousness. When she gave the throbbing erection a long lick from the base to the tip she smiled as he bowed so far off the bed they were both air bound for a moment. "You are not to break those bonds," she warned before sliding her lips over his throbbing need and taking him as far as her mouth would allow. When he began to murmur prayers, interlaced with homage to her beauty, she almost stopped to crow with glee.

Who said a dragon couldn't be tamed?

She could hear the sound of the bed cracking as Drake took a hold on the headboard and splintered the wood. Using one hand to encircle the part of his shaft her mouth could not swallow, and the other to cradle the globes beneath, she settled in for a very long inspection of the man who meant more to her than any other.

Drake kept repeating every prayer and piece of poetry he could remember to try and hold on. The pure unadulterated bliss he found under his female's ministrations had already blown out the few brain cells that were still able to function with the meager drops of blood he had left elsewhere.

His Sally-mine had been holding out on him.

Apparently his woman knew far more than he thought.

As he felt his body reaching a point of no return, he realized he would have to cut short this pure slice of ecstasy. "Love … please … ride me."

Sally shifted back so that she could keep him hanging over the edge, "No time for flying right now." She gave him another of those long, luscious licks once more, chuckling when his moan echoed around the cave. "I'm much more interested in seeing how far you can go."

"Not any farther," he rasped out. "Climb on top of me now, baby."

Her eyes dilated, her breath panting, Sally moved up his body, allowing her breasts to rub against his skin, her lids closing as the hair on his skin abraded her nipples and made her already throbbing core even wetter than before. As she positioned herself over his straining shaft she considered making him wait.

Rubbing her pulsating jewel over his heat and seeing if she could give herself an advance taste of what was to come.

Drake was not permitting her any such leeway.

He levered his hips off the bed to slide into her dripping sheath, both their voices filling the chamber with release as they connected. "Untie me," he commanded.

"I want to play more."

He could feel her interior walls gripping him, milking his body though they had yet to move. "Sally-mine," he growled at her. "Play later."

She pouted at him and rotated her hips, ripping an oath out of his mouth that blistered them both. "I wish to play now." Her beautiful lips made him remember just what she could do to him and he felt his body grow harder. He didn't think that was possible. Releasing his own binds, he grabbed her hips and took just a few thrusts before he forced them both over the edge. Sally threw her head back as he grabbed her breasts and massaged them while her body took every ounce of release from his that was imaginable. When she collapsed onto his chest, their bodies still joined, she seemed to purr with completion. "You cheated," she whispered as she petted his chest and nestled closer to his warmth.

He groaned as he used his magic to replace the ties around his arms. "We'll just have to keep playing until I get it right."

Her smile made his eyes cross and his balls tighten. With just that simple look on her face he was ready to go again. Sally's laughter danced over his body, making him pant as his cock bucked and hardened with the promising look in her eyes. "What a good dragon you are," she murmured against his skin.

Drake was grateful he was a strong one.

It would take everything in him to keep his mate happy.

And what creature could ask for more than that?

* * *

A trumpet heralded Tamarind's return with a number of smaller dragons the color of sunlight. Drake allowed them in, and as they bowed low to Sally he smiled at her discomfort for their formality. "Do you like your palace, your Majesty?"

"It's very nice," she assured him.

"We are so grateful that you agreed to return," one of the yellows informed her.

Sally shared a smile with Drake, "I am as well."

"Your transformation is complete," Tamarind eyed her with satisfaction.

Drake moved to her side, "How did that happen?"

"When the Queen healed us, the fuel came from the stored fat in her cells."

Sally's head fell forward, "So it's not eternal."

"On the contrary your Majesty, it is indeed. Our survival is linked to you now. It would be very difficult for your cells to accept what they did in the past."

His heart thundering with hope, Drake interrupted, "Does that mean she will live longer?"

"She is one of us," Tamarind explained. "She will live as long as we do."

Sally and Drake jumped into each other's embrace; the couple's laughter was music to the dragon's attuned ears. When Sally began to run biting kisses down his jaw, he managed to gasp out to the others, "Please excuse us."

"Of course, your Majesties," the dragons laughed.

Soon they did not care at all what kind of spectacle they had provided for the welcoming committee. Soon, all they could care about was one another.

CHAPTER THIRTY-FOUR

"It's official," Luke announced as he entered the room. "The Clan Lords are all returning."

"Even the ones in Europe?"

Luke shrugged, "If our enemies know where we are and what we are, there is no longer a reason for the separation. Better we stick together; there is far more protection in our numbers than there is in our isolation."

"We have news," Drake announced as he and Sally walked in, hand-in-hand.

Sally beamed at all of them and waved.

"You know," Mach opined. "For a chick who claims to be an ordinary Earth-girl, this is one female with continual miracles up her sleeve."

Turbo nodded, "True that. We figured you were worm food."

Drake wrapped his arms around her and twirled around in a complete circle. "That's my girl."

"So what's the news," Stealth asked.

"The portal is open," they crowed together.

"What?" all the brothers exhibited different levels of shock.

Drake beamed as he pulled Sally forward and wrapped his arms around her waist from behind. "It seems as if my Sally is the Queen of the dragons. Savior and protector to our kind. I am also forgiven for my treachery, by the way."

"Though probably only because I had the good sense to choose him," she teased.

Everyone laughed and clapped, Mach and Turbo pounded their fists. "Congratulations."

A blue elemental came in with a folded note and passed it to Turbo. "So what else is going on?" Drake questioned. He ignored Mach and Turbo slipping from the room, hopeful looks on their faces.

* * *

As Luke shared the news that they had decided to recall everyone, for once and for all, the cousins rushed outside.

There was a message from Blade in their hands.

On the farthest side of the property, hidden in the trees, were a series of caves. They were there in a matter of moments. As they stilled outside the shadowed world, they shared an uneasy glance. "Are you sure about this," Mach's nose twitched with the danger he could sense though not see.

"We've got no choice."

"I hate these situations." As they entered the cave both men separated, hugging a wall; the chamber went for twenty feet forward in a narrow corridor. There was an opening at the end where they could hear Blade groaning in pain. As they stepped over the line that marked the perimeter of the chamber they both heard a click.

* * *

Sally sat up and pushed away from Drake's hold. She had no idea how long she had been asleep. She remembered cuddling with Drake on the couch while he and the rest of the guys watched a game. She only knew that something had just happened that was very, very wrong. "We have to find the cousins," she gasped.

The men exchanged bewildered looks and rose with her. "We have to find Mach and Turbo," she repeated.

"Do you know where they are?"

She shook her head. "I can see a hazy picture."

Stealth and Luke both clasped each of her hands. "See it now, inside your mind."

The other brothers all grabbed some small portion of their bodies, so that when they got the picture and blinked out, they would all be taken with them. Sally looked around, bewildered. They seemed to have landed in a quiet wooded clearing with a series of treacherous sinkholes surrounding them.

One of them had a large puff of smoke coming out of it.

"Cave-in," Stealth announced.

Aquos leaned over the hole to breath in deep. "Explosion."

"Left over from the commandoes?"

He shook his head. "More recent."

Sally trembled as she moved closer to the hole, with her hands extended. "Mach and Turbo were inside," she told them. "There is more, though. Blade is trapped in there as well." The eyes she turned to Drake were pleading, "We have to help them. Please."

Luke, Stealth, and Aquos all disappeared. When they returned, they each had one of the Clan Lords in their arms. They lay them out on the ground, arranging their limbs with care. "Mach and Blade are badly injured," Luke explained. "Turbo is dead."

Sally staggered over to the first body. When she put her hands on his face he began to move. She turned to the last and did the same thing.

The men watched, amazed, as she healed Mach and then Blade.

She collapsed unconscious to the ground between the two cousins.

Mach pulled his body up and looked around, confused. "What just hit us?"

"Half the mountain."

When he looked at the others he saw remorse in their eyes. "What's wrong?"

"Mach," Luke cleared his throat as if it were blocked. "There is something we have to tell you. Turbo didn't survive. There was nothing we could do. We tried to get there as fast as possible but I fear we were much too late."

"No," Mach denied and turned to his cousin.

Sally woke up exhausted, then she saw the sheer naked grief on Mach's face. She moved to take Turbo from his arms, but Drake held her back. "No," he commanded her. "Sally you can't. You are already weak. It could kill you."

She cupped his face and shook her head. "I can't leave him like that."

He watched, terrified, as she took Turbo from Mach's embrace and began to rock him in her arms. They could all see the energy transfer from her body to Turbo's. Mach began to pray and was pleased when the other men joined their voices to his entreaties. Their distress was so great the Archangels Gabrielle and Raphael both appeared. As soon as they were sure that what was happening was only the Omega, they made the sign of a blessing to grant peace, and left them.

It felt like it took hours for the healing to finish, but soon Turbo's chest moved.

Then he took a loud gasping breath.

Finally his eyes opened.

Mach threw his body at Turbo's and gathered his cousin to him. "Welcome back, my brother," he gasped, tears shining on his face.

Sally collapsed to the earth. Drake knelt next to her, terrified that touching any part of her body might make her hurt more. His hands shook as they reached out to brush some tendrils of hair from her lips. "What did you do, sweetheart? Dear Oracle, what have we all done to you?" His eyes shone with more tears than Mach's as he picked her up. None of them knew what to say. None of them could try.

.

CHAPTER THIRTY-FIVE

Drake returned Sally to the limbo lands. He stood at the entrance of their cave looking out at the dragons' refuge. The mists were dispelling. As the dragons moved around and took over the guardianship of all that was magic and powerful for their world, the state of limbo was lifting. It was another sign that his people were truly on the way back to redemption.

What a state of hope to be in.

Sally moaned in her sleep. He flew to her side and wrapped his body around her. When she opened her eyes he was a breath away from her face. "Hello."

"Hi."

"I scared you."

"Almost to death," he confirmed.

"I'm sorry."

Drake rested his head against her hair. "I think it's time I took you back to your family."

Her eyes searched his, "Okay."

"You're alright with this?"

"Of course."

She hid her unease by turning her head from him. When she stood up, Drake conjured up clothing for her and took her flying over the dragon lands. His insides trembled as the other dragons trumpeted their blessings. He tried to freeze his eyelids so that his tears would not escape. When they landed in the portal room, Drake transferred back into human form and walked with his arms around Sally, not caring how awkward it made their gait.

She bided her time.

Sally knew him as well as she did herself now.

And the greatest lesson he had taught her was that you could have as little self-confidence as she did, even without the weight issue. When they reached the main gathering room the brothers were all lying across the seats and couches as if they were beyond exhausted. Sally was happy to see that her recovery had been faster than they thought it would be.

Mach caught her up in his arms to give her a tight hug as soon as she stepped in the room. "Thank you for Turbo's life."

"Same here," Turbo wrenched her out of Mach's embrace.

Blade was the next. "I have to offer my gratitude. If you had not encouraged the cousins to find me I would never have been released."

"Do you know who the traitor is?"

"No idea," he admitted.

Drake pulled her away from Blade and rumbled a warning sound at all of the men. "Stop squeezing her. She needs to go back to her family."

Sally took several steps away from Drake towards the others. "Mission accomplished."

"I meant your Earth family."

She tossed her hair over her shoulders, remembering that she was now transformed. There was no way this man was leaving her. She was almost as hot as he was. *So ha. Ha, ha, ha. Last laugh was on him.* "I have no Earth family."

"Your brothers and sisters will take you back," Drake growled. "I have plenty of money to save them. After a few hours of my threats, they will never think about threatening you again or not giving you your due."

Sally shook her head. "I love you."

"And I love you," he swore. "But being with me put you in jeopardy."

"A danger you could not foresee. My family, Drake, paid people to kill me. What safety do you think I'd find in that house?"

He roared his turmoil out. She ached for his pain for she understood it so well. *You finally find something wonderful; it takes everything in you not to start worrying when it might go away. When it could change into something ugly or mean. When it could see how small you were, how unworthy of having it in the first place.* It made her heart ache somewhere deep inside her soul, for both of them.

"Drake," she sighed. "I'm not leaving."

"Your family will keep you safe."

"Yes," she gestured to the men that were moving behind her as a gesture of solidarity. "They will."

Blade drew his weapon and held it to the center of his eyes, "Our sword is sworn for her."

Mach and Turbo both bowed low from the waist, "Our lives for her."

"She became one of my people when she drank the potion," Stealth shrugged.

Aquos eyes' glowed like sapphires. "She has my heart," he confessed.

Luke smiled, "My offer of protection was given in Sanctuary's walls. Sally belongs here as much as any of us now."

"I'm not leaving, Drake."

He stood before everyone he knew and loved, his fists opening and closing with frustrated helplessness. His head began to shake back and forth as his eyes filled with tears. *I can't do this*, he thought to himself. *I cannot risk losing her.* Not because of this stupid endless act of futile hope that the people of his world continued to indulge in. The despair began to build within him until it was a wave the size of a tsunami.

Sally stepped forward and put her hands on his chest. She slid them up until they were entwined around his neck and she could place a kiss on his chin.

Just that simple act made all his despair disappear.

He understood that turning her away was an act to protect himself, not her. "I love you," he gasped out.

"I know." She kissed his chin again, "And I'm not leaving."

His arms tightened around her like a vise. "No, you're not."

"Oh good," Mach observed. "I'd hate to see us erode into another clan war over who gets to keep her, just when we started to get along."

They laughed and the tension eased.

Sally put up with Drake seeming incapable of letting her go for the rest of the day. She had to be within a finger's width of his arms or his eyes glazed over and he'd start discussing his need to lock her into his tower for the next few decades. There was no way she was losing this feeling of brotherhood and kinship. Not today. Not now. It had taken her much too long to get to this point.

"If you run, you might be able to get out before he comes back," Mach quipped when Drake went to order their dinner.

Sally sat up and laughed when Aquos grabbed her hand and pulled her from the room.

He kept them moving through the empty hallways until they reached the entrance to the portal room. Sally pulled away from him when she saw the ancient piece of parchment hanging from the wall. Her hand trembling, she reached out to touch the frame with her mouth hanging open. "What is this?"

"It's the prophecy."

"Luke mentioned it to me ..."

"The prophecy?" When she nodded, he chuckled. "I'm surprised. He doesn't like talking about anything where the Oracle is concerned."

"What language is it in?"

"Our worlds. Did you want me to read it to you?"

"Yes, please," Sally's voice was a hushed awe.

Aquos read it out loud, "For the dragon it shall salvation be, happiness is found in three. Clearest sight is found below, what was gone, must start to show. Your armor will have to break, the last will cause the big mistake. Lay down your inherited power, do not stop in the final hour. Your lives will grow again here, when the Jewels provide the key to fear. For the one who is my very own, your greatest destiny is alone."

"It's beautiful."

Aquos leaned against the wall to watch her response to the truth. "The rumor is that once we answer all the questions and do all the things in the prophecy, we will be able to return home. That's all we want, really."

"Is to go home?"

"Yes."

"For the dragons it shall salvation be." Sally breathed the words with awe, her finger tracing over the line that for her was the herald of her arrival to these men's lives. Seeing his expression turn hungry, Sally tried to change the subject. "You realize that Drake is going to have a cow we left for even a minute."

"He owes them," he shared with his deadpan humor. "He used to eat cows by the thousands."

Sally shuddered. "Ick. Way too much information."

CHAPTER THIRTY-SIX

Drake went stomping through the woods, grumbling with every step he took. Sally had taken to disappearing with annoying regularity over the last month. He was going to have to kill whoever was helping her with these little escapes. *It was freezing outside; didn't they know how important it was for her to stay warm?* She was tired all the time, had taken to eating meat, and her body was continuing to change. The truth was, he was terrified by what was happening to her because he had no way of helping her through it.

He scowled as he remembered the day last week she had gone to the limbo lands without him. Drake had thundered at her for fifteen whole minutes before she changed his mood. His woman had one hell of a way of transforming his anger. They had ended up making love for four hours that night.

She didn't understand how dangerous his world could be. He was in a state of constant panic as he tried to keep her safe and protected.

Breaking into the clearing, he stopped short at the sight that awaited him. All the clans were there. Even the dragons were in human form, dressed in the gem-encrusted armor that indicated their warrior level and family loyalties. The scouts were haunting the trees; the Sanctuary Lords were in a loose half circle with Sally in the middle.

Who was wearing a pearl encrusted lace gown.

"Hello."

He had to use all of his strength of will to close his mouth. "You are incandescent."

Her smile brimmed with feminine pride. "You like my dress?"

"It is like you are clothed in a combination of moonlight and sunlight."

Mach looked at his friends, confused, "So he thinks her dress is just light? Cool. I'll enjoy seeing that."

Without breaking eye contact with Sally, Drake growled at Mach's implied leering. "One more word, octane-head, and I will tear you limb from limb."

The other dragons chuckled in approval.

"If you do," Mach shrugged. "Your mate will just resurrect me."

"Keep prodding my husband and I'll take a really long time before I do," Sally assured him. A harsh breeze whipped through the clearing and sent her hair dancing in the wind, getting caught on her lip before she pulled it away.

Drake looked around and felt a tremble that rocked his body. "Do you know how cold it is?"

"Tam taught me how to regulate my body temperature so I don't feel the cold."

"You were born on this world; there is no way you have that ability." He stalked across the clearing and wrapped his arms around her to make sure she was as warm as she should be. "And who the hell is Tam?"

"Tamarind," she gave him an impish smile that made him bite his cheek to stop from responding. This was a moment for a serious discussion, not jokes. "Drake, what's wrong? You've been stomping around the house so often it's beginning to wear out the floor boards."

"You must take better care of yourself."

"I do," she promised.

He gritted his teeth as he worked up his courage to add, "I think we should reconsider your family situation."

"I agree."

His jaw dropped open at her instant agreement. "You do?"

"Who knew the boy was psychic?"

Turbo shoved his cousin to stop him from saying more. Cleaning up a massacre was never fun for the elementals.

"What does he mean?" Drake asked, suspiciously.

Sally sighed. "I think it's time to make my being part of this world official."

"Luke's offer of protection is official. You don't get more absolute."

She brushed a kiss against his jaw. "I mean more official."

"Sally, I am confused." His eyes narrowed and his eyebrows went low. "I do not like it."

Her chuckle did little to assuage his tension. When he turned to leave she caught his hand. "Drake you are here to marry me."

"What do you mean?"

"People of this world believe in a ceremony where they declare their intention to be true only to one another in front of their friends and family."

Drake shrugged, "We have something like that as well."

"Tam told me," she gave him another of those impish smiles. "Which is why we are here."

"You cannot do the dragon ceremony if the female is not ready to bear young."

Sally glowed as she caught his hand and placed it low on her abdomen. When his eyes went wider than the moon, all the dragons in the area fell to their knees and lowered their heads. "What are they doing?"

He looked around to answer her whispered question, "They are acknowledging their King," she explained with a laugh that was part pleasure, part pride, and all seduction.

"I'm not the King."

The Sanctuary Lords joined her laughter. Stealth was the one who answered first, "You became King when you got her pregnant."

Tam stepped forward, a tall silver haired man with smoky eyes. Drake thought he looked like an Elvin cast-off from the *Lord of the Rings*, but guessed that saying that out loud might get him run through by the dragon guardian's very big sword. "Her Majesty does not have the dragon power of temperature regulation but your young does. When it became clear that the Queen was pregnant with the future Prince - you became King."

Taking his hand, she led Drake over to the altar that the dragons had helped them create. On it was a pile of substances they had brought with them.

When Sally knelt before the tree stump, Drake followed.

Tam brought over the first mound of soil. "To show he can provide for his mate."

Drake cupped it with his hand and it changed into a pile of multi-colored gems.

Luke stepped closer. A ceremony of this sort was unheard of for outsiders to attend and he did not wish to miss a moment of it. He smiled when he realized that everyone else had moved as well.

Next, Tam handed Drake a bottle of water. "So that you may show you can tend your mate."

Drake waved his hand and the fluid changed into a deep red wine color and then back to water.

A series of items was brought forth for Drake to transform.

When all the items had been made into something else, Drake next covered Sally's womb with both his hands. "To show that I can provide for the future of our race," he announced in a bellowing voice. A miniature transparent image appeared that made tears stream from Sally's eyes. Standing on the stump, amid all the gifts her new husband had created was a cross between Sally and Drake. A perfect little boy that made her heart swell larger than the universe. The child had his father's dark hair and his mother's pale green eyes, a real combination of their features. He wore the jeweled armor that the other dragons sported, and one hand rested on a miniature sword. He had such pride, and appeared to be around five years old.

Everyone in the clearing began cheering as the projection drew his sword and held it up to his nose, in a gesture of salutation and honor.

"Is that our boy?"

Reaching out a shaking hand toward the image, Drake wrapped his free arm around her. "It is," he promised as he kissed away the tears cascading down her face.

She covered her own womb as the image faded away.

"So, I don't get it," Mach intruded. "Is she having a human or a dragon?"

Tam turned to him and shrugged. "He shall be a bit of both. The child shall be born in an egg. Within the orb, he shall gain the rest of his powers over a period of one additional year, and then he shall live as any young."

"So I give birth to an egg and have to sit on it for a year?"

"Sitting is not required, and it is your mate's responsibility to safeguard the nest."

"But it takes a year for me to actually hold my child?"

Tam bowed to Sally's question. "It shall insure the child's health and vitality."

"That's fine," Drake gave him a nod, thanking him for the help.

"I guess I can live with that," Sally groused. "Though I'll probably hate it."

Drake hugged her close, "We will keep the egg as close as the boy."

"We'd better," she muttered.

Everyone cheered her possessive, protective qualities.

"Now," she took a deep breath. "There is more for us to do."

"What? We're mated by our customs."

She shook her head. "I belong to more families than just yours."

Luke came forward and helped them both to rise to their feet. This time it was the dragons who stepped forward as well, to witness the anomaly. Sally had given Luke the language that needed to be said. He was sad for her that she could not have a holy man of her society to officiate, but they would do the best they could for her concessions, since she deserved so much more. "Do you Drake take Sally to be your lawfully wedded wife? Do you promise to honor and cherish her for the rest of time?"

When he started to answer she quickly stopped him by putting a finger across his lips, "Not yet. Luke used my wrong name."

"What do you mean?"

"Sally is my nickname," she confessed. "The name given to me at birth was Salvation."

Her confession caused a susurration across the clearing in every clan except for the dragons. Drake knelt at her feet, holding her hands close. "For truth?"

"Yes."

The clans all knew the prophecy as well as they knew their own names. Cheering erupted throughout the clearing as they celebrated the beginning of their start on the road to redemption. After four thousand years of waiting they were finally going to start going home. There could have been no happier news for any of them.

"He still didn't say yes yet," Mach yelled.

"Yes," Drake wrapped her in his arms and picked her up. "Yes, yes, yes," he began to twirl her around, smiling with joy as she threw her head back with deep laughter. "I will cherish and adore you for all time, my mate."

"Ditto," Sally managed to holler before covering his lips with her own.

***

They partied for hours. The clans intermixed and shared stories with each other, gaining peace in the knowledge that their long exile was coming to a close. Each group had a reason to thank Salvation, and took joy in claiming her as their own. Luke was amazed that this meekest, gentlest soul could be the one who had brought peace to his people. It was near dawn when they found themselves in the living room, Drake and Salvation still wrapped in each other's arms, enjoying the glow of a people united.

"I don't get it," Sally looked around at the other men, "you've all made such a big deal over your hatred of each other. The rivalries and wars. It didn't seem like that today. Everyone was really nice."

The others chuckled. When Drake joined in, she poked him with her elbow, "What?"

"It's you."

"What do you mean?"

Luke shook his head. "Each of us owes you something, so we each took you as a member of our clan. You are what united us."

"How?"

Stealth shrugged, "You saved my life from the poison, and the mage appreciated you encouraging us to bring him into the building to talk to him."

"I would still be in the traitor's clutches if you hadn't encouraged Mach and Turbo to come after me together. The elementals all credit you with making them feel like a true part of our society and not just our servants. We know most of their names now."

Turbo gave her a gentle smile, "You saved my life."

"Resurrecting my cousin from the dead gave you all the points I needed, but even before that you were my friend."

Luke grinned, "I knew you were the one who would bring back our hope."

She looked around, still concerned, "How did the scouts feel?"

"Keva appreciated you expecting them to fight with us. Apparently we haven't been giving the scouts a great deal of respect."

She burst into laughter when all the men gave her rueful and guilt-ridden looks.

"It's not funny," Drake complained.

The others groaned when they passionately kissed. "Before you two leave to consummate the union, tell us how long we have."

"What do you mean?" Sally asked Mach.

Luke sighed, "He wants to know when you two are leaving for the portal."

"Why would we do that?"

"You're dragons."

"And," Sally prompted Aquos.

"Dragons always live by themselves."

She scowled. "I think I need to introduce you guys to the concept of integration."

"What does that mean?" Blade looked to the others for explanation.

"It sounds painful," Mach joked.

Drake shook his head, "It means that we will be dividing our time between both worlds. Tam is an established leader of the limbo lands. He does not need us looking over his shoulder all the time."

"And you guys do," Sally quipped.

They all cheered the announcement. When Sally turned her head into Drake's shoulder and softened to the press of his hold, he stood up with her wrapped in his arms. It was time they got a chance to start their honeymoon, and as far as he was concerned, there was no time like the present. The Lords of Sanctuary would have to function on their own for a while, so that he could tend his wife.

At the reminder that she was now his, body and soul, he began a passionate whirr sound that told her without doubt that they would be gone for a while.

Watching the lovers go made the men in the living room contemplative.

"So what's next?" Mach questioned his friends.

Turbo and Blade nodded, "We're going to find this enemy that is trying to pick us off."

Mach made a slow fist and smiled eagerly, "I'll help."

Luke sighed, "I have my own mission."

"What?"

He smiled at the single word that all his friends had chorused. "I need to find the woman that was here."

"The girl who asked for Sanctuary?"

"You didn't put a tracer on her?"

He nodded his head at Mach and shook it for Turbo's question. He had thought to have more time with the girl, and a tracer had never occurred to him. Of course she had only been here for half a day before they were attacked and she disappeared in the battle's chaos. She was haunting his thoughts. The fact that the mage had admitted that the female was the key to finding the gem warriors meant there was no question of the pressing need of hunting her down again.

Aquos leaned over, "When are you leaving?"

"With the dawn."

Stealth's jaw tensed, "I would like to accompany you."

"Nej. I need you and Aquos to stay and watch over everything. Try to remember, the scouts are still nervous and the rest of the clan leaders are coming home."

"Taking their sweet time about it."

Mach shrugged, "Most of them are used to the wild lands."

"This is hardly that."

"I wish you hadn't called them all back," Aquos said softly.

"We're about to be all full at the inn, my brothers," Luke tried to joke. "We need to keep the peace."

Mach said, "Since we never had peace before that shouldn't be too hard."

The others grew quiet as the thought struck them of just how impossible their future was.

In all their histories they had never had a moment when they could all be at peace.

Why should it start now?

They had no history or understanding of the state of rest and were terrified of its implications.

No one in the room slept easy that night, with the burden of their people's future weighing like cowls of nails they could not put aside.

.

Artemis Milchon

 Artemis is a time-traveling princess from a distant planet. She spent her childhood hopping worm-holes across the galaxy. Fluent in one hundred and seventy-nine languages, only one of them from Earth, she learned to speak English from a man made out of metal. Her traveling companion is a fire-breathing kitten who is also a gourmet cook. Love and romance are her passion, and she's thrilled to share it with you. Come and join her for a tale or two ... we promise the kitty won't set you ablaze.

Keep watch for more stories from Artemis.